There, across the ballroom,
was the man who had kissed her
in the stableyard of the King's Head!

His mere presence seemed to draw all eyes. To save herself from being flurried, Juliana swept very low into a particularly graceful curtsey, casting her eyes upon the floor to avoid that hateful gaze of his. She hoped that her fan would hide the rich blush that was already mantling her cheeks.

The Marquis gave a lazy bow and cast a thoughtful glance upon Juliana as if summing her up. "Miss Quincey, we have met before. I am delighted to have this opportunity for a more formal meeting. Our first encounter was so hurried, was it not? Besides, I have a commission to perform—something to return to you in the way of a token."

With these mocking words, he handed Juliana a small package.

For a moment she could not think what it might contain. She said in puzzled tones, "This is for me?" as she opened the paper. When she saw the contents, a wave of anger welled up in her heart. It was the glove that he had taken from her unresisting grasp that afternoon in the stableyard.

She did not pause to think. Forgetting the bystanders, forgetting all control, she took out the offending glove and cast it straight at those mocking eyes!

Novels By Caroline Courtney

Duchess in Disguise
A Wager For Love
Love Unmasked
Guardian of the Heart
Dangerous Engagement
Love's Masquerade
Love Triumphant
Heart of Honor
Libertine in Love

Published By
WARNER BOOKS

CAROLINE COURTNEY

Libertine in Love

WARNER BOOKS

A Warner Communications Company

WARNER BOOKS EDITION

Copyright © 1980 by Arlington Books (Publishers), Ltd.
All rights reserved.

Cover design by Gene Light

Cover art by Walter Popp

Warner Books, Inc., 75 Rockefeller Plaza, New York, N.Y. 10019

Ⓦ A Warner Communications Company

Printed in the United States of America

First Printing: August, 1980

10 9 8 7 6 5 4 3 2 1

Libertine in Love

One

The King's Head was bustling with activity in the late spring afternoon, when a traveling coach drew up in its stableyard. The head hostler cast a knowledgeable eye over the two sturdy horses that drew it, and over the vehicle's lumbering and far-from-fashionable design. Everything about the conveyance bespoke the country gentleman's establishment—comfortably circumstanced, perhaps, but certainly not fashionable. Sighing, the head man gestured to one of the stable lads to take the horses out of the traces; ever-hopeful visions of golden guineas faded from his mind. These were guests who would give a shilling or two, not guineas.

He turned his attention to a spanking racing curricle, driven into the yard at a highly dangerous pace, by some young gentleman of fashionable attire and noisy behavior. From these he might get the generous tips he hoped for. He set his nut-brown wrinkled face into a servile smile and started forward. The King's Head was having an unusually busy day, with vehicles of many descriptions arriving hourly, thanks to a prizefight which was to be held the next day in the neighborhood. With half the young bloods from London currently clamoring for stabling and rooms at the inn, there was little time for a mere traveling coach from the country.

Had the head hostler stayed to watch the coach's occupants descend, he would have been even less impressed. For from the solid vehicle alighted two females, neither of them dressed stylishly. Indeed, the elder might have seemed an upper servant but for the unmistakable gentility of her garments. There was something fussy and spinsterish about her crimped hair, tightly stretched back underneath the sober hat. The younger female—little more than a slip of a girl—was less easy to classify. Bright eyes of gray danced beneath chestnut curls which poked from under a plain straw hat. She wore a demure gray traveling cloak, almost Quakerish in its sobriety, but the richness of the fabric and something about her confidently inquiring gaze suggesting a young lady of quality. The buckles on her neat black shoes were real silver, and she carried a pair of equally plain gray soft leather gloves.

"Oh, Miss Humphries," she said with a wry but enchanting smile, "I am positively aching in every limb. The roads are so full of ruts!"

"When you have traveled to the Metropolis as frequently as I have, Miss Quincy," said her severe companion, "you will know that the roads are, on the contrary, excellent. London is so commodiously seated that it has high roads to most great towns for the convenience of carriages and cattle. I assure you, Miss Quincey, there are far worse roads in this country of ours. But let us not stop here chattering idly. Where is the landlord, pray?"

There was no sign midst the bustle of stableboys and clatter of horses of this worthy. After a moment while the two ladies turned inquiring gazes around them, the younger one said anxiously, "I trust that our chambers have not been taken by some other guests. This inn seems to be prodigiously busy, Miss Humphries." With a complete lack of self-consciousness, she turned to a groom who was loosening the harness of one of the horses. "Pray, can you tell us the reason for such activity?"

"Come Miss Quincey, we have no time for such inquiries," said her companion impatiently.

" 'Tis the fight, miss," said the stableboy, looking down at the innocent gray eyes of the girl below him. "The Marquis put up a fifty-guinea purse to match the Black against Harry Ruck. All the Lunnon young gentlemen is here to watch."

"Thank you, my boy," said the young girl with a quaint kind of dignity, as she placed a coin in his hand. He tugged his forelock gratefully and went back to his task.

"Come, Miss Quincey," said Miss Humphries for the second time, her voice taking on a peevish note. The girl obediently followed her, toward the back door of the inn, where the stout figure of the landlord, looking extremely harassed and red in the face, had now appeared from the kitchens.

"I am Miss Humphries," she said to him patronizingly. "We ordered two bedchambers and a private parlor, my good man. Please take us to the parlor."

"I am very sorry, ladies," said the landlord firmly. "You may have the bedchambers which I have saved for you though many wouldn't. But as for the parlor, I am unable to oblige. It has been already taken, and, as you see, I am at my wits' end what with every young blood anxious for a room and us full to the brim already."

"But a letter was written to you weeks ago," said the young Miss Quincey indignantly. "A parlor was particularly requested."

"It's the Marquis of Peterborough, Miss." The landlord shrugged his shoulders, as if no further explanation need be given.

9

The young lady was obviously not impressed and was about to argue further, when she noticed her elderly companion shaking her head. "Come, Miss Quincey," said that formidable spinster, "We will retire to our chambers. As it is quite out of the question for us to eat in the common inn parlor, we will have supper brought to our chambers."

"Right, if you say so, Miss. I will get the maid to show you your rooms." The landlord had scarcely finished speaking, before he turned away to greet more guests. It was evident that he had spoken nothing less than the truth when he had said that the inn was full to the brim.

In Miss Humphries's chamber, her young charge lingered before going to her own room. "Why did you shake your head at me like that, Miss Humphries?" she asked directly. "That rascal of a landlord knew very well that we had reserved the parlor. Why should he give it to some marquis or other? It is just not right!"

"My dear Miss Quincey, it is not ladylike to insist upon such matters," said her companion. She spoke with the authority of a woman accustomed to laying down the law. "There is something very unbecoming about a young lady who puts herself forward, and besides, nothing but harm can come in crossing the path of the Marquis of Peterborough. It would be quite improper of me to animadvert further upon that nobleman's character. Suffice it to say that he is wild to a fault, a reckless libertine, and that no young woman is safe in his presence. It is for a lady to withdraw, Miss Quincey, I shall expect you to keep to your bedchamber this evening. Do not fail to remember that we are in the vicinity of a vulgar prizefight that will no doubt attract the attention of undesirable persons. Discourtesies and other difficulties are likely to occur if you do otherwise than retire early."

"But, Miss Humphries, I must have a word with the coachman before I retire. He was worried about the horses, and I know he would feel happier if I listen to him about it tonight."

Miss Humphries looked down her pinched nose at the girl, who was sitting on her bed, swinging the demure straw bonnet by its gray ribbon. "Be ruled by me, Miss Quincey. I am in *loco parentis* for this journey. True, you are not my usual charge, but as a governess of many years standing I have been asked to look after your welfare during this journey. I cannot command your obedience, but I can caution you. Propriety and good sense demand that you should keep to your chamber."

"Thank you for your advice," was the polite reply. "It is kind of you to look after me and I am grateful to you for your chaperonage. But, as you say, you are not in command of me. I believe that my duty to the servants requires that I should talk to the coachman. I shall not be more than a few minutes. I will content myself with just a few words with John."

Having delivered this ultimatum in quiet but decided tones, she stood up to go. Juliana Quincey was of diminutive stature, daintily made, but with a decided air of self-possession. Gray eyes, widely spaced under delicate eyebrows, looked firmly at Miss Humphries with a distinct twinkle of rebellion in them. A small turned-up nose, and a rosy button mouth in a heart-shaped face, gave further character to her looks. Chestnut curls, glowing with health, which tumbled round her cheeks completed the picture. Miss Juliana Quincey lacked the Grecian profile, tall figure, and golden locks of an acknowledged beauty. But there was charm enough to make up for that.

It was with a firm tread that she left the room, ignoring the irritated sigh that came from Miss Humphries. As she ran down the inn staircase toward the stableyard, Juliana pondered the penalties of being Miss Humphries's companion. For a whole day she had been shut up in a coach with the elderly governess, who had beguiled the passing hours by reading from an improving volume, titled *The Antiquities of London,* which was described as "being an account of whatsoever is ancient, curious, or remarkable as to Palaces, Towers, Churches, Exchanges, Halls, and all Public Edifices."

In between a succession of these very dreary facts about the buildings on London, she had been forced by politeness to listen to anecdotes about Miss Humphries's career as a governess. She had been told unendingly of the exquisite gentility of the Milgrave household in London, to which Miss Humphries was bound. She had heard of the beauty and sense of the eldest Milgrave daughter, the only one who was out in society, until she could almost want to scream at the mere mention of Miss Milgrave's name. Indeed, the governess's whole conversation had seemed entirely to consist of a series of names, rich fashionable and genteel, which were dropped into every sentence. By Miss Humphries's account, it seemed that she was intimate with many of the most noble families in the country.

Having never before come into contact with a governess, Juliana was in no position to know whether such intimacy was likely. But a kind of native shrewdness told her that it was not very probable. No, doubt, Miss Humphries had been a conscientious and talented preceptress in many great families, but it seemed unlikely that she had stood on such intimate terms with them all; after all, the position of a governess was not much respected.

With such thoughts in her mind, Juliana arrived at the stableyard, which was still bustling with activity. She looked round inquiringly for her coachman but could see no sign of him. Perhaps he had already left for his lodgings. However, something else caught her eye. In a nearby corner of the yard, just outside the kitchen, a small rather grubby little girl dressed in servants' clothes was crying as if her heart would break. A huge white cotton apron, not altogether clean, was thrown over her face, and her thin shoulders poking out of a somewhat large frock were heaving with sorrow.

Without a second thought, Juliana felt in her purse for a coin. Her worthy father, Sir Basil Quincey, had not been in favor of indiscriminate charity, but he had been fully conscious of the power of money to aid the distresses of the poor. He had brought up his daughter to take an interest in charitable works, for he had held the view that it was the duty of those fortunate to be born into comfortable circumstances to aid those less well placed. Sir Basil had never knowingly passed by human distress without attempting to apply aid.

Sir Basil's daughter had quite naturally grown up with the same compassionate feelings as her father. Crossing the yard, dodging a scurrying groom and stepping over a heap of discarded harness, Juliana made her way over to the pathetic little sobbing figure. Gently tapping the scullery maid on the arm, she inquired in her soft voice, "Pray tell me, what is making you cry so? Can I help you?"

A frightened none-too-clean face looked up at her. The maid dropped a hasty curtsy. A sniff followed a couple of sobs, while the tear-stained face tried to pull itself together. "Please Mum, 'tis naught," was all the little girl could murmur. She looked more alarmed than comforted, and glanced hastily over her shoulder in the direction of the kitchen.

"Has somebody been angry with you? The cook perhaps? Is that what is making you weep?" Juliana persisted.

The small girl remained mute, merely looking more terrified than before. A harsh female voice from the kitchen floated out into the yard, and obviously added to her distress. Juliana decided that further interrogation would be useless. Taking a coin out of her purse, she pressed it into the small maid's hand. "There my dear. Spend it prudently."

The small girl glanced hurriedly down at the coin with pleasure which rapidly turned to surprise. Her tears vanished. Her mouth widened into a smile and her whole smudged face took on an expression of seraphic bliss. She bobbed another curtsy, then a third and looked as if she wanted to utter words that would not come out. Instead, she made a dive at Juliana's hand, snatched it up, kissed it hurriedly, and turned to flee back into the kitchen.

Juliana smiled to see her go, and was about to turn herself, when a hand touched her on the shoulder. Surprised, though not alarmed, she swung round unselfconsciously to face whomever it might be. It was with amazement that she saw the elegant figure of a man of fashion standing in front of her. He was wearing the plain riding breeches, frock coat and top boots of a sportsman, but nobody could have mistaken him for a country gentleman. His buckskin breeches were impeccably cut and his boots shone with a gleam which betokened the hand of a master valet. A plain white stock, fastened with a single large diamond pin, girded his neck. He carried a riding crop.

"Pray, sir, how can I oblige you?" she asked him, with a slight shy smile.

"Sweet Quaker, you can oblige me with a kiss," came the astonishing reply. The young man had seized Juliana's hand, and stood there grinning as if his outrageous demand was the most natural request in the world. His eyes glittered in an odd way which made Juliana wonder if he were entirely sober.

"Pray let go my hand, sir," Juliana said, stammering slightly. She supposed she should pull back her hand and flee, like the kitchen maid, into the safety of the inn kitchen, but she was held back by the thought that she would be making a spectacle of herself. Perhaps the man was mad, and she should humor him. The stableyard was a public place, and she knew that rapid retreat would only draw all eyes toward her.

"Come now, sweetheart, whence such prudery? Such

14

sober dress makes me wonder whether it hides a loving heart." The man must be mocking her. She found his raillery inexplicable. As he spoke, he was pulling her closer until he swiftly put his arm around her waist, drawing her so close that she stood panting against his powerful body.

"You must be mad," protested Juliana vigorously. "Is this some hateful joke? I am no serving wench, you know. I am a lady of quality."

"Bravo, my dear. I see that you are a woman of fire and spirit. I have wagered I shall kiss the first pretty female I see and you are she. And devilish pretty you are too. It will be a pleasure to win my bet. See her, Ponsonby? Look what the fates have cast my way?" With a gesture he swung Juliana around, and, to her shame, she noticed that the whole encounter was taking place in front of an audience. Against a sporting curricle lounged a young dandy, with a gaudily dressed female on either arm. From their direction came a strong and unmistakable smell of brandy.

"You are drunk, sir," she panted furiously at him. "Unhand me, pray. I shall scream." Her tormenter just laughed and with a grip of iron drew her even closer.

"Drunk with your beauty, fairest. And now let me sip from those tempting lips." Very slowly and deliberately he bent down to kiss her. A mocking smile was on his lips. Juliana made desperate struggles to escape, but could not slip out of the strong encircling grip. At the last minute, realizing that her struggles were undignified, she stiffened into immobility and tried to shrink into the folds of her traveling cloak. She could not fight against this tormenter. All she could do was to suffer his vile attentions with an attempt at dignified detachment. It would be no use screaming. That would simply create a scene that she was desperately hoping to avoid. There was nothing she could do.

His lips were brutal upon her mouth. They seemed to demand . . . to search her very being.

She stood rigid, disgusted and ashamed. She could feel the blood drumming in her veins, mounting toward her hot cheeks into a blush. Her heartbeats sounded like thunder. She was horribly conscious of the tall, strong male body, pressed against hers. For a moment she thought she would swoon. And, then, somewhere, in the inmost depths of her heart—she shuddered with the sensation—her flesh was responding to those insulting, those demanding lips. It was as if the heat of them seared her whole body, melting it into a kind of humiliating surrender.

Just as she thought that body and soul could bear it no longer, and that she must faint or die of the disgrace, the lips released her. She could see his mocking smile, and those dangerously glittering eyes above her face. Once again, she feebly tried to wrench herself out of his grasp, only to discover that he still held her tight.

"Where are the screams you promised, my beauty?" he said mockingly.

She looked at him in silence. Her hands tightened into fists involuntarily, and she longed to hit that jeering face. But she remembered that there were onlookers. It could not suit the Quincey pride in her to make such a scene publicly. She could not bear that they should hear her pleading with him. Dimly she thought of the painted women, lolling on the arm of the young man by the curricle. Somehow she knew that they were unlikely to be women of fashion. They would not come to her aid. They would more likely join in the taunts.

"Do you need further provocation?" he said deridingly, and made as if he would kiss her again.

Juliana had had time to get herself under control before replying. She stiffly turned her face away. Still blushing furiously, she managed to say: "I must bear with your insults, it seems, since you will not let me go. You mock me to make your companions laugh. You have won your vile wager, sir. You can have no further interest in tormenting me."

"You underestimate your charms, my dear," came the hateful voice. "Even those Quakerish clothes cannot hide your beauty."

"Sir, surely you have beauties enough, and willing ones, I dare vow," she could not help herself retorting. "Keep your kisses for them, and suffer me to be on my way, if you are a gentleman."

"I am a nobleman, not a gentleman," he replied. "I am somewhat tired of my dashers. I have a mind for another Quaker kiss, my dear."

"I am no Quaker, sir." Juliana was losing her self-possession. She found herself horrified by the tangle she was in. What on earth would all the people in the yard think? By now, there must be a sizable crowd, including every stableboy employed at the King's Head. The shame of it was awful to bear. "I beg you, sir," she said, close to tears, and by now willing to sink her pride. "I beg of you ..." The violence of her humiliation overcame her, and she could not speak on.

The man showed no immediate signs of releasing her. Steadily he gazed at her face as if lazily deciding whether he would take further sport at her expense. The intent look of those glittering eyes frightened Juliana.

She was saved by his companion. "Auberon, for the love of God, leave the girl alone." The young man near the curricle shook off the arms of the two women, and lounged over towards his companion. His gait was unsteady, and it was clear that he was drunk. Juliana's tormenter loosened his hold somewhat on her. If she had had the strength, she could have torn herself from his arms, but by now she was too seriously upset to try such a move. She was fighting not to lose her senses.

"My Lord, come away," whined one of the women. "I vow we are neglected by you! Leave the wench. We have better tricks to show you than these country trollops." Her female companion uttered a somewhat raucous laugh.

Juliana got the unmistakable impression that it was

the woman's jeers, rather than the man's words, that halted the man who was holding her from kissing her a second time. "I will leave you, my dear, but I must have a love token before I go," he said. "What will you give me? A lock of that pretty chestnut hair? Your pearls?" He continued teasing her. "I see that your tongue has quite deserted you, and that you will not reply. Well, I will content myself with one of those gloves you are carrying. Perhaps I shall wear it as a love token like a true knight-errant."

Juliana stood her ground, unmoving, while the strong arms released her and without resisting she let him take one of her gloves from her grasp. She fixed her eyes upon the flagstones beneath her feet, just waiting for the torture to come to an end. She dared not look up, for she was sure she would meet the jeering hateful glances of the two women. As she stood there, she was conscious that the little party had now turned away from her, and, with a flurry of gaudy petticoats, they were making their way into the inn.

When eventually she looked up, she saw the other young man, the one he had called Ponsonby, still standing awkwardly near her. "My heartfelt apologies, ma'am," he said with an attempt at a low bow. "It's the devil in him which will have its way. Any service I can do for you . . ."

"The only service you can do for me is to leave me well alone," said Juliana sharply. "Just follow those friends of yours. All I want to do is forget this whole shocking encounter."

The fair-haired man looked as if he would have liked to explain or apologize further, but then thinking better of it, he shrugged his shoulders and took Juliana's advice. Simultaneously, the little knot of stableboys and idle bystanders who had stood round melted away. Work in the stableyard returned to normal so that Juliana might have thought nobody had ever noticed, except that she knew better.

A timid hand on her arm made her jump round nervously. It was only the little kitchen maid, whom she had helped earlier. She had reemerged from the kitchen. The small child bobbed a curtsy, and Juliana saw that she was blushing in a sort of sisterly sympathy. "If you please, mum, I will come back to take you to the chambermaid," said the lass rather tentatively.

"Thank you, my dear," said Juliana gravely. The child's obvious anxiety about her somehow steadied her nerves. "I have no need of aid. I will retire to my chamber now, I think."

"I'll help you, mum," the maid insisted. And resolutely turning her back on the kitchen and the noises of conflict within, she led the way back into the inn hall.

A subdued Juliana followed her, barely conscious of her surroundings. The emotional turmoil within her breast could not be quieted. Her agitation was extreme, and it was an effort for her to walk with an even step. Still clutching her remaining glove, with her cloak wrapped even more firmly round her, she obediently followed the girl up the stairs.

"That is Miss Humphries's chamber," she managed to say, pointing at the door.

The small girl opened it, and she walked back into the room to the side of the governess whose advice she had so recently spurned. Almost fainting, she sank down upon the bed. "Thank goodness . . . you are here, Miss Humphries . . ."

The governess had been examining her gray hair, at the mirror, and prinking at stray hairs that had come loose. She turned with amazement to see Juliana's agitated arrival. For a moment, her impulse was to scold, but the girl looked upset enough to faint.

Miss Humphries reached for the smelling salts which she always carried with her. She waved them vigorously under Juliana's nose. They had the desired effect. The girl sat upright, choking slightly, then sneezed. "Oh thank you, Miss Humphries, but I do not need salts," she said.

"I beg of you to take the nasty things away! I cannot abide them!"

This graceless refusal of what was a kind gesture offended Miss Humphries. Not for the first time, she regretted having offered to take charge of the girl. Thank heaven, Juliana was not one of her pupils. Until this journey she had never set eyes upon the minx. The Hallidays, with whom she had been employed, had had some slight acquaintance with Sir Basil Quincey. It had only been slight, because Sir Basil had been practically a recluse, content to spend his time looking after his estate, running several charitable good works on it. He had been so busy with a Sunday school, a row of almshouses, Sunday readings for estate workers, and a soup kitchen for the indigent during winter that he had not visited his neighbors very much. Really, thought Miss Humphries, his dauhgter had been deplorably neglected.

Miss Humphries had merely been asked by the Hallidays whether she would be willing to accompany Juliana to London. Regrettably, the Halliday family had grown too old for governesses, and therefore Miss Humphries was to take up a new post with the Milgrave family in London. All she was required to do was to look after Juliana for the journey. The child had recently lost her father, and would have to go to live with her old grandmother in London. Miss Humphries readily agreed, since she was to receive a handsome sum for this small duty, besides having all the expenses of the journey paid. Indeed, she was grateful for the chance of traveling in a private coach, even if the journey was being made slowly with no changes of horses. Miss Humphries was not fond of traveling upon the common stagecoach, where the companions on the journey might include such vulgar people as farmers' wives or even tradesmen.

She had soon concluded that the girl she was to accompany had developed a very unbecoming willfulness, probably as the result of being too often alone with just a father. Miss Humphries could not conceal a snort of disapproval, when she thought of how her kind advice about staying in the bedchamber had been flouted. Now something very bad indeed had happened. The girl still looked pale, though color was beginning to come back in to her cheeks. *She had obviously had an unfortunate experience with a man,* thought Miss Humphries. In Miss Humphries's knowledge of girls, which was very wide, all unfortunate experiences were connected with men. Usually Miss Humphries was able to control the high spirits, childish giggles, and other undesirable character traits possessed by her young charges—thus minimizing the chances of such things occurring.

But somehow Juliana Quincey was different. For one thing, during the journey she had never acknowledged Miss Humphries's authority, but had made it plain that she considered herself too grown-up to take orders from a governess. It was not that the child was rude, thought Miss Humphries. Nor did she exactly behave badly. There were no giggles or flirtations. But she was incurably independent, with a tendency to what Miss Humphries considered over-emotional passions. Miss Humphries shuddered when she remembered what difficulty she had in preventing Juliana leaving the coach in order to interrogate some gypsies who were ill-treating a wretched donkey. After a brisk disagreement the girl had agreed that the coach should continue without stopping. "Papa would have wished me to stop, but I will allow that your superior knowledge of the road suggests that we do not have the time," the chit had said. There was something disagreeably pert about the remark, thought the governess.

Now the girl looked as if she had a sharp and unpleasant lesson. Miss Humphries displayed a thin acidulated smile, bending over the girl. "What is the matter Miss Quincey, pray. Why are you so agitated?"

"Oh, dear Miss Humphries. I fear I owe you an apology. I should have heeded your advice and stayed in my chamber. The most terrible thing occurred . . ." Juliana's voice trailed off into sobs, as she recalled her humiliating experience.

"Calm yourself, Miss Quincey. Pray take five deep breaths and count to ten. Then perhaps you will have regained your self-control enough to tell me exactly what has happened," said Miss Humphries bracingly. "Now then. I await your tale."

Painfully Juliana took the five deep breaths and counted to ten. Somewhat to her surprise, this seemed to do the trick. Her sobs ceased and she felt calmer. "Miss Humphries," she whispered earnestly, "I am almost too ashamed to tell you. I was in the stableyard, looking for the coachman, but I could not find him, I think he must have gone to his lodgings, when this strange young man, a gentleman completely unknown to me . . . well, he . . . insulted me. I fear it was the man that the landlord mentioned . . . the Marquis."

"The Marquis of Peterborough! In what way did he insult you, Miss Quincey?" asked Miss Humphries with equal urgency in her tones. "Come, you must hold nothing back from *me*. If you will not tell me, then I am quite prepared to interrogate the landlord. Depend upon it, he will know all about it. I must have the truth!" Miss Humphries had had more than twenty years of experience with girls, and there was nothing she did not know about how to worm a story out of them.

"Oh, please, Miss Humphries. Don't ask the landlord. I should die of shame," cried Juliana with alarm. "I will tell you, myself. That is, if I can only find a way of putting it. You see, he insulted me by . . . he embraced me! And that is not all. There were people about who could not fail to see it, and there were these friends of his—a gentleman who was, I think, in drink and two females of a very odd appearance."

"What kind of females?" asked Miss Humphries genuinely puzzled by this extraneous detail. She had not been expecting *females* to occur in the story.

"What kind of females?" Juliana paused and tried to

22

think of a way of describing them. "They were not ladies, if you understand. Indeed, I do not think they were . . . women of virtue, even."

"There is no necessity for you to say more, Miss Quincey," said Miss Humphries in shocked tones. "I am happy to say that I have never encountered females of that class, and I am confident that their very existence is best forgotten. Young girls, Miss Quincey, do not talk about such things. They do not *know* of such things. But I feel it my duty to point out to you that this encounter was the disagreeable consequence of your disobedience. For this journey I have been put in charge of you, and I am obliged to do my best for you, Miss Quincey. Unless you are obedient to me, I must wash my hands of you. Consider what must be the reproaches of your grand-mama, when she hears of this distressing episode. She will surely point the finger of disapprobation at *me,* for failing to chaperone you properly."

"I am sorry, Miss Humphries, really I am," said Juliana penitently. She added with dismay, as Miss Humphries knew she would: "Is it really necessary for my grandmother to know about this . . . this encounter? I should so much prefer for it not to be known by anybody."

Miss Humphries allowed herself another thin smile. She was pleased to see that the girl was falling into line. She had had a very unpleasant fright, and now at last perhaps she would listen to her elders and betters! "It could be thought, Miss Quincey, that it is my duty to tell your grandmother of this misfortune. On the other hand I do not hesitate to tell you that I feel partly to blame for not insisting on accompanying you to the stableyard. I was fatigued from the journey, but I should not have let my natural feelings of weariness overcome my sense of what was proper." As she expected, Juliana began to feel very uncomfortable and guilty when she heard about the governess's tiredness.

"But I should also prefer this unfortunate episode to

23

be forgotten," went on Miss Humphries. "I believe that I can promise not to mention it to your grandmother on one condition—that you promise to obey me for the rest of the journey. What do you say, Miss Quincey?"

"So you won't tell on me? Oh, thank you. You are so kind!" The girl jumped up enthusiastically and hugged the shrinking governess.

Miss Humphries drew back with alarm and dismay. In an exaggerated way, she tidied her clothes where the girl's embrace had disarranged them, and said, "My dear Miss Quincey, you forget the proper demeanor of a young lady. A young lady never shows wanton enthusiasm. True elegance of mind never gives way to mere impulsiveness. You should never deviate from calmness and moderation. I am told that Miss Charlotte Milgrave, the eldest daughter of the family to whom I am bound, is a pattern of good behavior. I fear that you should learn from her example, Miss Quincey."

Juliana privately considered that Miss Milgrave sounded a terrible bore. Once again she gave thanks secretly that her father, Sir Basil, had never inflicted a governess upon her. It seemed—from Miss Humphries— that governesses were always talking about propriety and calmness and duty, and other disagreeable virtues. Her father, Sir Basil, had educated his only daughter by himself. She had a tolerable command of French, a respectable grounding in the classics, and a background of wide reading in the Quincey library. From her slight acquaintance with Miss Humphries, Juliana could not help thinking that the governess was rather ignorant in such subjects. Miss Humphries, it seemed, knew little about Latin or Greek though she excelled in polite accomplishments such as fine needlework, piano playing and sketching. These accomplishments, alas, Sir Basil had been unable to teach.

But he had made up for this by educating his daughter in charitable works. Juliana had helped him run the almshouses and could say exactly how much a week should be set aside for an aging pensioner. She knew too, how to run a Sunday school, and how to organize Bible readings among the poor. She had supervised the winter soup kitchens and helped relieve the wants of numerous cottagers upon the estate. Sir Basil had not talked of propriety and duty so much, but he had certainly *acted* upon these and other Christian virtues.

Juliana sighed, when she thought of her father. She missed him so much. Sir Basil would have wanted her to be kind to Miss Humphries, who was really rather a pathetic figure. "Thank you, Miss Humphries, for looking after me," she forced herself to say. "I shall promise to obey you for the rest of the journey. I feel rather fatigued myself, so I will take myself to my bedchamber for the night."

Going to her bedchamber was one thing; getting some rest was quite another. Juliana took a mouthful or two of the meal brought up by a harassed chambermaid, but found she had little appetite for it. Somehow she could not help dwelling on the unfortunate incident in the stableyard. It all seemed not only disgraceful and embarrassing, but also exceedingly odd. Back in her quiet country home, she had known little of how fashionable people behaved. Her father had not been interested in social life, nor had she. They had been a close and loving couple, so happy that they had not needed outside distractions. As a result, Juliana had no way of knowing how young gentleman behaved. She had never really met any. Was it usual for them to make senseless wagers on kissing the first female? Was it normal for them to behave so badly?

Juliana had been brought up to think that she might one day meet a young man and fall in love. Sir Basil had approved of love. "I loved your mother, Juliana," he would often say, "and we made a runaway match of it. I have never regretted it." Then he would fall silent, thinking of the lovely young wife who had died so tragically in childbed. Juliana had never known her mother. But Sir

Basil's words had made her dream of falling in love, herself, one day. And in those dreams, she had thought . . . had thought of kissing.

Yet the behavior of the man in the stableyard, those hard demanding lips, those mocking taunts . . . surely this could be nothing to do with love? Juliana tossed and turned in her narrow bed, as she thought of it.

Her restlessness was not helped by the noise from the inn. From her chamber, she could hear the steady murmur of the taproom, and outside in the stableyard, there was the occasional snort of a horse or a clatter of hooves as some animal walked round its loosebox. But there were other noises, too.

These seemed to come from the private parlor on the floor below. At one point a door opened, and a woman's high-pitched laughter sounded down the corridor, laughter which broke off into muffled giggles as if somebody had . . . had embraced the laugher. Juliana could hear the clink of glasses, the deep voices of the men, and the higher voices of the women. It was a lively evening that was going on. Juliana remembered the gaudily dressed women who had been in the stableyard, shamelessly flirting with their eyes.

She blushed when she remembered how they had seen her embarrassment, and her hot flush mounted when she thought of the remarks they might be making about her in the parlor. Or would the incident have been wholly forgotten among the evening's merriment? Was it just a trivial passing whim of the marquis? A whim that was so common that he, and his intimates, would forget about it!

It was a dark-eyed, subdued Juliana who took her place in the coach the next day with Miss Humphries. The governess's demeanor made it clear that she expected her charge to behave docilely. Juliana had no spirit of rebellion left in her. After such a sleepless night, watchful hours and worried dreams, she was anxious only to shake the dust of the King's Head off her feet.

They left early before most of their fellow guests were stirring. In the stableyard, the grooms were rubbing down some of the fine blood horses that had been driven in curricles and carriages by fashionable young men. But there was no sign of their owners. Nor was there any sight of the two gaudy women or the marquis. Juliana supposed that, having reveled all night, they must still be abed.

In the coach, Miss Humphries immediately took up where she had left off with *The Antiquities of London*. She droned: "There are three principal fountains or wells in London, to wit, Holy-Well, Clement's Well and Clark's Well . . . The river of Wells on the West runs under Holborn Bridge and Fleet Bridge and is of such breadth and depth that of old ten or twelve ships laden with merchandise were wont to come from the Thames . . ." By the time Juliana had learned that the river of Wells was another name for the Fleet river, which had a bridge over it near to the Fleet prison, she was heartily sick of the little guidebook. The only interesting fact it seemed to mention, she noted, was that the prison was famous for its clandestine marriages of those couples who wished to marry in haste.

She wondered if she might plead a headache as an excuse to stop the reading. Then she looked gloomily out of the window and tried to shut her mind to the horrid rollcall of boring facts that Miss Humphries was reading: "These conduits used to be in former times visited, and particularly on the eighteenth of September, 1562, the Lord Mayor, Aldermen, and many worshipful Persons, rode to the conduit heads to see them, after the custom . . ." Would it never end?

Juliana plucked up courage to interrupt. "Pray help me, Miss Humphries. I am so ignorant of the fashionable world, that I wondered if you might put aside your

27

interesting volume for a moment and enlighten my ignorance. I am interested to know if there is much gaming in fashionable society? Papa disapproved of gaming, and, as you know, I have been much withdrawn from the world until now. What should I expect when I come out into society? I know, that, having lived among the people of highest *ton,* you will be able to set me right."

Her ploy worked. The governess, at first annoyed at the interruption, began to soften under the compliments. It was just the sort of inquiry that Miss Humphries enjoyed answering, giving her the chance to roll fashionable names round her tongue, and to show off her intimacy with the great and the mighty.

"My dear, Miss Quincey, what a country mouse you are, to be sure! Such a question to ask! Why, I am sure that the rage for gaming is ridiculous! Among the young bucks, there is nothing more talked of and practiced. They will wager fortunes, thousands of pounds, upon any small occurrence. Dear Lord Halliday told me an interesting anecdote about the gentleman's club, White's, which illustrates this perfectly. A passerby in the street dropped dead outside and was carried in to be revived. All the gentlemen present laid bets on whether he were dead or no. When a surgeon came to bleed him, he was countermanded by some of the young bucks present. His actions would affect the fairness of the bet, they said."

"How very heartless it all seems," said Juliana doubtfully. "If all the young men behave like that I fear I shall never meet a man I can esteem. I could not love a gamester."

"Love, Miss Quincey?" Miss Humphries sounded quite shocked. "What romantic folly is this? Love is for the playhouses and for romances. But I am sure it is not at all the sort of thing that a young girl should be thinking of. Why, I always tell *my* girls that love is for the lower orders of society. In their class of life, love can play no part in their marriages."

"Papa said he believed in love. He told me never to

give my hand unless I could also give my heart," said Juliana with a touch of her old rebelliousness.

It was soon crushed. "Your papa may have *said* such things," said Miss Humphries snubbingly, "but then your dear papa, Miss Quincey, was a recluse." With this final statement, she picked up the volume of *The Antiquities of London.*

Two

"Sir Basil Quincey was more than just a recluse. He was a quixotic idiot. No, don't defend him, child. I am sure you were very fond of your papa and that he was an excellent man. But nothing will make me agree that he had the right to keep you locked away in the wilds of the country."

Lady Talboys was rather overwhelming, thought Juliana. She had expected to find an elderly lady, probably with invalid habits, leading a retired life. She had not expected this kind of grandmother. Lady Talboys was in excellent health, and vigorous both in mind and body. True, she was in her eighties and needed the help of a silver-topped cane to negotiate stairs or surmount obstacles. But that, and a formidable quizzing glass which she put to her eyes whenever she wanted to inspect a person, were her only weaknesses. She was dressed in the height of fashion.

When Juliana had arrived at Curzon Street, having said a polite, if not fond, farewell to Miss Humphries who had been earlier dropped at the Milgrave residence in Audley Street, Juliana had been amazed by her first sight of her only surviving grandmother. She had been shown into Lady Talboys's drawing room expecting to see the little old infirm lady of her imagination.

At the far end of the room, perched bolt upright on a very fashionable Sheraton settee, was Lady Talboys. She was wearing a very fine purple and white sacque dress, finely adorned with elegant French trimming, with tippet, stomacher, sleeve knot, and ruffles all of the same purple color. The trimming, which was mainly of lace, was of the finest Juliana had ever seen, and had been further beautified by the addition of silver thread at both sleeve and bodice. The old lady was wearing a matching lace cap, and a very fine diamond necklace gleamed at her throat. Her shoe buckles were resplendent with further diamonds. Her bony hands were almost covered with three or four huge diamond rings, and she wore several patches on her face.

Juliana also suspected that her glowing color owed something to art rather than nature. In a word, Lady Talboys *painted*. Nothing could have been further from the harmless sickly grandmother of Juliana's fancy. Altogether her finery was astonishing to the girl who had just come up from the country. Juliana hardly knew whether to be shocked or amused.

She was also slightly embarrassed by her own apparel. At home with Sir Basil—with little prospect of visitors —it had been her custom to do without the hooped petticoat, which was necessary for more formal wear. Thinking that traveling upon the road was both tiresome and often dirty, Juliana had contented herself with wearing one of her simple gowns in a dove gray lutestring, with a white cotton apron, only slightly trimmed. Now, in the formal surroundings of her grandmother's house, she realized that she was dressed in shockingly simple style.

Wondering whether she ought to apologize, she dropped a polite curtsy and waited.

"Come here, child," Lady Talboys said, "I expect you're thinking that it's a fine thing to see an old woman like me wearing patches and rouge. No don't deny it. I saw you looked astonished, and who shall blame you. Didn't your papa tell you that I was outrageously fashionable?"

"To be frank, grandmama, he hardly ever spoke of you. When my mama died he was so upset that sometimes he would go for months without mentioning her name. He told me how beautiful she was, of course, but not about her family. I knew that I had a grandmama in London—that was all. I don't agree that he was a quixotic idiot, but it is true that we led a very rustic life."

"Did he tell you that he and I didn't see eye to eye?"

Juliana paused delicately. "He never said exactly that, but I had supposed that you two did not agree so I did not ask."

"Fiddlesticks, girl. It's no use beating about the bush. I don't believe in being mealy-mouthed like this new generation. I didn't like Sir Basil and he didn't like me. I opposed the match, and then your mama ran off with him and married secretly. She always was a headstrong girl. She took after me, I dare say. I liked her the better for it. I suppose that Sir Basil and I would have come to terms, too, had she not died in childbed. But with my only daughter dead, I saw no need to eat humble pie to him. Are you angry that I didn't rescue you sooner?"

"What do you mean by rescuing me?"

"Get you away from that damp hole in the country. No visitors. No proper clothes, as I can see for myself. Nowhere to go and nothing to do. You must have been bored to death, poor child."

"I was very fond of Papa," said Juliana stiffly. "I know that he was not exactly *sociable,* but we loved each

33

other and we were very happy. There was plenty to do." Her voice quavered when she thought back to those happy days before Sir Basil's sudden death, when it had been just her father and herself. Golden days they seemed now. No worries, no anxieties—just the two of them passing quiet hours together.

"Humph!" said her grandmother rudely. "I can see that you may have enjoyed it, child, but it's no way for a young girl to go on. Now it's time for you to discover what you've been missing all those years. If I'd had my way, you'd have come down two years ago for a London season. I wrote to your father, but he would not let you go. He said you were too young! At seventeen! Lud, I was engaged to be married at seventeen, and a mother at eighteen! How old are you now, child?"

"Nineteen last December, grandmama," said Juliana. Then with a flash of spirit she added, "I am glad Papa kept me with him for an extra two years. I have had two extra years of happiness with him to keep in my memory."

"Well, your loyalty is very proper, no doubt, but there's no denying that your education has left a lot to be desired. From the look of you, I'll wager you haven't a thing worth wearing. You've no idea of how to go on in the world, and I'll hazard a guess that you cannot dance. Is that so?"

"It's true I cannot dance, grandmama, but I can speak French and Latin and some Greek, and I have been reared in the principles of economy. I can run a house, supervise the stillroom, keep accounts and look after the estate. Papa taught me all these things."

"Lud, child, these things will get you nowhere. Can you hold a fan? Can you sketch and sing? Can you *play*?"

"You mean can I play cards? I have played whist with Papa sometimes, but he did not approve of gaming, grandmama. He said 'twas the ruin of society, and that no child of his should play for money."

"Fine words. Heaven's child, you've been brought up to be a veritable country cousin. Not play? 'Tis the main amusement of society! Everybody plays! I am very partial to games of chance, myself, and you will find me at the card table almost every evening. So, you cannot play loo or brag, or basset or faro? I can see you have never heard of hazard or roulette. How provoking, to be sure!"

On that note their first interview had ended, and a troubled Juliana had been shown to her bedroom. Her grandmother's outspoken views had worried her, but something about the old lady's bluntness, her directness and her honesty had reassured her too. It might be that Lady Talboys was a gambler and an addict of fashion, but Juliana was also convinced that she had a kind heart. There were small touches which suggested this. Her bed-chamber had had a bunch of flowers set on the polished chest of drawers, and though the spring evening was not cold, a fire burned in the grate. In Sir Basil's household, fires in the bedrooms were lit only when there was illness in the house, or in particularly cold weather. Juliana, warming herself in front of the blaze, had to admit that it was a very agreeable luxury.

The next morning other signs of luxurious living greeted her. A deferential housemaid woke her with a cup of chocolate, and told her that she would act as her lady's maid for the time being.

Sipping the warm liquid—another treat for the country-bred Juliana—the girl thought how pleasantly her grandmother lived. She was amazed to discover that it had been nine o'clock before anybody had thought fit to wake her. Back at home, Sir Basil and his only daughter had risen at seven every morning. Sir Basil had argued that early rising, and early retiring were essentials for good health. No doubt he had been right, thought Juliana, but for all that it was delightful to be allowed to lie in bed without any hurry to rise. And, when she did go downstairs, she found that Lady Talboys was still abed so that she might—had she chosen—have lingered longer between the sheets.

When Lady Talboys did finally emerge from her room, Juliana was interested to see that she was still finely dressed. The diamonds that had glittered from her the night before were no longer there, but, even so, her morning dress was of a dark red silk cut with a very full skirt over a slightly smaller hoop. Juliana, who was wearing one of her better gowns, a green and white linen one, still felt unduly plain. She had been in the habit of having very little trimming on any of her dresses—a habit which she could now see might do in the privacy of Sir Basil's home but would not pass muster in the fashionable world. Most of her dresses were what the fashionable world called "nightgowns," full skirts worn without a hoop. Obviously in Lady Talboys's circle, the rule was that indoors, when company was expected, hoops were *de rigueur*.

Lady Talboys brought up the subject almost immediately. She asked Juliana whether her gown was the best that a provincial dressmaker could manage, and shook her head when Juliana confessed that all her dresses were made by the housemaids at home.

"This will never do, child," said Lady Talboys firmly. "I can see we must start afresh. It is unfortunate that the Reddingtons must see you in such dowdy rags; but I'll wager that the admiral will not notice, and Lady Helen is far more interested in your fortune than your looks. They are your relatives, too, child."

"Are we to have visitors? Papa never mentioned any relatives to me except for you. Shall I like them?"

"Sir Basil never knew them, child. They are cousins on *my* side of the family. To be exact Admiral Reddington is a nephew of mine, and his children are therefore your cousins. I am sure you will like the admiral, though Lady Helen may not be altogether to your taste. But I will say this for her—she's a sensible woman and means to do the best for her children."

All this meant very little to Juliana who was not yet familiar with her grandmother's prejudices. Obviously, thought Juliana, Lady Talboys must approve of the Reddingtons otherwise she would not have invited them. She was agog to see what her new relatives would be like.

"You know, it is exceedingly odd to find that one has a whole family," she confided. "I had thought that papa and I were almost alone in the world."

She liked what she saw when the Reddingtons arrived a few moments later. The admiral, a man in his fifties, was bluff and hearty—as befitted a sailor. He chucked Juliana under the chin, called her a pretty little puss and forecast that she would have plenty of admirers. He made proper condolences on the death of her father, but confessed that he had not had the pleasure of being acquainted with Sir Basil.

Lady Helen Reddington was completely unlike her husband. Where he was informal and hearty, she was formal and restrained. She smiled graciously enough when Juliana curtsied, made some polite remarks about her father's death but said little with any feeling. "I am so sorry to hear about your sad loss," she said to Juliana. "It is to be hoped that your papa left a will, and put his affairs in order."

Rather bewildered by Lady Helen's concern, Juliana thanked her kindly but said that her father had left all in order. "The will was read out after the funeral," she said, "but I was crying too much to remember what it said."

"The girl's worth at least ten thousand a year, Lady Helen," said Lady Talboys bluntly. "There's the estate, and a further fifty thousand pounds in the funds. Sir Basil was prodigiously rich. So now you know."

Lady Helen looked upset by Lady Talboys' frankness. She did not like her conversational maneuvers being so easily shown up.

"I must be glad for Miss Quincey's sake that she is so comfortably circumstanced," Lady Helen said, "but I am sure that was not on my mind! Still, you are quite an heiress, you know, Miss Quincey. Pray let me introduce to you my daughter Elizabeth and my son, James—your cousins. I hope that you will all become the closest of friends."

Juliana curtsied to her two new cousins. Both were attractive. Elizabeth Reddington was a tall willowy girl, with curling black locks and sparkling brown eyes. She stepped forward, offering her hand.

"Let us not stand upon formality," she murmured. "I am known as Lizzie by the family, and I hope you will call me that. I am sure that we will be good friends."

Her brother James was more stockily built and formal in his politeness. Without being particularly handsome, his face was pleasing and his figure neat. Juliana noted that Lizzie, like her mother, was dressed in a silk sacque dress that was the height of fashion, but that James Reddington was more subdued in his dress. He wore a tie wig, rather than a full-bottomed version, and his only jewelry was a plain signet ring.

"Charmed to make your acquaintance, Miss Quincey," he said formally, bowing over her hand. "It must always be gratifying to meet new relations, and I hope that you will think of me as one of the family. I understand from my mother that this is your first visit to the Metropolis and that you have up till now lived retired in the country. If there is aught I can do for you in town, do not hesitate to call upon my services."

"Thank you very much," replied Juliana. She was pleased by his frank and open manner, and she liked his restrained clothes. At last, she thought, here was a man who did not dress like a tailor's dummy, a man she could respect. Perhaps she was going to enjoy her stay in London after all. She looked again at James Reddington and told herself that he did not have the air of a gamester. Not all the young men were of the kind she had so unfortunately encountered at the King's Head.

"I expect the city seems rather strange to you, Miss Quincey," James Reddington was saying in kindly tones.

"I must condole with you for the death of your parent. I have never had the pleasure of meeting him, of course, but I have heard that he was a great philanthropist. The Quincey system for almshouses has been much admired among some of my acquaintances who take an interest in ameliorating the condition of the poor."

"Oh, Mr. Reddington, you don't know how glad that makes me! I had not realized that dear papa's charities were known, and I had feared that in fashionable circles they would not be rated at their true worth. It seems to me that to be in the mode, one must talk of gaming and cards rather than of doing good." Juliana felt an enormous sense of relief. Here was somebody who shared her interests, somebody who would understand her thoughts and feelings. Everybody so far she had met—Miss Humphries and Lady Talboys—had merely dismissed the late Sir Basil as a recluse. Here was a person who had heard of his life's work, and who seemed to value it correctly. She afforded Mr. Reddington her sweetest smile.

James Reddington returned it and said, "You must not judge the fashionable world too harshly, Miss Quincey. Not all of us are fribbles. I own that I am not of that set which is in vogue. I am no gamester, though I enjoy a hand at whist. I will not hazard my fortune on the fall of the dice, and that alone is enough to cast me out of the inner circle."

"So I have been told; I have heard amazing stories of the huge sums which are hazarded nightly at White's Club," said Juliana in troubled tones. She felt she might confide her worries to this sober young man. "I was dismayed to hear that gaming was so prevalent. And yet it seems that it is all the fashion to belong to White's. I find that difficult to understand."

Lizzie Reddington looked as if she would liked to have made a remark, but her brother spoke before she could utter a word.

"They play deep at White's Club," he said. "The vice and ruin for which White's has been responsible should be condemned, in my opinion. Yet, when I express my views upon this matter, I am not listened to. I could tell you such tales, Miss Quincey, of reckless extravagance, or inordinate prodigality...why only last year Sir John Denbigh flirted away his whole fortune at hazard. He lost near enough two and thirty thousand pounds to the Marquis of Peterborough in one hour at the table. In such fashion he was eventually ruined."

The mention of money seemed to stir Lady Helen's interest. For she looked up from the comfortable conversation she, the Admiral, and Lady Talboys had been having together. "What is this? Two and thirty thousand, you say?"

"I was telling Miss Quincey of Sir John Denbigh's losses," he replied, pressing his lips together in disapproval at his mother's interruption.

"What folly! I expect you already know that Lord Albemarle leaves not a shilling to his family. When he married he had near ninety thousand pounds and my lady brought him twenty-five thousand. Now all this is dissipated to a mere fourteen thousand—and that entailed away to a cousin. I am prodigiously pleased, James, that you have inherited what I flatter are my instincts for economy. How sad it must have been to have a mere gamester in the family!"

"I am decidedly fond of play, myself," said Lady Talboys rather crossly. She was irritated by the turn in the conversation. "There is a great deal of pleasure to be gained at the card table, let me tell you, Lady Helen. Besides to hazard all upon the turn of a card may be reckless folly, yet it shows, at the least, a disregard for the vulgar matter of money."

An awkward pause ensued on this pointed rebuke to Lady Helen. It was broken by the admiral saying gruffly, "Well, well, we cannot all agree on our pleasures and it would be a dull world if we could. I must go to the War Office. Will you accompany me, James? We can leave the ladies here for a comfortable chat, I am sure." Having thus broken up the conversation, he rose to go and it was with real regret that Juliana said good-bye to him and to her cousin, James Reddington.

For his part the stocky young man gave an impression of equal regret as he bent over her hand. Punctiliously he said, "I look forward to furthering my acquaintance with my newest cousin, Miss Quincey." There was a note of sincerity and warmth in his voice.

Lady Helen Reddington looked on at this bit of byplay with obvious approval, which embarrassed Juliana. "I can truly say, Miss Quincey, that dearest James has never given me a moment's worry," she went on when the gentlemen had left the room. "I am happy to say that he is of a serious disposition, and has never shown the slightest interest in the vices that are now fashionable. His principles are so firmly based and his good sense is so evident, that you will look in vain for follies in his life."

This speech was partly spoiled by Lady Talboys who wickedly interjected, "Yes, my dear Juliana, you can see that James is no rake. It is too sadly obvious."

Lizzie Reddington by Juliana's side gave an unmistakable giggle which she quickly changed to a cough. To cover up this lapse, she exclaimed, "Can I be of use to you, dear cousin? I believe that if I were to look through the clothes which you have brought from the country, I might advise you which are suitable for London wear."

"That is an excellent scheme," said Lady Talboys. "I have been telling poor Juliana that she has nothing fit to wear. I shall rely on you, Elizabeth, to help her. You and your mother have such excellent taste."

Lady Helen smiled graciously at the two girls. "I'm afraid you will find Lizzie is such a frivolous little thing, Miss Quincey. She has been too much in the world of fashion, I fear. If your influence can bring a certain gravity to her, I should be so grateful. Lizzie has need of a friend who combines good sense with an amiable disposition."

Juliana hardly knew what to reply to this, and so

remained silent. With a sinking heart she followed Lizzie Reddington upstairs. When they entered her bedchamber, she was astonished to see her companion fling herself upon the bed, sprawling with a complete lack of decorum. "Phew," said Lizzie. "What a tedious bore my brother is! I wanted to further our acquaintance, so I thought of offering to look through your clothes. James proses on so boringly. I cannot think where my brother gets it from. Papa is a dear, and even mama, though she is amazingly mercenary, is not so everlastingly full of morality!"

Juliana was shocked at these outright remarks. "I liked your brother," she said with a blush. "It seemed to me that he felt just as he ought. I have been dismayed to see how cruel and heartless young men of quality seem to be, and so it has come as a pleasant change to meet Mr. Reddington."

Lizzie Reddington gave her a glance which suggested she thought Juliana was joking. Then, as if she had decided she was serious after all, she merely said, "Well, I am glad James has found a willing listener to his orations. My mother would be glad to hear you speak well of him. She is very pleased with you, though I do not scruple to tell you that she would be pleased with any girl who had ten thousand pounds a year and thousands in the funds. Mama believes that a fortune is what is needed to make any girl acceptable. Or young man for that matter," she added with a note of gloom in her voice.

Juliana felt that some further questions were expected from her. "Do you share her sentiments?" she asked cautiously.

"Oh no, not in the least. I think it is hateful to think only of money. Why shouldn't younger sons be as eligible as their older brothers? It seems very wrong to me that an estate is always entailed to the older. What is more I am sure that a younger son is far more romantic than an older son who is always being chased by heiresses!"

These remarks, though general in their application, were uttered with such conviction that Juliana guessed that they must have some bearing on Miss Reddington's own circumstances. "Is your brother an older or younger son?" she asked. "Does he have other brothers?"

"No, you are safe there," said Lizzie bitterly. "James is the oldest in the family, and I am his only sister. He is comfortably circumstanced enough, though mama naturally hopes that he will make what she calls an advantageous match. That is what she hopes for me too. I am to have fifteen thousand pounds, which is comfortable, you see, though I am not an heiress. Mama says that I must do my best to marry well."

Juliana began to get a glimmer of what this was all about. "Forgive me," she said bluntly, "am I to understand that your heart is given to somebody of whom your mama does not approve?"

Lizzie looked frightened. "If I tell you, you will not let mama or Lady Talboys know, will you? I am in trouble enough! Even my own brother will not help me. He says that I should not be so romantical in disposition which is just the sort of hatefully moralizing thing he would say."

"I swear I will not betray your confidence," said Juliana slowly. "You know that, though I am of a serious nature, I am romantic too. My own mama ran away and eloped for love, and I am the child of that marriage. My papa believed in love. He always told me never to marry unless my affections were engaged."

"Did he really?" asked Lizzie in surprise. "My papa might let me marry whom I choose, only he is so ruled by mama that he dare not. And mama thinks that love is just so much nonsense! All she cares about is that the marriage settlement should be a large one."

"How very unpleasant for you, dear Lizzie," sympathized Juliana. "I am learning more and more about fashionable society every hour, it seems. I had not realized that its dealings were so mercenary. I can see that my poor papa would never have enjoyed himself in London. No wonder he stayed in the country. I think he must have worried a great deal about me. Perhaps that is why he wanted me to stay by him. But pray tell me of your own circumstances? Have I guessed aright?"

With a deep breath, Lizzie launched out into her tale. She did not mention names, but Juliana gathered that her outburst about younger sons had been the outpourings of a suffering heart. Lizzie had fallen in love with one of them—a younger son whom she described in dazzling terms as being both handsome, charming and kind, though unfortunately as poor as a church mouse. His family was more than respectable; it was of the highest breeding. But the family estate was to pass in its entirety to his older brother, and he was left to make his way in the world by his own exertions.

"So far mama has warned me about encouraging his attentions, but she does not know that he has offered marriage or that I have accepted," Lizzie said. "She would be furious if she did. I fear that my brother has his suspicions but he does not know anything for certain. If only, I dared tell papa, I know that *he* would allow me to do as I wish. He only wants me to be happy."

"Why do you not confide in him?" suggested Juliana.

"Why not indeed? Papa is a dear but he is the most gentle of men in the world and he tells mama *everything*. It would be useless to suppose that he could support me against her. He might try. He might even agrue on my behalf for a day or two but then soon he would tell me that he knew mama had my well-being at heart." Lizzie imitated the admiral's bluff way of speaking so perfectly that Juliana had to smile. "No," Lizzie concluded with a sigh, "there is nothing I can do. I am at my wits' end. All that is left for me is to go into a decline and die, and then mama will be sorry."

Juliana could not help laughing at this last remark. Lizzie looked such a picture of health as she said it. She wondered if the girl had been exaggerating her mother's hardness of heart, but reluctantly came to the conclusion that she was not. Lady Helen gave the impression of being a just woman, but not one of any great sensibility. And, it had already been clear from her conversation that she valued fortune and money above all else. There was something a little bit vulgar about that, thought Juliana. She did not know how to comfort her new cousin and asked, "Is there anything I can do to help you?"

Lizzie looked at her suspiciously. "I don't know that I can trust you, Juliana, just yet," she declared frankly. "If you are going to make a match of it with James, then I fear you must become my enemy."

"Marry your brother! Surely that is rather premature?" said Juliana laughing. "I have just arrived in London, remember."

"I can see that you do not know how marriages are arranged," said Lizzie with gloom. "I know for certain that my mother would like to secure your fortune for James, and James, himself, seems to have taken a liking to you. Why, you must be aware that he cannot abide gaming and frivolous pursuits. You are just the sort of girl of whom he would approve—serious-minded and not scatterbrained like me."

"Well, nobody has consulted *my* sentiments on this," said Juliana uncomfortably. "I am sure that Lady Helen can have no such plan in mind! Why, she scarcely knows me! But I can assure you, Lizzie, that your secret is safe with me. Why, I could not tell, even if I chose, for you have not told me the name of your young man."

"No," agreed Lizzie naively. "I could not be sure of you. Perhaps if we become good friends, I shall feel able to confide in you further, but it is more than I dare for the present."

Juliana changed the topic of conversation. "If we are to be friends, then you can help me, as you suggested, by looking at my clothes. I fear that the ones I have brought with me will not do at all. Perhaps you would advise me."

Lizzie Reddington agreed with alacrity. Juliana was

amused to see how seriously she took the task, carefully looking through armfuls of every kind of garment, pondering an apron here, looking carefully at a petticoat there. At last she had put on one side a small heap of four dresses. "There," she said with firmness, "those are the only ones that are wearable, and they all need extra trimming. The others simply will not do, my dear Juliana. They are quite out of vogue and you would only be laughed at, if you wore them."

"This means I shall have to spend hours and hours in shopping for materials and having dresses made," said Juliana gloomily. She had not realized just how accurate her grandmother had been when she said that she had not a rag to wear.

"How delightful," said Lizzie. "I should enjoy having new clothes. For you cannot be pinched in the purse, and it means you can have all the pleasure of being entirely in the mode. How provokingly fashionable you will be."

Lizzie then lectured Juliana on the importance of being in the mode, and by the time the two girls went downstairs again Juliana felt she had learned a great deal. She would need, she had heard, special dresses for court functions with extra large hoops and feathers in the head-dresses. She would need at least a dozen ballgowns for assemblies, ten or so silk sacque dresses for receiving or paying visits, and nobody would think her in vogue unless she wore at least part of her fortune on her back.

For outside wear, she learned she might forgo her hoop, and content herself with panniers and slightly shorter walking-out dresses. For traveling or for riding, at least one, and perhaps two, riding habits would be required—a jacket and waistcoat to be worn over a special petticoat. A special cocked hat, or a so called jockey cap, would be worn with the habit. Hats, indeed, would be very important. The influence of the French court had meant that the *bergère* or shepherdess style was much in vogue. Hats of straw, chip, or cane were in fashion, worn either plain for informal wear or "dressed" with silk and ribbons for the more modish. Finally, it was *de rigueur* to have at least one masquerade dress, which should preferably be a magnificent fancy dress in the historical style. Lesser females, Juliana heard, hired theirs from Jackson's Habit-Warehouse in Covent Garden. Lady Helen—and therefore it was to be assumed Lady Talboys, also— would not have felt happy with such economical straits.

As well as discovering that she would be expected to spend a fortune on her clothes, Juliana had learned about her behavior. Sir Basil had brought her up very simply to believe that flirting was wrong. Lizzie Reddington laughed at this and said that every girl indulged in a little flirtation. " 'Tis not to go too far," she warned, "for a reputation may soon be ruined." But she went on to describe ways of looking with the eyes, laughing softly, and tender smiles, that made Juliana blush. One thing her cousin said made Juliana uneasy. "Of course it would not do to be discovered in a compromising situation," said Lizzie seriously. "It is one thing to let a gentleman kiss your hand, but I, for one, think it too great a liberty to give my lips to anybody."

"Not even to your lover?" asked Juliana, teasing Lizzie, but also anxious to discover her answer.

"Oh Lud, no. I have no mind to be ruined," said Lizzie, "and ruined I should be if those hateful cats of chaperones discovered such conduct."

That last remark made Juliana apprehensive. She could not help thinking that perhaps the encounter she had had in the stableyard was more serious than she had thought. Could it be that her reputation was in jeopardy? She thought of Miss Humphries and prayed that the elderly governess would keep her promise not to mention the fact.

"Are you sure that if a girl were found kissing somebody, she would be ruined?" she asked Lizzie.

"Ruined is perhaps too harsh a word," admitted Lizzie, "but she would be thought fast and that would never do. Let us say that I should not like to be caught in a compromising situation myself. It would be a hard thing to have to live down, unless one might immediately announce one's betrothal."

Back in the drawing room there were further ordeals for Juliana to undergo. She had to sit quietly and try not to blush while Lady Helen Reddington told Lady Talboys how much she approved of Juliana's modest demeanor. "She will take very well," said Lady Helen in a way that made Juliana want to squirm. "Yes, my dear, you have my fullest approval. I am sure you will be a good influence on my dearest Lizzie. And I can see that dearest James is quite taken with you."

When Lady Helen had finally taken her leave, not without further remarks about Juliana's fortune including a query of whether she had any trustees, Juliana could not help heaving a sigh of relief. "I am not sorry they have left, grandmama," she admitted. "Indeed I do like both Mr. Reddington and his sister very much, but I wish their mama would not talk about me so. Lizzie says that she wishes her son to marry me, because of my fortune."

"Lizzie is correct," said Lady Talboys with her usual frankness. "I cannot like James Reddington, myself, but then I always was partial to a rake, my dear. That is why I did not like your father, I suspect. But there is no denying you could do worse. There is bad breeding on Lady Helen's side, but the Reddingtons are comfortably circumstanced and Mr. Reddington must have large expectations. I'd lay ten to one that he would be a pattern card of virtue as a husband, too."

"Must I be married off so soon?" reproached Juliana. "Why, I have not so much as tasted the pleasures of high society yet."

"I am glad that you look forward to them," said the

old lady with satisfaction. "I was beginning to fear that you were a milk-and-water miss who was going to complain about the frivolity of the world. There is no haste to betroth you. With your face, and your fortune, there will be plenty of offers, I have no doubt. But not if you wear the clothes you brought from the country! That must be our first task! What Sir Basil was thinking of to let you go around dressed as if you were a Quaker or one of those newfangled Methodists, I do not know! I must not speak ill of the dead, but I hope you will take note of what I say, Juliana. I am a better guide to such things as clothes than your papa was, even if I am a disagreeable old woman who is no better than she ought to be."

With these stirring words, she swept off Juliana for a long consultation with her dresser, Miss Pinkerton. Miss Pinkerton, who had been Lady Talboys's personal maid for the last forty years, was formidable—thin, elderly, and none too polite, thought Juliana. "Pinkerton knows everything about clothes," said Lady Talboys, preparing herself for an afternoon nap. "She will supervise your purchases. Follow her advice and you will not regret it. Now Pinkerton, I trust you to turn out my granddaughter like a lady of quality. The girl's fresh from the country and has nothing to wear."

"If you will forgive the liberty, Miss," said Pinkerton, staring carefully at Juliana's modest gray dress, "I think you need an entirely new look. We have a lot to do."

They were prophetic words. Three or four hours later, Juliana's every limb ached with standing around to be measured. She felt she was almost cross-eyed with the effort of examining materials in the various mercers' shops. Silks, flowered tabbies, satins, paduasoys, lutestrings, damasks, camlets, crepes and calicoes—she had admired and examined them all, to the accompaniment of Pinkerton's expert advice. An enormous quantity of packages had been carried into her grandmother's carriage from the mercers.

Then came the matter of buying some made-up dresses from the mantua-makers. "For you cannot wear the garments you have with you, Miss," warned Pinkerton. "Not without them all being unmade and re-trimmed." Finally, they visited two or three milliners. Several charming straw and chip confections were bought there and then; others, dressed with the silks and ribbons they had purchased at the mercers, were ordered. It seemed as if milliners and seamstresses would be burning the midnight oil all over London.

Juliana had ventured only one protest. "Is it really necessary to purchase quite so many silks?" she had asked the grim Miss Pinkerton. "Do I truly need a dozen pairs of white stockings? At home I only possessed three, and those were not white."

"I should be failing in my duty if I told you otherwise," said Pinkerton grimly. "What we have purchased is hardly adequate. It is just a start."

Only one other incident marred the harmony of the afternoon. Pinkerton had shown the utmost disapproval when Juliana had attempted to distribute pennies to some ragged children who were clustering outside one of the milliners' shops. Pinkerton had not said anything, but she had sniffed in such a way as to make her views perfectly clear.

Obviously she had mentioned this to Lady Talboys. For the old lady had said to Juliana, "I am satisfied that we are now beginning to set you up as a young lady of fashion. But how am I to persuade you to give up these very odd habits that you have no doubt picked up from your philanthropic papa? In the country, you may have been accustomed to handing out pennies to the workers' children. But it will not do in London. They will cluster around you and draw attention to you in a way that is very improper for a girl who is not yet married. Gentle-men, in particular, a child, do not like a girl who gets herself talked about. It may be proper for a married lady to exercise herself in good works upon her husband's estate —though I by no means favor too much exertion, myself —but nothing could be more deplorable than for you to get a name for making an *exhibition* of charity."

Juliana hardly knew what to reply. After a pause she had said quietly, "I apologize, grandmama, if I embarrassed Pinkerton. It was thoughtless of me. But I do not think that I can give up all attempts to ameliorate the shocking conditions of the poor. Papa brought me up to think of others less fortunate than myself, and I consider it nothing less than my duty as a Christian so to do."

"Well, child," said the old lady brusquely, "all that is hoity-toity. You can do your duty as a Christian in private. There is no need for you to show it off to all the world in the public street. I am sure that I make a point of looking after my servants and their dependents, but I do not puff it off so that everybody knows."

Juliana felt like making a retort, but what was there to say? She contented herself with adding, "I will try to do my good works in secret, but I think it is a poor sort of world where such good works have to be done in secret. I really do."

"You may think all you like, child, but you'll do well to think twice before making a show of yourself. Come, I will not lecture you further. Instead, I plan to teach you how to play cards this evening. You have naught fit to wear, Pinkerton says even the made-up dresses must be altered. What better way to spend the evening than to teach you how to gamble a little?"

Juliana wanted to protest but she saw the sense of it. If society was full of gamesters, she must at least know what were the games they played. To her surprise, she discovered that she quite enjoyed them. True, some of them required little skill, depending mainly on chance and what hand was dealt. Others demanded the exercise of judgment, foresight and quick wits. She found that she was quite absorbed by the fall of the cards, and that occasionally she could beat her grandmother. Possibly Lady Talboys was losing to encourage her protégé, but all the same it was fun.

To teach her how to bid, Lady Talboys had borrowed a large box of buttons from the formidable Pinkerton. "I shall not fleece you for real coins yet, my dear," she explained. "But 'tis necessary you should learn to game a little. Cards may be required of you. I, myself, am very partial to 'em and receive many invitations to afternoon card games with other ladies. I should wish to take you along with me, and that I cannot do unless you know a little about the games. There is nothing so helpful to a young girl than an acquaintance with London's hostesses, and that you will get if you accompany me."

"Thank you, grandmama," said Juliana submissively. She discovered that she could play a trick with trumps and could not resist an exclamation of pleasure.

"You may not wish to be a gamester, child," said the old lady, amused by Juliana's sudden enthusiasm. "But I vow that with a little more practice you would be a veritable faro's daughter. That is what they call the true female gamesters, of which I am not yet one, I thank heaven. I vow that skill at cards must be in your blood. 'Twas no doubt inherited from me. Say what you will, Juliana, you are a gamester at heart."

Three

Juliana felt distinctly nervous. All around her were the pink of the *ton*—men and women of the noblest, richest, and ablest families in Britain—beings from a different world, she could not help thinking. Everywhere she looked, she could see glittering jewels—diamonds, rubies, emeralds, and pearls shining from rich fabrics, or from the powdered hair of the ladies, or winking from shoe buckles. There was a king's ransom in jewels, alone, in this ballroom, she thought. And the men, in their knee breeches, embroidered waistcoats, and richly colored coats were as fine as the ladies, with their elaborate wigs, their lace at the throat and at the wrist, and jewels flashing from their fingers.

Juliana, herself, was beautifully gowned. Under the aegis of Miss Pinkerton, she had chosen a heavy white satin, embroidered with silver thread at both hem and bodice. Its rich folds parted to reveal a blue embroidered silk petticoat. Small seed pearls had been sewn into the silver embroidery scattered over the petticoat, the bodice, and the hem of the skirt. Round her neck Juliana wore a delicately made sapphire and pearl necklace, with matching small earrings. Her ripe chestnut curls had been powdered, as was the fashion, and among the powdery locks glinted small sapphires and pearls.

By her side, Lady Talboys was dressed *en grande dame*. For this night, she had chosen a black heavy silk with startling red embroidery. Fine Brussels lace at the old lady's wrists and bodice softened the austere effect of the black. She was wearing the Talboys rubies, a matching necklace, bracelet, and earrings which were the envy of all her acquaintants. With her silver cane, and her jeweled quizzing glass, she looked extremely fashionable. "You may think I look a sight all dressed up so finely, and me an old woman in her eighties," she said to Juliana with mock ferocity, "but I tell you that is the only way to go on. My beauty, such as it was, vanished years ago and now I dress up my wrinkles with rubies and lace. They are not stones for you young girls. The bloom of youth has no need for rubies, but they suit us harridans, who must dazzle with jewels where we can no longer dazzle with beauty."

Once again, Juliana hardly knew how to give a polite answer. She was only just beginning to get used to Lady Talboys's rather disconcerting remarks. It was with relief, though, that she saw the familiar figure of Lady Helen coming toward them. Like Lady Talboys, Lady Helen was glittering with jewels—in her case, diamonds. Her tall rather over-powering figure was dressed in a stiff brocade with elaborate embroidery. She looked a fine figure of a woman but not the sort of person, thought Juliana, with whom you would be comfortable. She was all grandeur and graciousness. Juliana couldn't help noticing that her diamonds were a little less fine than the ones Lady Talboys had been wearing the first evening of her arrival.

"Dear Miss Quincey," said Lady Helen with condescension, giving Juliana three rather lifeless fingers in salute as the girl curtsied. "This must be your first ball. You look very becoming, child."

"She's a taking little thing, is she not?" said Lady Talboys. "No height, of course, but that can't be helped. Let us hope the gentlemen call her a pocket Venus."

"I am sure James will think so," said Lady Helen with a meaning smile at Juliana. The girl did not care for the smile. It implied that there was an understanding between her and her cousin. She liked James Reddington. She approved of him. In a fashionable world where it seemed that most young men were wastrels and rakehells, James Reddington must come as a pleasant change. But she was not happy with Lady Helen's matchmaking efforts.

Fortunately the two women had other things to talk about, and they both engaged on a course of gossip which Juliana found uninteresting. "Lady Mary Coke was robbed t'other night under the very noses of the lamps in Hyde Park . . . a new fashion which My Lady Hervey has brought from Paris. It is a tin funnel covered with ribband, holding water to keep bouquets fresh . . . Lady Lincoln gives a prodigious assembly but she has not invited the duchess . . . 'Tis said she will make a little opposition dinner . . ."

The flow of names gave Juliana time to look about her. She had never before seen such a display of wealth, enough—she could not help thinking—to put right the condition of every pauper in the kingdom. The women, with their fine clothes, were what she had expected from London society. But it was the men who astonished her. They were so unlike the country gentlemen who had hitherto filled her life. Sir Basil had been in the habit of dressing soberly. During the day he would usually wear breeches, riding boots, and a sober colored frock coat. In the evening, though, he always changed into satin knee breeches, he was not in the habit of wearing jewels, other

55

than a single fine signet ring. Juliana had not been ready for the sheer magnificence of the men around her.

She knew it was the fashion for men of vogue to wear embroidered coats, waistcoats, lace ruffles, and precious stones amidst that lace. But these men simply dripped with jewelry. Gem stones of great price gleamed from the lace at their neck, or sparkled from their fingers. These were men of a world Juliana knew nothing about. She might have thought such finery effeminate but for the jeweled swords carried by many. Already she had learned that these brightly plumaged birds of fashion were not what they seemed. If a quarrel should break out, then swords or pistols would immediately be brought into play and a duel fixed. A man of fashion might look like a mannequin, but underneath he could as well be a man of violence. Under the surface finery ran a strong current of recklessness, outrageous behavior, vicious practices, and what seemed an almost pointless extravagance.

She had been warned by Lady Talboys not to show how the fashionable world shocked her. In particular, the old lady had cautioned her about any utterance which might give an impression that she was interested in philanthropy and good works.

"Nothing could be more disastrous, child," she said, "than a reputation for being a bluestocking, as they are known. Gentlemen do not like to be reminded of their follies or lectured about their duties, and I am sure that is not surprising. I should not enjoy it, myself. So, no words of censure! Put those thoughts of your papa's quite out of your mind, child. They have no place at a ball. You are here to enjoy yourself, not to think on disagreeable subjects like poverty."

Juliana had accepted what Lady Talboys told her, though not without some inner rebellion. But she did not, at this moment, feel much enjoyment. Seated beside her grandmother, who was busy talking across her to Lady Helen, she felt very much an outsider.

She could see other young girls who were chattering

to young bucks, flirting with their fans, using their eyes to charm and tease; others were on the dance floor, swaying with their full skirts, curtsying and suiting their steps to the music. Juliana had had some hurried lessons in the dance figures, and she yearned to try them out with a real partner.

In particular, she could not help noticing one young lady who seemed the cynosure of all eyes. She was a dazzling blonde, and her hair had been left unpowdered to fall in golden ringlets on her bare shoulders. Tall, slender, and very stately, she stood with graceful unconcern like a Greek statue, her perfect profile almost immobile, accepting homage from a variety of men. Eventually, unable to smother her curiosity, Juliana broke into her grandmother's conversation to ask who she was.

" 'Tis our reigning beauty, child—Charlotte Milgrave. She has broken hearts everywhere, and it is said that even the Marquis of Peterborough is taken with her. She is universally acknowledged to have pleasing manners and great priority, and I personally find her a dead bore."

"Come, come," said Lady Helen Reddington with disapproval. "Such criticism of Miss Milgrave is hardly fair. I own that I cannot think that the Marquis of Peterborough will be such a good match. Of course, he is immensely rich, but so wild! A better behaved young woman than Miss Milgrave I have never encountered. I would have been glad if . . ." She broke off what she had been about to say.

Maliciously, Lady Talboys finished the sentence for her. "You would have been glad if your son James had had success with the beauty, but unfortunately the Marquis, who is a bigger catch, intervened. Is that not so?"

Charlotte Milgrave is not only amiable; she has a marriage portion of forty-thousand pounds which you will acknowledge, Lady Talboys, is not to be ignored. That alone must make her a good match for any fond mother. But she is modest and sensible, and in addition has not let her head be turned by the admiration she receives. In short she is a paragon of all the virtues."

"In short, she is a bore, as I said," put in the outspoken Lady Talboys. "She may have every virtue, but she has little wit, few brains and, I think, not the slightest inkling of a sense of humor. What is more, Lady Helen, you know that. Not that James has noticed, and if he did, he might think it no drawback."

As she spoke, Juliana noticed Mr. Reddington making his way toward them. He was dressed more elaborately than when she had last seen him, but even so, he was not remarkable for finery. His coat was of carmelite brown velvet and his breeches of matching brown silk. The only touch of opposing color was his waistcoat which was green silk, embroidered with brown and yellow. He wore only a single ruffle of lace at the wrist, and a modest fall at the throat. A modest diamond ring on his right hand and a small pin at the neck were his only jewelry.

Everything about him denoted a certain solidity, as if to say: "Here is a young man of solid worth and serious tastes." There was nothing extravagant either in his clothes or his air, though the neatness of his dress argued care in its choosing. Juliana had no doubt that James Reddington, like other young men, could use the sword he wore at his side, but she could not imagine him taking part in a duel at dawn. The undercurrent of recklessness and danger, that she could sense in others, was lacking. She told herself that she liked him the better for it. He was a young man of whom she felt her papa could have approved, and that must make her feel a liking for him. She smiled at him with a sincerity which the sharp-eyed Lady Helen did not fail to note.

Mr. Reddington bowed over her hand, and asked if she would like to take her place in the set which was just forming on the dance floor. Pleased that at last she would have the chance to try out her steps in the glittering assembly of the ballroom, Juliana accepted with enthusiasm. She was grateful that he had asked her.

At first she had to concentrate on not forgetting her steps, and it was only possible for her to make very desultory conversation. But it did not seem to matter. Mr. Reddington kept up a flow of small talk, mostly of information about the London season which he considered she ought to know. After a few minutes Juliana began to regain her confidence and was able to look round a little more. James Reddington, she noticed, performed his part in the dance with propriety rather than grace. He was a correct, but not a dashing dancer.

He had changed his conversational approach, and was now asking her about her home, the scenery there, and whether she missed the familiar places where she had lived. Thinking of such things, her eyes filled with tears, and she said with a sincerity that she could not hide, "I must confess, Mr. Reddington, that I feel a stranger here in London. I was not expecting such magnificence as I see this evening. The splendor seems odd to me."

"I believe that it must be counted a virtue to be a stranger to extravagance," said James Reddington, making a ponderous little joke. "If your upbringing has failed to teach you the vices and follies of the fashionable world, you are to be congratulated on your ignorance, Miss Quincey. I for one am delighted to think that you are not wholly bent on frivolity, as are so many of our young ladies."

Juliana was emboldened by his approval to ask, "Is it true, Mr. Reddington, that I must learn to play like a gamester? My papa abhorred games of chance, and he was opposed to habits which he thought encouraged wasteful expenditure whether among rich or poor. Yet Lady Talboys tells me that I shall be considered simply gothic and ridiculously prudish, if I do not play."

"I would not for the world criticize Lady Talboys," said Mr. Reddington solemnly. "I am sure that there can be no opposition to the *rational* enjoyment of the occasional game of cards. But I should be deceiving you, if I did not tell you that the reigning fashion among both men and women of quality is to indulge in all kinds of gaming —cards, wagers, and lotteries. These last encourage a spirit of speculation and gambling not only among the better sort in society, but also among the lower orders of people. Thousands have their morals corrupted and fall victim to the insinuating and tempting allurements of such places like cockpits, gambling dens, and other low places."

"And is it true that men of quality will wager sums on the most unlikely occurrences?" Juliana asked timidly. Mr. Reddington seemed a fund of information, even if he was rather long-winded in his replies. She was anxious to know if the kiss that had been stolen from her at the King's Head was part of the normal misbehavior of the gambling set.

"My dear Miss Quincey, there are men of quality, of good breeding, and otherwise of respectability, who will bet on anything, however trivial," said Mr. Reddington with distinct disapproval. "I am not one of the gaming set. I will occasionally wager a few guineas at cards, when conviviality demands it, but I do not sit up all night hazarding a fortune like George Selwyn or the Marquis of Peterborough."

"Are both those gentlemen known for their gambling?" asked Juliana cautiously. Now at least, she might discover more about the odious marquis.

"Selwyn is an eccentric. Peterborough is the leader of the wildest set of all. In his company you will find not only reckless folly and extravagance, but a complete lack of morality and temperance. He is, I fear, a libertine of the first order."

Juliana longed to ask more but prudence suggested it would not be a good idea. Something told her that further questions might make Mr. Reddington wonder why she took such an interest in the marquis. James Reddington, she thought, had a habit of talking rather like Miss Humphries. He would go on about such horrors as immorality and intemperance, without explaining exactly what the Marquis of Peterborough had *done*. She supposed it was nice to meet somebody who shared her outlook on gambling and fashionable folly, but she wished that James Reddington would be a little less pompous.

As she moved in the steps of the dance, she cast her eyes round the room to see whether a different topic of conversation might present itself. To her delight, she noticed Lizzie Reddington, beautifully gowned in pink silk with a white embroidered petticoat. Lizzie was looking unusually pretty. A soft flush was on her cheeks, and her dark eyes shone like stars. Juliana could not help noticing that she looked up into her partner's face with an adoring expression. Was this the young man Lizzie had told her about? Certainly he looked the part. He was tall and slender, dressed in the dashing costume of an officer in the Grenadier Guards. His face was pleasant and his features were agreeable. Juliana thought she had seen more handsome men, but she could not deny that he was very good looking.

"Why, there is your sister," she cried out with pleasure. "Who is the young officer with whom she is dancing, pray?"

James Reddington did not reply directly. He was obviously not pleased by what he saw. Juliana wished she had stayed silent about Lizzie's partner. Eventually he said, "If you would like to further your acquaintance with my sister, I will endeavor to bring her over to you, if I may find a minute when she is not engaged to dance. Elizabeth is still young and finds a natural pleasure in frivolity which I hope she will outgrow. Her lively spirits sometimes overwhelm her natural good sense, I fear."

This daunting description of the gay and chattering Lizzie Reddington silenced Juliana for a moment or two. Then she said carefully, "I am sure that your sister would never let her lively spirits overrule her good sense, Mr.

Reddington. I find her delightful company, and I hope we may become firm friends."

"I hope so too, Miss Quincey," said the earnest young man at her side, as they left the dance floor after the music had stopped. "A closer relationship between you and my family is what I most ardently desire. I will bring Elizabeth over to you late in the evening, but now I see that Lady Talboys is anxious for you."

Lady Talboys had, in fact, procured a partner for Juliana—and a startling figure he was too. "This is Sir William Goring Pelham," said the old lady with a distinct twinkle, as she introduced him to her granddaughter. "Sir William is always anxious to make the acquaintance of new young ladies, my dear. I am sure you will find him a charming partner. He is a great favorite among the ladies." Juliana thought that the last sentence was uttered not so much as a compliment to the young man, but more as a *warning* to her. She curtsied low, giving herself time to look up under her fluttering lashes at the astonishing man in front of her.

Sir William Goring Pelham was certainly strikingly dressed. He wore coat and breeches of striped yellow silk shot with green, with a white waistcoat. All were embroidered with gold foil in wreaths of flowers round the borders and seam, and the silk ground was covered with single brilliants and spangles. Juliana guessed that the outfit must have cost him hundreds of pounds. It was unmistakably noticeable, and all eyes were drawn to him. He had taken such evident pains with his toilet, that Juliana wondered if he were a little effeminate.

"Ravished to make your acquaintance, Miss Quincey," said Sir William with an affected drawl. "You're new to the *haut ton,* what? It pleases you, I hope? Not too terribly fatigued by it all, I hope?"

"Not at all, sir," answered Juliana submissively. She did not much like Sir William's way of speaking, and could not for the life of her think of any topic of conversation. With mincing steps Sir William led her back to the ballroom floor. In desperation, as the silence seemed to stretch from minute to minute, Juliana looked round and caught sight of the young man with whom Lizzie Reddington had been dancing. He was standing in a group, laughing at some remark, but Juliana noticed that his eyes kept straying back to where Lizzie stood talking to Lady Helen. "Who is that young man, pray, Sir William?" she asked. "You will understand that I am a country bumpkin. I do not know half of the people here tonight."

"The young man in regimentals?" drawled Sir William, taking a quizzing glass, heavily encrusted with jewels, out of his breast pocket, and fixing his gaze upon Lizzie Reddington's former partner. "Oh *him!* A veritable nobody, Miss Quincey. Handsome enough, I'll allow. Regimentals give a man an air, even when he's of no importance. Robert Torrington's his name. Younger son, you know. I vow he's not the sort of fellow would add to your consequence."

Despite his sneering tone, Juliana persisted. "I am afraid that the gentleman's name means very little to me, Sir William. But I have a particular interest in knowing more about him. Is the Torrington family a respectable one?"

"Respectable, but hardly more. Older brother's an acquaintance of mine. Fine fellow, Gerald. One of my dearest friends. Has a decided air of fashion. But young Robert's a nobody, I assure you, Miss Quincey. But lud . . . allow me to suggest that your interest in that particular sprig is rather singular."

Juliana felt embarrassed. It must indeed look rather particular for her to be inquiring so closely, but of course she could not explain to Sir William. Her reasons for wanting to know were simply that she hoped to learn more about Lizzie's lover. She could hardly tell him that! Somewhat rattled by his evident disapproval of her inquiries, she said to him: "Pray, Sir William, is the state of the poor in this city always so wretched? I have been most shocked by the hordes of ragged children in the streets."

As soon as the words left her mouth, she realized they had been a mistake. In the confusion of not being able to explain her interest in Robert Torrington, she had forgotten Lady Talboys's warnings about being a blue-stocking. Sir William Goring Pelham's reaction left her in no doubt that the warning had been well founded. His mouth pursed with disapproval, as if she had brought up some indecent topic. He raised his eyebrows, and gave her what she could only describe as a withering stare.

"Truly, Miss Quincey," he drawled, "I know nothin' at all about the poor, save that I am told that they are always with us. That sort of thing's left to my man of business. Very much better to deal with it than I am. See no sense in settin' myself up as a philanthropist. Always considered that sort of thing a dreadful bore."

"I am sorry to remark on it, Sir William," said Juliana in what she hoped was a casual tone. "My papa was most interested in charitable works, you see."

"Very worthy of him, to be sure," tittered Sir William with an ill-concealed sneer. It was the last remark he made before the dance ended. He took her back to Lady Talboys's side, thanked her with a few murmured commonplaces and made his way back to a throng of other exquisitely dressed men. Juliana could see him laughing and joking among them, and she could only hope that she was not the subject of his mirth. But a suspicion lingered that she was. Something about the way Sir William let his quizzing glass pause on her, and the way the men round him subjected her to intense stares, made her think that he was already telling the tale of her uncouth interest in the poor.

"I fear that Sir William and I did not see eye to eye, grandmama," she said to Lady Talboys. She rather hoped that the old lady would be sympathetic.

"That fribble is a frightful creature, my dear, but there's no denying he has a certain influence. You may think in private that he is not worth a moment's thought, and I may agree with you—in private. But his good opinion is worth having, and his bad opinion worth avoiding. A man like that makes a great deal of mischief if he so chooses. The power of the creature lies in his malicious tongue. I only hope that you were not rude to him. I tried to give you a hint."

"I was not rude," said Juliana slowly, "but I believe I bored him."

"Well, there's no use crying over spilt milk. Sir William is not the only power in society," said her grandmother bracingly. "He's known as the Golden Exquisite, for his riches and his fine clothes, but he is not yet the ruler in society. You will survive his bad opinion, child, though I had hoped to avoid it. I am sure that with your entrancing looks, other gentlemen will not be put off by by Sir William's remarks."

Other gentlemen, it seemed, were not put off, and Juliana found herself with several partners. She was beginning to feel that perhaps the evening was not such a terrible ordeal. Some of the young men made encouraging compliments, and it seemed that—as long as she kept off dangerous subjects—she was quite an acceptable partner. Her confidence began to blossom, and she felt more kindly disposed toward the fashionable world.

Seeing that the girl was launched, her grandmother had escaped to the cardroom, leaving Juliana in the care of Lady Helen. It was with pleasure, therefore, that Juliana saw James Reddington fulfilling his promise and bringing over his sister Lizzie toward them both. Lizzie, flushed and happy, was obviously enjoying herself, and if her eyes did stray towards a certain young gentleman, she was discreet enough to try to conceal her glances. Juliana only noticed because her attention had already been drawn to the couple.

"My dear Juliana, what a lovely dress!" chattered Lizzie. "Why, you look even lovelier than Charlotte Milgrave. What is more I think she knows it! She's been looking down that aristocratic nose of hers all evening at you."

"I'm sure I can't compare with her," replied Juliana modestly. "She's such a lovely blonde. Mind you, Lizzie, I think you are looking perfectly ravishing, yourself."

"Both of you look exceedingly well," said James Reddington seriously, "I hardly know which bears the palm, though I must rebuke you, Elizabeth. I am sure that Miss Milgrave is too high-principled to look down her nose at anybody. Now, if you two young ladies will excuse me, I shall fetch you both a glass of lemonade."

Lizzie Reddington made a little grimace as her brother moved off. "James approves of Charlotte," she said. "I thought at one point he was going to propose to her. I'm glad he hasn't. She is too chilly for my liking. I'd much prefer *you* as a sister in law."

This frank remark made Juliana smile. "Well, Lizzie," she said daringly, "I have seen your young man, and I think him very handsome. It is Robert Torrington whom you love, is it not?"

"If only we are allowed to marry! Oh, Juliana, what shall I do? It is so heartbreaking only to be able to have one dance with him, and to have to pretend that I do not care for him! You have no idea how perfectly horrid it is to fall in love and not to be able to tell anybody about it!"

"You know, I think I ought to meet Mr. Torrington," said Juliana thoughtfully. "Not for my own enjoyment, Lizzie, but because it might be useful if I could make a friend of him. After all, I might be able to act as a sort of go-between. I could pass messages between you, and people would think he was paying attention to me, rather than to you."

Lizzie Reddington clasped her hands. "That's a marvelous idea! I will tell Robert just as soon as I get a chance and I know that he . . . Oh!" The exclamation was forced from her, as she noticed a tall dark figure walking towards them. "Why, Juliana, how droll! I vow 'tis the Marquis of Peterborough, coming toward us! His eyes are fixed on you, my dear! Well, what a conquest, to be sure! I did not know he was your admirer!"

"Hush, Lizzie!" Juliana whispered hurriedly. "He is no such thing."

She stole a look at the man who so casually was walking toward them. He was undoubtedly the man she had last met in the stableyard of the King's Head. The Marquis of Peterborough was approaching with cool confidence. She had met him when he had been wearing the buckskin breeches and riding coat of the country gentleman. Tonight he was all magnificence. His silk coat and breeches were in midnight blue, embroidered with silver thread. Silver lace, of a kind Juliana had never before set eyes on, trimmed his impeccably cut coat, and fell in several ruffles at the wrist and throat. His waistcoat was white silk, with more silver embroidery, and the same embroidered theme was taken up by the clocks on his tight stockings. A single diamond glittered at his throat. Compared with the spangles and brilliants of Sir William's clothes, the marquis was plainly dressed. Yet he conveyed an impression, thought Juliana, of magnificence which quite outshone poor spangled Sir William.

His mere presence seemed to draw all eyes. To save herself from being flurried, Juliana swept down very low into a particularly graceful curtsy, casting her eyes upon the floor to avoid that hateful gaze of his. She hoped that her fan would hide the rich blush that was already mantling her cheeks. She could sense Lizzie Reddington agog with curiosity beside her.

The marquis gave a lazy bow. He cast a thoughtful glance upon Juliana as if summing her up. "Miss Quincey, we have met before. I am delighted to have this opportunity for a more formal meeting. Our first encounter was so hurried, was it not? Besides, I have a commission to perform. Allow me, Miss Reddington," he added, casually nodding to Lizzie.

Juliana straightened up to meet those mocking eyes for the second time. She took a deep breath to steady her fluttering nerves. "We have not yet been formally introduced, I think, sir," she said with icy politeness, affecting not to know who he was.

"Why, Juliana, I will perform the introductions," said Lizzie Reddington quickly and eagerly. "This is the Marquis of Peterborough . . . Miss Quincey, my cousin," she said, turning to him.

"Thank you, Miss Reddington, for observing the proprieties for us. I am your obedient servant, Miss Quincey. Now perhaps you will feel free to give me a moment of your time. For I have something to return to you in the way of a token."

With these mocking words, he handed Juliana a small package with a flourish.

For a moment she could not think what it might contain. She said in puzzled tones, "This is for me?" as she opened the paper. When she saw the contents, a wave of anger welled up in her heart.

It was the glove that he had taken from her unresisting grasp that afternoon in the stableyard.

She did not pause to think. Forgetting the bystanders, forgetting all control, she took out the offending glove and cast it straight at those mocking eyes. It hit the marquis on the cheek, and fell at his feet.

The man in front of her was perfectly still. Only his eyes and the way that his face seemed to drain of blood, showed how great was his anger. There was a pause during which Juliana felt that she wanted the ground to swallow her up. "I am sorry that the return of your glove should have so offended you, Miss Quincey," said the marquis in quiet tones. There was infinite menace in his words. Then with a faultless, very formal bow, he turned on his heel.

From behind a mist of unshed tears, Juliana saw him walk away and join a group of young men who had Miss Milgrave in their midst. The hum and chatter of the assembly, which had seemed for those few seconds to be entirely hushed, started up again slightly louder than before.

Somebody tapped her on the shoulder. Half-blinded with emotion, Juliana turned round to see James Reddington. He had stooped to pick up the offending glove, which he had placed in his own pocket. Without saying anything he swept her on to the floor where a dance was forming.

Juliana could not trust her own voice for several minutes. It was all that she could do to take her part in the dance, without bursting into sobs. As she wrestled with her emotions, she could see the men and women round her looking at her with sly curiosity. She fought for mastery over herself. Eventually, she attained a modicum of calm, and was able to say to her partner, "Thank you, Mr. Reddington. I believe I should not have lost my temper, but the Marquis of Peterborough was teasing me so." It was not much of an explanation. But it was the best she could manage. She assumed that it would be overheard and reported as part of the gossip.

James Reddington looked very solemn, but he started a flow of small talk for which she was very grateful. It gave her time to recover. He was doing his best to help her get over a very difficult moment, she knew. As she took part in this parody of unconcerned behavior, she could not help noticing that the marquis had just brought the beautiful Miss Milgrave into the dance. For once the statuesque beauty looked almost animated and even seemed to blush at her partner's obvious complimentary remarks. Well, thought Juliana, I wish her luck of him; nothing in the world would persuade me to dance with the odious marquis. It seemed the final humiliation.

At the end of the dance, it was with relief and true gratitude that Juliana said to her cousin, "Thank you, Mr. Reddington, for looking after me. I am truly very obliged to you."

As they walked back to Lady Helen, Mr. Reddington said solemnly to her, "I am convinced that you were provoked beyond endurance, Miss Quincey. But I would not be doing my duty by you, as one who is older and more at home in the world than yourself, not to tell you that your hasty reaction has invited widespread attention. I fear that you will find the consequences tiresome."

Lizzie Reddington immediately came up to them both, and started making a fuss of Juliana. "It wasn't your fault. I am sure of that though I did not understand a word of what he said, I could see that the Marquis was teasing you! Though why you should be so upset over a glove, I vow I do not know! I cannot wait to hear the tale behind it."

Juliana had greater difficulty raising her eyes to meet those of Lady Helen's. That formidable matron looked disapproving but was obviously far too well behaved to allude to the little scene which had been so widely noticed. "I am so sorry, Lady Helen," faltered Juliana repentantly. "Perhaps grandmama could take me home . . ."

"That would provoke just the sort of attention that we must endeavor to avoid, Miss Quincey," said Lady Helen frigidly. "I rely on you not to do anything to draw further attention to yourself."

There followed a nightmare for Juliana. She had to sit fanning herself, trying to keep up a conversation with her two cousins, conscious that all eyes were on her. Lizzie was sympathetic. James Reddington also rallied nobly to her aid. He talked to her on a wide variety of subjects, telling her about a very interesting sermon he had heard the previous Sunday at St. Margaret's, Westminster. He outlined some of the principal churches of London, and told her that he hoped she and Lady Talboys would be attending morning service at St. Margaret's, which he considered a very superior church. Such was the flow of his information, that Juliana found she hardly had to say more than yes and no. It was not as soothing as it was designed to be, but she had to acknowledge that Mr. Reddington was being her friend.

It seemed as though the evening would never end. Juliana was not entirely left to the goodwill of the Reddingtons. One or two young men danced with her, but she feared they were motivated as much by curiosity as by admiration. She was excessively cautious in what she said to them, confining herself to polite nothings. She found their conversation insipid and feared they must feel the same about hers.

At last, after midnight, Lady Talboys came back from the card tables. She was in a grumpy mood, having lost several hundred guineas. Juliana tried not to listen while Lady Helen gave her grandmother a quick outline of the scene in the ballroom. The marquis, himself, seemed to have vanished. As Juliana left with her grandmother, she looked round. But his tall figure was nowhere to be seen.

The Marquis, as any man of fashion could have told her, rarely stayed long at balls and assemblies. It was his custom to go on later in the evening to White's, the London club most patronized by the heavy gamesters of the town.

This evening he had settled down to play hazard, and it was at the gaming table that Jeremy Ponsonby found him after midnight. The candles were guttering in the candlesticks by that time, and next to the marquis, George Selwyn was slumped across the table asleep with a heap of guineas in front of him. His companions were staking for him; and, as he slumbered peacefully, the pile was slowly diminishing.

The marquis was fully alert, though the night had passed into the small hours of the next morning. He had loosened the lace at his throat, which now fell askew to one side, and he had rolled back the ruffles at his sleeves the better to play. A bottle by his side, one of many that evening, was half empty. He was sprawled on his chair in an ungainly fashion. Nothing else about his figure showed that he was drunk, unless it was the wild glitter of his eyes. "The devil's in him tonight," thought Ponsonby, as he took his place in the table.

He looked round at the assembled gamesters, including Sir Francis Dahswood, Charles James Fox, and Lord Mountford—all deep gamblers. Stakes were high. Already thousands of pounds had changed hands. Charles James Fox had been scrawling IOUs all night from the look of the paper which littered the table. The largest pile of it was in front of the marquis.

"Auberon has the devil's own luck tonight," complained Fox. He, too, was drunk and his words were slurred. Yet he was not quarrelsome. Charles James Fox was a man of charm and sweetness of temper. He was known to walk home in the morning, having gamed and drunk all night, and then spend the morning reading Horace in the original Latin in his bedchamber.

"Auberon may be lucky at cards," came an affected titter from the other side of the table, "but does his luck hold in love?" It was Sir William Goring Pelham. Ponsonby looked at him with frank dislike. The Golden Exquisite was not a favorite with him—nor with the marquis. He hoped there would not be trouble.

Mountford stood up from the table. He was a tall, heavily built man of middle age. Rumor had it that he was gaming away his whole fortune at the tables. "I can play no more, Auberon," he said. "I grow weary of it. I must find some other amusement. Hazard palls."

Sir William rose with him. The Golden Exquisite was not a heavy gambler, taking part in gaming merely as a fashionable exercise. He lacked the will to win and the recklessness to lose more than a few hundred pounds at a sitting.

"Are you bored with play, too, Sir William?" mocked the marquis. The men round him smiled. Sir

William had a reputation for leaving the table when he was losing.

"I cannot compete against your luck," said Sir William peevishly. "But I will wager that you cannot do so well in love, Peterborough. I will lay odds that you cannot conquer the new heiress as easily as you win at play. Girl seems to have taken a dislike to you."

Before the marquis could speak up, Lord Mountford spoke. "Done, Sir William," he said. "I will take on the wager. Let us leave Peterborough out. He cannot wager on his own efforts. Two hundred guineas, Sir William, that Peterborough will win the heart of this girl . . . what the devil is her name?"

"Miss Quincey," tittered Sir William. A club servant hurried up with the betting book.

Ponsonby looked at the marquis with apprehension. He did not like the way things were going. Of course, Auberon could not object to the wager. Absurd bets of all kinds were placed daily in the famous gaming book. But he knew that this would not please his friend. Ponsonby knew—as others less close to the marquis could only suspect—that the Honourable Auberon Marcus St. John, Fifth Marquis of Peterborough, was not enamored of being in the public eye. He had a damnable sense of pride.

The Marquis had hardly seemed to notice the byplay between Sir William and Lord Mountford. He was still sprawled at his seat, and had just drained another glass of red wine. He was very, very still. Ponsonby knew that stillness. It was a danger signal.

The other men had gathered round to see the wager inscribed. Lord Mountford's name had already appeared several times in the last few days in that book. "Lord Mountford wagers Sir Desmond Stanhope twenty guineas that Lady Mary Coke has a child before Lady Kildare . . . Mr. Fox wagers Lord Mountford five hundred guineas on number two against number four in the lottery."

Carefully, the latest wager was written in. "Lord Mountford wagers Sir William Goring Pelham two hundred guineas that . . ." Sir William paused. "How shall we frame it?"

Impatiently Lord Mountford took the pen from him and finished writing, ". . . that the Marquis of Peterborough will conquer the heart of Miss Quincey. The wager to be decided by marriage or the lady's decline within six months."

" 'Tis damned irregular," grumbled Charles Fox looking over his shoulder. "Why, Auberon has the power to decide this as he chooses. Should he favor you, Mountford, he has only to ask the girl."

"Oh, I do not despair! 'Tis my belief the chit would refuse him!" tittered Sir William. "I have nicknamed her the Fair Fury. Did you not see how she cast the glove?" His voice trailed off into silence.

The marquis sprung up from the table. He stood over Sir William menacingly, and the Golden Exquisite quailed under his gaze. "I do not choose that you should spread tales of me, Sir William," he said and his voice was icy. "I cannot stop this wager, but I do not wish to hear that you have been talking about me. I should have to silence you." He patted the hilt of his sword with an unmistakable gesture.

Lord Mountford intervened. "I am happy to forgo the bet," he offered generously. " 'Tis only a frolic, after all, Auberon, but if it offends you . . ."

The marquis shook his head. "No, my dear Mountford, I would not in the world stop my fellow men enjoying themselves. Let the wager stand. Besides, it is of no importance. I shall not let it rule my conduct. Now if you had wagered that I might drive from London to Peterborough with record speed that might be a different matter . . ."

Four

Lady Talboys was propped up against a huge pile of down pillows, while a cup of steaming hot chocolate stood on the tray in front of her. Her nightcap, an extravagant concoction of lace and ribbons, was slightly askew, and the very elegant shawl which she had draped over her shoulders was getting in the way of her breakfasting. Lady Talboys shrugged it off with an irritable sigh. She had wakened in a bad mood, and in the way of old ladies who are thoroughly cross, she was going to make sure that those around her knew of her bad temper.

"Pinkerton, why are you fussing with those pots on the dressing table, woman?" she grumbled. "Where's my gown for this morning?"

"I have laid out the green gown, my lady," said Pinkerton, tight lipped. Pinkerton knew all about her lady's bad moods, and, when provoked, was capable of giving as good as she got. But that was rarely. She knew that the bad temper would not last forever. You could not work as a lady's maid for more than half a century with the same employer without knowing how to cope with her moods. Pinkerton had her methods.

"Rubbish, woman. The green frock is only suitable for a fifty-year-old. Do you want me to look like mutton dressed as lamb? I shall wear the black brocade."

"Very well, my lady. I am sure if you say so it is the right choice, not but what I think it is rather a sad sort of gown for such a lovely day."

"Lovely day? My good woman, no day is lovely when you wake up and remember that you lost two hundred guineas at the card table. That odious Mrs. Milgrave had a run of good fortune and cleaned me out. I swear that my luck was out all evening." Lady Talboys felt like adding that it could hardly be a good day, when one recalled how one's favorite granddaughter had made a fool of herself. That scene with the marquis must have drawn all eyes. She wished that just for once she had eschewed the delights of the card table, and had instead kept an eye on Juliana. The girl was so naive. She had no idea how to go on in the fashionable world. And obviously Lady Helen had been no help at all.

"Lady Helen has only one thought in that disapproving head of hers, and that's pound, shillings, and pence," she said aloud to Pinkerton. The maid knew better than to say anything back. Often, Lady Talboys would voice her thoughts out loud, saying the most outrageous things with utter frankness to her maid. Pinkerton always kept silent. It was best. Sometimes she wondered if Lady Talboys were even conscious of her presence. But after all, talking about such things probably helped Lady Talboys get them off her mind. So much the better, thought Pinkerton.

"Where is the girl?" asked Lady Talboys impatiently, as if Pinkerton should have known she would want to see Juliana.

"I will ask Miss Quincey to step up, My Lady" said Pinkerton submissively. Well, she thought, the girl is going to get a proper talking to! The old lady's as cross as a Tartar today. Already the household staff were aware that their new guest was rather a rustic, though obviously a favorite with Lady Talboys. Lady Talboys was known by all to be the sort of old woman who scolded her favorites unmercifully, browbeating them and bullying them—all for their own good. If she liked people, then she was often disastrously rude to them. If she disliked them, then she was icily polite or ignored them altogether. Miss Quincey was in high favor, a position which meant that she would have to get accustomed to her grandmother's scoldings.

"Well, you've made a fine start in society, I must say," said the old lady abruptly, as soon as the girl entered her bedroom. "Your first ball, and you all but caused enough scandal to last you the whole season. Why did you do such a thing, miss?"

"It wasn't my fault, grandmama," said Juliana defensively. "Well, at least it wasn't *altogether* my fault. You see, the marquis and I have . . . met before. I had an unfortunate experience with him, when I was on my way to London. We were staying at the King's Head." And she launched into the tale of that ruthless embrace in front of the stableboys. By the time she had finished, she was hot all over, blushing from the embarrassment of having to recall that horrible afternoon.

"That dratted young man is never content except when he's causing trouble of one kind or another," said her grandmother crossly. "If it isn't mounting some of the most expensive mistresses in the world, then it's fighting duels, and gambling for stakes high enough to ruin him. But why should he pick on *my* granddaughter? That's what I object to. And why were you so foolish as to let the world see that he had discomposed you?"

Juliana hung her head. She was conscious that her behavior in the ballroom had been gauche. There didn't seem much she could say to excuse herself, so she stayed silent.

"Well, it doesn't surprise me," went on her grandmother when the girl said nothing. "That young man is just like his father, and like his grandfather for that matter. The third marquis was a dreadful rake, to be sure. Why I remember when . . . but he's been dead for these twenty-five years or more, and nobody but an old woman like myself remembers . . ."

She paused for a moment. Then, recollecting that such reminiscences were hardly useful for the occasion, changed tack. "You say that there were others with him? That young fellow Ponsonby and two women?"

"I think that they had all taken drink," added Juliana cautiously. She was not sure if that made it worse or better.

"Well if he was in his cups, he would not hesitate to ravish any maid," said Lady Talboys thoughtfully. "I dare swear that we should be grateful. 'Tis lucky 'twas no worse. Can you trust this governess woman to keep her mouth shut?"

"Miss Humphries promised that she would not breathe a word," said Juliana.

"I vow I put no trust in promises from shabby genteel females, but we must hope," said her grandmother bracingly. "Lud, 'tis enough to madden me! Had I only known I might have kept closer watch on you, Juliana. Nobody would have thought twice if the marquis paid you attentions, but now you have shown your own anger, 'twill be the talk of the town. Still, there's naught we can do now, save try for a little discretion, however belated. What's done cannot be undone! What's more I'll wager the marquis has had a nasty shock. He's had every fool of a debutante languishing over him for these past ten years, simpering, flirting, and making eyes at him. I'll lay ten to one that the marquis has never had such a reception before. It will do him a great deal of good, though I fear it must do *you* harm, my dear."

I know grandmama. I am truly sorry," apologized Juliana. "It is my temper which is at fault. I have these violent rages, when I do not pause to think. Papa used to say that I should endeavor to control my feelings. He said that it was the business of a young lady to restrain any public show of feelings, though I must own that he never did tell me *how* I could achieve this."

"Did your papa really talk like that?" asked Lady Talboys disagreeably. "I consider his conversation must have been very tiresome, though no doubt full of worthy sayings. It sounds just like James Reddington. No wonder you have taken a liking to that young man. He can prose on forever using words in a way which makes me want to slumber."

"I like a man with a serious mind," said Juliana springing to the defense of both Mr. Reddington, and of her father. "Besides I have reason to be grateful to Mr. Reddington. He was excessively kind last night. Had it not been for his prompt action, I believe I might have been involved even more disastrously with the marquis. But he swept me onto the ballroom floor in such a way as to prevent further scenes."

"Well, there's no accounting for tastes," grumbled the old lady. "For my part I've always had a weakness for rakes. I had a positive affection for the third marquis. He was prodigiously handsome. It stands to reason that a libertine knows how to charm females, else he wouldn't be a rake in the first place. All the St. Johns are charmers, though I'll admit that both the third and the fourth marquis became quite staid once they were married. Still, it's not easy marrying a rake. Where's that Pinkerton? Where is the woman? She's laid out that odious black brocade. I've determined I shall wear the green after all . . ."

Juliana slipped quietly out of the bedroom, and motioned to Miss Pinkerton who was waiting outside, that her mistress wanted her. "She's in rather an uncertain mood," she warned the maid.

"You mean, she's as cross as crabs," said Pinkerton with a kind of resentful satisfaction. "Well, that's nothing unusual and I am sure it is my duty to bear it." With these stoical words, she went back into the room, bracing herself for reproaches about the black dress.

Later, clad in green watered silk cut so as to reveal a petticoat of paler green, the whole trimmed with blond lace, Lady Talboys made her way into the morning room.

"I have decided that what we need is a plan of campaign, child," she said firmly to Juliana. Her voice was less grumbling than earlier and it was clear that she had recovered her good humor. "If we are to make sure that the little fracas last night is not to do you harm, we must show we are not in the least disconcerted! We must be seen to be enjoying ourselves. Carry it off with an air—that's my idea—and damn the consequences. I've lived out more scandals than you've seen ballgowns, my dear, and it's always the same: if you hold your head up high, give the impression that you know nothing about it, and make 'em think that you're too superior to care, then you brush through it without too much ado. That's what we'll do. We must parade you around, child. Show the world that you're in fine spirits. We'll start by a drive in the park."

"Is it really so serious that we need to brazen it out?" asked Juliana with dismay. She was alarmed by her grandmother's militant words. It seemed her position was much worse than she had thought. She knew that Lady Talboys was annoyed about the scene last night, but she had not thought there would be other consequences. "Surely the Marquis of Peterborough does not have that much influence? If he is well known to be a gamester, and a libertine . . . then surely he cannot be of good standing in the fashionable world?'"

"Nonsense, child! Where did you get such gothic ideas? Since when did gaming or wenching make a man unfashionable? Mark my words, Peterborough is top of the trees. He may be a tiresome young puppy to an old woman like myself, but even I know that he wields power. Besides, it's perfectly good *ton,* however immoral, to kiss a wench in an inn yard, and it's perfectly good *ton* to return your glove. But it's not good *ton* to make a scandal, as you did, by throwing it back in his face in front of all the world. You won't get mealymouthed sayings from me, Juliana. In a nutshell—the world will forgive a modish young man any number of mistresses, mad pranks, and debaucheries; but it will not forgive a young woman evident rudeness."

Juliana felt crushed by this plain speaking. "If that's the way of the world, then I don't like it," she said, with a mulish obstinacy hovering round her mouth. "Still, as you say, we must fight a campaign against it, and I will do as you say, grandmama. Only I still think that things were better ordered back home."

"Better ordered, perhaps, but less agreeable," was Lady Talboys's caustic comment. She liked people who stood up to her. "Now, miss, let me look at your gown. It is of the greatest importance that you should look well today. You're a taking little thing, even if you're not a beauty."

She subjected Juliana to a long hard stare. The girl had put on one of her new gowns, a cherry pink silk worn without a hoop. Her first thought was that Lady Talboys would insist on a hoop being worn. But the old lady did not seem to mind. "For outdoor wear, child, padding is enough," she explained. "But where is that new hat with the cherry ribbons you were having dressed? Is it finished? 'Tis just what you need. With gloves, of course, and white stockings. How many times have I told you that white stockings are in vogue. Take off those dowdy black ones immediately, child. Then come down and show me again."

Even after Juliana had changed her stockings, found the hat with the cherry ribbons, and put on white gloves, Lady Talboys had a further inspection. This time she contented herself with suggesting white leather half-boots, instead of buckled shoes. "We may wish to stroll a little on the grass," she murmured. " 'Twill be easier in that way to greet people."

The drive in the park reminded Juliana just how predictable was the fashionable world. It was as if everybody who mattered was there. Carriages, mostly open ones, thronged the road. Coats of arms on their sides showed which belonged to noble families. Those who did not have a carriage were on horseback. Juliana thought she had never before seen such a wonderful collection of hacks. Gentlemen showed off the paces of glossy blacks or bays, while the ladies seemed to favor grays and chestnuts. Looking at them, riding sidesaddle with ease and grace, resplendent in their riding habits, Juliana decided she, too, would like to ride, rather than drive, in the park.

Quite a few people were also walking. The day was fine, if not very warm. The sun was out, and only a few white clouds in the sky threatened rain later. A spring wind whipped the horses' manes and tails, caught Juliana's own locks, and tugged at her cherry trimmed hat, setting its ribbons fluttering. She was glad she was wearing gloves for the extra warmth they afforded.

As the carriage went round, at a gentle pace so that Lady Talboys could wave at her acquaintants, Juliana recognized some familiar figures walking near the beds of spring bulbs. "Grandmama, may we stop? There is Lizzie, and her mother and Mr. Reddington. I should like to thank Lady Helen for her care of me last night, if you are agreeable."

The Reddington family, like the rest of their circle, were taking the air. They had left their carriage and were strolling quietly along the greensward. Lizzie was very prettily dressed in blue. James was in the top boots and breeches which showed he had been riding. He carried a riding crop in his hand, and a hat under his arm. Lady Talboys signaled to her coachman to pull up near them, and the two ladies left the carriage, the better to great their friends.

The two elder ladies walked on ahead, after the proper greetings and courtesies had been exchanged between all the company. Juliana rather thought that Lady Talboys wanted to explain things to Lady Helen, and so she was happy to linger behind with brother and sister.

"Juliana, there is awful news," burst out Lizzie, as soon as they had got out of earshot of the two older ladies. "James has discovered that bets are being placed upon the marquis's hopes of conquering your heart. Is it not so, James?"

"My sister pelts these things out in such a hasty fashion; I had hoped to tell you at some quieter moment, Miss Quincey," apologized Mr. Reddington solemnly. "I am sure that you will be gravely shocked, as I was, to hear that your good name is the subject of such idle talk. I have told my mother about it. 'Twas no less than my duty to warn her, and she will, I have no doubt, warn Lady Talboys. You will have to summon all your good sense to bear with it, cousin. Let circumspection be your watchword."

"What does this mean? How can such wagers be made? I fear that I am being foolish beyond belief, but I find it difficult to believe. Surely this is an idle rumor?" said Juliana imploringly.

"I regret that the report is substantially true, Miss Quincey. I have felt it incumbent upon me, as your nearest male relative, to check with a reliable gentleman who tells me that your name appears in full in the betting book at White's Club. 'Tis there for any idle buck to read, Miss Quincey. I am sure I do not have to tell you what that means? You will now be the subject of ceaseless conjecture, and even those who do not know you, will be speculating on whether you are the Marquis of Peterborough's latest flirt. For your sake, I hope that the man does not start paying you any exceptional attentions, but I fear that he will. He is so reckless, that such a wager will no doubt provoke his pride. He is not a man who is like to refrain from conquest, Miss Quincey."

"James is correct about the speculation and gossip," Lizzie added, gently confirming her brother's more solemn utterances. "It is odious for you, Juliana. But there is one thing that I, for one, find funny. I am sure that the news will make Charlotte Milgrave as mad as fire. Everybody knows that she is setting her cap at the marquis, and she will be jealous as a cat to know that your name is being linked with his, even though it is a mere gossip and mischief."

"But my name should *not* be linked with his," objected Juliana. "I do not properly understand this wager. Do you say that they have wagered that the Marquis of Peterborough will win my affections? He has placed money on *that?* And there were men of fashion who have aided him in this degraded transaction?"

"I had hoped to spare you the details," said James Reddington ponderously. "They can only distress you. But I see that I must risk shocking you further. The money is wagered that the marquis will conquer your affections, and it is to be paid either on the announcement of his marriage to you, or on your decline from a broken heart."

"But that is the most horrid thing I have ever heard!" exclaimed Juliana with amazement. "Suppose that I had an affection for the marquis, which I am happy to say that I do not in the least? Indeed I think he is detestable, as this betting proves! But suppose that I did feel a liking for him, why these gamesters would be placing their horrid guineas upon my feelings! I am deeply shocked, Mr. Reddington. Can this really be true?"

"I fear that it is," said Mr. Reddington. "The cancer of gaming is rotting society, destroying all morality and delicacy of feeling. And, I fear that the marquis is no stranger both to the evils of gambling, and to the vice which so often accompanies it. He is a man whose tastes I deplore."

Juliana smiled at him tremulously. Although James Reddington *was* rather solemn, she was relieved that he at least entered into her feelings. He seemed to understand the dismay, and disgust she felt at the uncaring follies of the fashionable world. Lizzie Reddington was a dear, of course, but she did not think very deeply about such matters. Her brother, on the other hand, had showed that he had solid principles and, if perhaps he was a little dull, well then it was better than being wild and thoughtless like so many of the young men around him.

She was rather less enthusiastic about his mother. Lady Helen, Juliana sensed, was a little more standoffiish than she had been before. A certain reserve was evident in the way she treated Juliana. There was an impression that she was waiting to see whether she could give her *full* approval. The scandalmongers must already have been at work, thought Juliana, and then she remembered that James Reddington had told his mother about that hateful bet at White's.

Lady Helen gave her hand to Juliana after just a second's hesitation, saying gravely, "I have been telling your grandmama, child, about the regrettable consequences of last night's affair, Miss Quincey. I am sure that you do not need me to tell you that from henceforth, you must be discreet in all that you do and say. Even the least hasty word or ill-considered jest could rebound against your reputation. People will be watching you to find fault, if they can. I fear that this is a harsh lesson for you, but one from which I am sure you will profit."

Juliana's first reaction was to defend herself vigorously. After all, it was not *her* fault that a set of rakes and gamesters had contrived such an ill-considered wager. But she could see Lady Talboys giving her a warning look, and so with difficulty she held her tongue. "Thank you, Lady Helen," she managed to say docilely. "As you say, it is a lesson for me. I shall endeavor to learn it. I can see that I have many harsh things to learn about how the world wags, and I am grateful to you for your kindness to me."

At these words, Lady Helen began to thaw. "Well, you are a pretty child," she said with a little more graciousness in her voice, "and you have a good fortune to bring to marriage. I see no reason why you should not live down this minor scandal. If you will forgive me for saying so, my dear, one of your difficulties is that you have too much sensibility, too much feeling. Take your tone from Miss Milgrave. She has excellent good sense. I have never seen her show unbecoming warmth on any topic."

"Mama, you know that Charlotte Milgrave is completely inhuman and has no feelings at all," protested Lizzie. "I should not like any friend of mine to become like her. She is not flesh and blood; she is nothing but a marble statue."

"Elizabeth's right," said Lady Talboys bluntly. "I shouldn't like a granddaughter of mine to go round looking as if she had been stuffed and put in a glass case. Not but what you speak wisely, Lady Helen, when you tell the child not to let her emotions get the better of her. There is a happy medium in everything, but for the moment we must contrive to undo the harm that has been done. Last night was bad enough! But after this wager every tongue will be wagging, and the scandalmongers will be agog to see if they can't make more out of it.

"Don't think I'm not grateful to you, Lady Helen. You and your son and your daughter will be doing a lot for Juliana if you stand her friends, and show the world that she is not deserted. Come, Juliana, we must parade some more, I think. Lud, I'll make everybody I know bow to us this morning! I vow I'll discover who are my friends today! I never thought I'd have to test it out, but I dare say the experience will do me a power of good."

Climbing back into the carriage, Juliana could not

help thinking it would be a great deal more comfortable if only she could just go home and give up this charade. She hated the idea that she had put Lady Talboys to all this trouble, ignoring the fact that the old lady by her side seemed to be enjoying it. Lady Talboys loved a good fight.

For the rest of the drive, the old lady ordered the coachman to put the horses at a walk. As they proceeded through the park this way, being overtaken by more dashing vehicles whose horses were at a trot or even a canter, Lady Talboys busied herself in waving and bowing to all her acquaintances. There were a formidable number of these, and for the first time Juliana realized just how well-connected her grandmother was. To those who seemed disposed to halt, she would introduce Juliana. Soon the girl felt her head buzzing with names. All the time her grandmother kept up a running commentary. "That's Lady Betty Coke, a nice woman though a dreadful gossip . . . Lady Archer . . . I suppose I must bow but she would not do to introduce you to, Juliana . . . she's one of a gaming set which plays too deep even for me, though I have been to her card parties . . . Lady Sefton . . . She's one of my dearest friends, and very good natured. Runs to fat, of course, but a kind woman as long as she don't have to put herself to any inconvenience . . . Lord Mountford . . . He's gambling away his whole fortune . . . I'm surprised to see him here . . . Usually he's in some gaming den . . ."

The worst moment came when their carriage passed a group of young bloods, which included Sir William Goring Pelham. The Golden Exquisite obviously had been amusing his cronies with some kind of joke, and when the carriage passed by they all looked up with such knowing glances, that Juliana feared she had been the subject of their mirth. Sir William raised his quizzing glass, and after a very long stare at the carriage's occupants, favored them with an exaggerated bow. It was studied insolence, thought Juliana, and she looked at

Lady Talboys at her side. The old lady had returned the bow with a dignified acknowledgment of her head, and a smile.

But obviously she too had noticed Sir William's insolence. For once they were safely past, she said crossly, "That little wretch of a man makes me very angry indeed. He has a poisonous tongue and I fear he's been exercising it at your expense, child. Perhaps he is one of those who has laid money upon the marquis's chances. If only that pompous James Reddington had listened to gossip a little more carefully, we might know their names . . . It is too bad that you should have given Sir William the opportunity to class you as a rustic female full of good works."

"Sir William has no cause to dislike me, grandmama, save that he might think me a bore. I was perfectly courteous to him last night," objected Juliana.

"Child, you are too naive. The Golden Exquisite does not *need* provoking to malice. For malicious gossip is his chief amusement, and the only quality which makes him tolerable. Though he is a man of fortune, he cannot make his way in society by his own natural parts—for he has neither the manly virtues, nor the manly vices! He neither games deep, nor wenches. His only interest is clothes, in which he affects a very singular taste, and gossip. He has no *feeling* of dislike for you, Juliana! Why should he? You are merely another subject about whom he may amuse the world by saying malicious things! Since he has no wit, he must season his talk with malice if it is to be enjoyed."

"How unpleasant," sighed Juliana. She felt utter depression settle on her. It seemed as if all things conspired against her. She had unwittingly given a poisoned-tongue gossip ammunition against herself. She had then lost her temper with a rake. There seemed nothing so very shocking about either action, except that both the gossip and the rake were apparently important people in society. It was most confusing!

While suffering from this feeling of depression, she was introduced to yet another fashionable matron. This lady was younger than Lady Talboys, more of Lady Helen's generation, Juliana judged, as her grandmother exchanged salutations. Juliana took only a passing interest in the woman, who was also in an open carriage. She was middle-aged, with a pleasant face, and quite plainly dressed. Perhaps the only thing remarkable about her was the evidence of once-great beauty in her face. Juliana recognized quality in that face and figure.

"Juliana, my love, this is the Dowager Marchioness of Peterborough," said Lady Talboys at her side. Juliana's wandering thoughts came back to the present with a bump. She almost fell off the carriage seat. This, then, was the odious marquis's *mother*. It simply could not be! But when she looked again, she could see a definite resemblance. She was aware that her surprise must be showing in her face and immediately blushed.

"Come, child," said the lady in the carriage, which had pulled up next to the Talboys' vehicle. "I would talk with you. Can you spare Miss Quincey, Lady Talboys? I should like her company for a moment." The voice was low and gentle, and the eyes were kind.

"Yes, my dear," said the dowager, as Juliana clambered into the carriage and sat beside her, "I *am* like my son to look at, and, no, I am not nearly as fashionable as he is. Was that not what you were thinking? Or near enough?"

Juliana blushed again. "You are very acute," she said.

"No, I am not so much acute, as used to interpreting the astonished look that all young ladies who have met my son first and me second give me," said the marchioness agreeably. "Come, child, tell me what my son has been doing to cause you such distress? I have heard garbled rumors from more than half the gossips in town, and I do not believe them. Auberon is occasionally thoughtless, frequently rude, and always wild. But he is not usually cruel. But perhaps you have reason to think otherwise?"

Juliana was amazed to find herself talking quite freely to the woman beside her. She kept nothing back—though she blushed even deeper when she told of that shocking kiss in the stableyard. "And I dare say that it was nothing to him but the merest bagatelle. Gentlemen are such odd creatures; I know that they have their fancies and that they behave in the most odiously amorous way to any female at all. But it was not like that for me. I am not a gentleman, and I am not even fashionable. I detest his way of life, and the misery to which it leads."

The marchioness by her side was silent for a moment. Juliana noticed for the first time that she had, sitting close to her ankles, almost covered by her skirts, a tiny, rather shaggy mongrel. "Is he not ugly?" the marchioness said. "I was forced to rescue him from some children who were ill treating him, and somehow I have not had the heart to give him away. Besides, he is so very loving."

Looking at the small terrier, Juliana had to admit that the marchioness was right. He *was* ugly, besides being the most unlikely dog for a woman of fashion to have accompany her. "Do you take him *everywhere?*" she asked doubtfully.

"No, I have not the courage, Miss Quincey. I fear his appearance does me so little credit . . . Miss Quincey, we have more serious matters to discuss. Leaving aside Toby dog, for so he is called, it is my son that I wish to talk about.

"I do not usually apologize for Auberon, but in this case I believe I must make an exception. You have been shabbily treated by him, and indeed I am astonished by his behavior. I vow he is not normally so rude to ladies. Indeed his behavior is often the reverse. He usually is all charm and soft words, and I have often wondered whether these do not show how little he cares. But in your case, his charm seems to have deserted him and I do not know what to make of it."

"Perhaps your son thinks I am just a country bumpkin of no account," said Juliana. She could not keep the bitterness out of her voice.

"I do not think so," said the Marchioness coolly. "Of course, he has the devil's own temper. You were not wise to throw that glove at him. I have never known a man less able to stomach an insult—unless it was his papa, before I married him. A hot temper runs in the family, my dear. All the St. Johns are wild to a fault when they are young. The fourth marquis, my late husband, was a rakehell. My mother told me not to marry him, but I would not listen to her. Yet we were very happy. I do not think he ever looked at another woman after we married, though before I met him he had had scores of mistresses. I can only hope that my son will follow the same pattern."

"Then I can hardly wait for your son to marry," Juliana commented with biting irony. "For in the meantime, he is like to ruin my reputation and plunge us both in scandal."

"My dear, you have a right to be bitter," his mother said apologetically. "In the meantime I will have a word with him and see what I can do. I cannot silence the tongues of the gamesters, though. Sir William Goring Pelham, for one, will not be silent. He has already given you a cruel nickname which I would not repeat save that I think it best you should know. He calls you the Fair Fury, and I fear the name will stick."

Juliana was taken aback by the extent of anger she felt. It seemed as if her troubles would never end. Like a stone in a pond, whose ripples drift ever outward, her one moment of foolish temper seemed to be producing all kinds of disagreeable consequences. First that shocking wager! And now Sir William was making up hurtful nicknames! "I suppose that not *all* the young men will follow Sir William's lead," she found herself saying in a small voice. "If they do, then I for one do not think much of them, and so perhaps I do not care." But, she knew that she did care.

The marchioness did her best to be comforting. "I am sure that it is not as bad as it seems, child," she said. "At least our drive round the park may do something for you. Of course, the gossips will notice it, and it will at least show that I do not hold your outburst of temper at my son against you. It is little enough, I know. But there is not much I can do. If I show pleasure in your company, then some of the older matrons, at least, will follow my lead. And I shall have a word with Auberon, though I cannot promise he will listen. He has such a bad temper when he is roused, that sometimes I fear for him. If only he could find a female he could truly love . . ."

Juliana could think of nothing to say. It seemed to her that the marquis had found too *many* females to love—but it would be cruel to point this out to his mother, who was trying to be kind. Juliana was conscious that she owed the woman by her side a debt of gratitude for helping her. "I am truly grateful," she ventured to say. "It is not everybody, ma'am, who would have bothered to be so kind to me."

"Well, child, it is my pleasure. I vow that I have never *had* to apologize in this way for my son before. His dealings with females are, as I say, usually of a different kind. I do not like to see somebody suffering because of his thoughtlessness. Besides, when I was young I was perhaps a little like you. I had a hot temper, you know. I fear that Auberon's temper does not come solely from his father's family."

On their return to Lady Talboys' coach, the old lady joined her thanks to those of Juliana.

"You were always kind, Anne," Lady Talboys said gruffly. "I don't want you to think that I hold it against the boy. I know what it is to be young and wild. He'll sow his wild oats, you'll see, and then settle down like his father did. Like his grandfather did, come to that. I haven't forgotten the scandal when the third marquis ran off with one of the maids of honor! All of us young girls were green with envy! What an uproar there was, to be sure! Yet they lived happily together, and I vow he never so much as looked at another woman. Ah, well, 'twas so long ago! But you'll understand, I have my granddaughter to think of. I can't let your wild son ruin her chances of a good marriage."

As the dowager marchioness drove off and Juliana returned to Lady Talboys' carriage, the old lady continued, "There are not many woman I could name who would do for you what she's done today. She must have taken a liking to you, though why I cannot think. Let us hope it helps quell the rumors."

They were just going to turn the horses' heads for home, when a handsome young man on a showy bay mare rode up to them. "Lady Talboys," he said tentatively, "will you be so kind as to introduce me to your granddaughter? I am anxious to meet the latest beauty."

Juliana, after a moment's doubt, recognized him as the young man in regimental uniform who had been dancing with Lizzie Reddington. So this was Robert Torrington. She glanced at her grandmother, and saw that Lady Talboys did not look overjoyed at his interest, though she made the introduction.

Robert Torrington looked rather downcast at the old lady's evident disapproval, but he persevered nonetheless. Walking his horse by the side of the carriage he engaged the ladies in polite conversation. He asked whether Juliana had enjoyed the ball, and regretted that he had not had the pleasure of a dance with her—"an omission that I hope to right on a later occasion," he concluded gallantly.

His words were balm to Juliana's soul. She had a shrewd idea that he had been put up to this introduction by Lizzie Reddington, but she did not care. After the difficulties she had had to endure, the sneers and the jokes at her expense, the attention of any tolerably personable young man was a nice change. She smiled at him, and said that she too hoped to dance with him in future assemblies.

"I hope you are not going to encourage that young man!" said Lady Talboys, attacking in characteristically forthright fashion directly Robert Torrington had ridden off. "He is nothing but a younger son. The Torringtons are perfectly respectable, and the estate is quite a nice little seat in its way, I am told. But it has been entailed upon the eldest brother. This Robert Torrington is penniless save for his own exertions in the army."

"I thought him extremely charming," Juliana said teasingly. "Besides, I need not marry every young man who says a few civil words to me."

"No, and not every young man will ask you, child, you may be sure," countered her grandmother blightingly. "But younger sons have a way of being charming when they are seeking a fortune in marriage. If they do not have money, then they must seek it by marrying. And I am sure I need not tell you, Juliana, that with your face and your fortune you can look a great deal higher than Robert Torrington. To be encouraging him cannot add to your consequence."

"You sound rather like Sir William Goring Pelham," Juliana grumbled. She sighed. She would have liked to explain to Lady Talboys that she did not have any particular interest in Robert Torrington. But she had said that she would be of service to Lizzie Reddington, and by setting up a flirtation with the young man, it might help. Under cover of her own interest, Lizzie's relationship with the young man might not be noticed. "Anyway," she continued, "I do not see anything wrong with Mr. Torrington. At least he is civil to me, and I am so circumstanced, grandmama, that any civility to me is something that pleases."

She had just finished speaking, when something caught her eye. The carriage had turned out of the park, and was going at a quick pace toward the Mayfair house of Lady Talboys. The road was crowded with other fashionable carriages and riders, as well as the carts, wagons, and horses of tradesmen and other working folk. On the paving stones near the houses, the town was bustling with pedestrians—footmen running errands, serving girls, city aldermen, a passing clergyman, and scores of men and women selling goods from either barrows or baskets.

It was none of these busy people that caught Juliana's attention, but a pitiful waif in the gutter. Ragged and dirty, he was lying face down in a pool of muck, where he had obviously fallen or been pushed. His heaving shoulders were the only evidence that he was alive rather than dead.

"Oh, pray stop at once," cried Juliana to the coachman, "I must get down." The servant obeyed, thinking some terrible accident had occurred, and the horses came to a sudden halt.

"Juliana, what is this distempered freak? Pray sit still, girl," cried the old lady at her side, as Juliana, clutching her skirts, leaped wildly from the carriage even before it had stopped.

Ignoring her grandmother's cries, she ran back down the road keeping her hat on her head with one hand. She could hear Lady Talboys exclaiming in a very improper way, "Drat the girl. Turn the carriage round. What a devilish performance . . ."

But by this time Juliana had no further time to listen. She had reached the small urchin, who was pulling himself painfully into a sitting position among the muck and mire of the roadway. He was crying and his tears made little rivulets of cleanliness down his otherwise filthy face. His waiflike features were sharp with lack of food. Altogether he was a pathetic sight.

Forgetting her fine clothes, Juliana helped him rise and stood by rather helplessly while he made ineffectual attempts to wipe some of the mud off his rags. Putting her hand gently on his shoulder, she asked him in a soft voice, "Are you badly hurt?"

The child's immediate impulse was to jump away from her touch, as if it had been a blow. Juliana could only think that he was more used to kicks and cuffs than to caresses. She repeated her question: "Are you much hurt, child?"

The boy looked up at her suspiciously. A small crowd was beginning to collect round the two of them, with some of the bystanders making vulgar remarks and unhelpful suggestions. The urchin began to look frightened. "I ain't 'urt, miss," he muttered. " 'Twas one of them big wagons knocked me down."

"I am sure you could do with something to eat. You look hungry. Come with me, and I will see what can be done," said Juliana, forgetting everything but the boy's need.

At the word "eat," the boy looked up eagerly, but when she suggested he come with her, a look of sulkiness came over his face. "Thanks, miss. I don't need 'elp. There'll only be trouble."

He was correct in his assessment, for through the bystanders a portly-looking shopkeeper pushed his way to the front. He was wielding a large stick, and he looked far from kind. "Is this 'ere varmit troubling you, miss," he said, waving his stick in the direction of the small boy. "The thievin' little beggar should be locked up."

"I'll 'ave to go, miss" said the urchin desperately, looking round in dismay.

"I'd like to help you," Juliana said quickly, accepting that he knew best. "Do you know Curzon Street? Number twelve is where I live. You ask for me, Miss Quincey."

The boy nodded. His eyes were flicking from side to side, and he was growing more fearful by the minute. "Shall I chase 'im off, miss?" boomed the interfering onlooker. "Just say the word, and I'll give 'im something to remember you by! Thievin' little rascal!"

"Oh pray be quiet, you horrid man," Juliana

snapped at him. She was thankful to see that her anger had temporarily deprived him of speech. "Look here, child," she said rapidly to the small boy. "I should like to be your friend. If I can help you, you will find me in Curzon Street, at Lady Talboys's house. Have you got that?"

"Curzon Street at Lady Talboys," repeated the small boy. Then without saying more, he slipped through the crowd like an eel, and darted off as fast as his legs would carry him up the street, weaving through the people like lightning. To the astonishment of the small crowd that he left behind, he then disappeared up a small alleyway out of sight.

"Now look what you have done. I particularly wanted to help the poor child, and you frightened him off," Juliana turned upon the stout shopkeeper in anger. "I hope you are satisfied. The child needed help and all you offered was a beating. You sicken me."

There was nothing she could do. With a parting fierce look at the fat man, she walked crossly back to the carriage. The small crowd trailed back with her, eager to see whether further amusement might be provided for them. The coachman was open-mouthed with astonishment, and Lady Talboys looked both disgusted and cross. But neither said a word, as Juliana climbed back and the carriage set off again towards Curzon Street.

Five

In Curzon Street, Lady Talboys broke her silence and a vigorous disagreement followed. It was to be the first of many. Lady Talboys in vain portrayed the foolishness of jumping down from the carriage, risking life and limb for an urchin in the gutter. Juliana agreed that her actions had been dangerously impulsive but that was all. She refused to promise better conduct in the future, and she set her face willfully against her grandmother's opinion that street urchins were best left where they were. "Papa would have wanted me to do my best," was all she would say about her charitable intervention.

In the days that followed, Lady Talboys found herself feeling quite angry against the late lamented Sir Basil. Juliana's papa had been a thoroughly bad influence upon the girl, she concluded. In the old lady's opinion, Sir Basil, having been a pompous bore all his life, now exerted an equally boring influence after his death. For the incident with the child was not the only moment when Sir Basil's influence seemed to reach beyond the grave.

Lady Talboys was horrified to learn that Juliana had questioned Hitchens the butler who presided over the Curzon Street establishment about the wages paid to kitchen maids. "I am sure miss means well," said this old retainer, keeping his face impassive, "but I felt it was my duty to tell you, my lady. Such inquiries I understand to be of a sympathetic nature and springing from a wish to do good, but I need hardly tell you that other members of the staff might fail to understand, and might see in them opportunities for grumbling and discontent."

When Lady Talboys remonstrated with her granddaughter, Juliana apologized for any discourtesy, saying: "Perhaps I was at fault in not asking you, grandmama. But I did not wish to bother you." She entirely failed to see the force of Lady Talboys's argument that such inquiries would only unsettle the household servants, who, heaven knows, were flighty enough. "Surely it is the duty of you and me to inquire into the well-being of the servants?" said Juliana wide-eyed and innocent. "I am sure that you have always taken this kind of interest in their welfare, grandmama. I should not like to think otherwise of you."

"Stuff and nonsense," the old lady said, and apparently that was all she could say. Lady Talboys stifled a desire to tell the girl that she had never in her life felt the slightest interest in the well-being of her kitchen maids. But for the occasional report by the French chef about the need to hire or fire such menials, she had little or no knowledge about the existence of such lowly beings as kitchen maids. She was not seriously worried about Juliana's intervention, since she had perfect confidence in Hitchens' ability to deal with the matter. Hitchens had worked for the best part of half a century in the Talboys household, and was the unquestioned dictator of the house—to whose decrees, indeed, Lady Talboys herself sometimes was fain to bow. Quite often she was not entirely aware how the butler ruled, since it was both benevolent and usually too tactful to be noticed by his superiors who thought *they* ruled him.

Hitchens might be able to deal with Juliana well, but there were other uneasy moments. There was the time—Lady Talboys shuddered when she thought of it—when Juliana had insisted on bringing home a very small bedraggled cat which she had found in the gutter. Miss Pinkerton, who had accompanied her to do some shopping for trifles, had arrived home rigid with suppressed disapproval. Lady Talboys had had to cope with Pinkerton's outburst. It had involved listening to an offer of resignation ("Quite out of the question, Pinkerton," the old lady had said), followed by a diatribe against the foolishness of a country upbringing for young ladies of quality. Lady Talboys had been much in sympathy with this, but she had felt it her duty to try to explain the unfortunate influence of Sir Basil on his only daughter. She had not entirely succeeded. "If it wasn't that miss is a lady, which I am sure anybody can tell," sniffed Pinkerton, "I would say she was downright eccentric."

What had happened to the cat, Lady Talboys hardly liked to ask, in case it produced another outburst. She was again indebted to the excellent Hitchens for his management of the whole affair. He told her discreetly that he had disposed of the animal that Miss Juliana brought back.

"It is in the care of the second coachman who has assured miss personally that he will care for it well," Hitchens said. "I knew that the chef would never have taken it, Lady Talboys, and so I told miss when she suggested it should live in the kitchen. Besides, I told Miss Quincey that it would be happier in the stables."

"I do not know what I would do without your help," sighed Lady Talboys to her butler—not for the first time.

As well as these trying experiences, there was another test of Lady Talboys's patience. She had been prepared for gossip about Juliana and the Marquis of Peterborough—the scene at the ballroom, and the subsequent wager in White's betting book made that inevitable. But what had shocked her was that somehow, somebody had told the world about Juliana's encounter with the marquis at the King's Head.

Lady Talboys had been told of this by Lady Helen. "As you can imagine," said this formidable matron, "I was at first quite dismayed but further reflection led me to suppose that Miss Quincey had been unwise, rather than at fault. Her deplorable upbringing has meant that she is often unconventional, as I have had occasion to warn her. Any lady of quality, in particular one with ten thousand a year *and* fifty thousand in the funds, cannot be too cautious about her actions in public."

Lady Talboys, usually so outspoken, managed with difficulty to refrain from asking Lady Helen what difference an income of ten thousand pounds might make to a lady of quality's public actions. She needed Lady Helen's support, and she knew that her usual frankness might not help her in gaining this. Instead she contented herself with saying, "I know all about it, Lady Helen. A storm in a teacup! The child told me just as soon as she arrived in London." (This was a lie, but Lady Talboys trusted that nobody would discover it.)

The old lady then added, "These young rakehells will stop at nothing when they are drunk, you know! I suppose you know that the marquis was quite disguised with drink. I was able to assure Juliana that no blame attached to her." With that second lie, Lady Talboys hoped she had secured Lady Helen's approval.

In public the old lady maintained this firm line and did her best to damp down the fires of scandal. But in private to Juliana and to the ever-present Pinkerton, she confided her worries. "I cannot think how *this* particular piece of scandal reached the gossips," she asserted. "I can't think that Peterborough is to blame, nor Ponsonby. Why, whatever foolish pranks they have committed, both are gentlemen after all. Peterborough would never kiss and tell. At least till now he has never done so! I can only wonder whether you, dear Juliana, may have been indiscreet. We were brushing through so nicely, too, until this came to light."

"I told the Marchioness of Peterborough," said Juliana cautiously, "but I feel sure she would not have told anybody. No, grandmama, I feel sure somebody else is the culprit. Have you forgotten the governess, Miss Humphries, with whom I traveled to London? She promised she would not tell anybody, but perhaps she did not keep her word. I should not be surprised if she has confided the whole story to one of her charges—as a dreadful warning. She did not like me, you know. Once the tale was out, it would not take much for it to spread further."

"Trust an underbred female like a governess to tittle-tattle," barked Lady Talboys savagely. "Shabby-genteel women! I've no time for 'em myself!"

"There's another thing," added Juliana. "You see, Miss Humphries was going to work for the Milgrave family. Not as Charlotte's governess, of course, since she is out in society, but for the younger girls. When I was with her, all her conversation was about the families she knew, and so perhaps she mentioned my name and told about our journey."

"The Milgraves! Of course. Why did I not think of it before? I'll lay odds that that governess female told Charlotte or even perhaps her mother. She thought to curry favor, no doubt. Mrs. Milgrave is as mad as fire about you, of course, for all that she's asked us to her assembly. She fears you may be spoiling her girl's chances. She wouldn't hesitate to pass round any story which casts discredit upon you, Juliana. I'll wager my diamonds that *she* is the source of this."

"Why should Mrs. Milgrave wish to do me such harm?" asked Juliana, puzzled. By now she had been introduced both to Charlotte and her mama, and both had been polite if not enthusiastic about her acquaintance.

"Because that Milgrave girl has had her eye on the Marquis of Peterborough all this season. Everybody knows that Charlotte Milgrave is ambitious. She has the face of an angel, and a fortune, and if only she was a little animated, I daresay she might have had the marquis at her feet weeks ago. It looked very promising. Now, I am not saying you rival her Juliana, for you don't. You ain't pretty enough for one thing, and for another you've no idea of how to behave. Charlotte Milgrave never puts a foot wrong, and you are always doing the wrong thing, despite all my efforts. But there's no denying that the marquis has taken an interest in you. It may be very shocking and all tied up with some senseless wager, but for all that, I vow Mrs. Milgrave must be worrying. She hopes by spreading scandal about you to disgust the marquis and keep him for her own daughter."

"It seems rather odd to me," commented Juliana. "After all, I shouldn't have thought that any amount of scandal would have disgusted the marquis. After all, his whole life is just one scandal after another. Or so it seems to me."

"That's your opinion, child, but I tell you there is a great difference between the scandal attaching to a gentleman and the scandal attaching to a lady. The marquis may enjoy having amours with scores of females, but he will nevertheless wish to marry a lady of unimpeachable reputation. It is unfair, but it is how things are."

"Is Charlotte Milgrave engaged to be married to him? She certainly has an unimpeachable reputation," asked Juliana. She was conscious of a sinking feeling. Somehow the idea of a marriage between those two upset her a great deal. "On the other hand, I shouldn't have thought they would suit very well. Miss Milgrave is a pattern of correct behavior, and the same cannot be said for the marquis."

"That is just why he may choose the Milgrave girl,"

said Lady Talboys. "So far there has been no engagement, but Mrs. Milgrave has had high hopes. Charlotte knows how to conduct herself, and that alone may attract the marquis. There would be no ill-bred scenes from her if he mounted a mistress—as heaven knows he probably will! Charlotte Milgrave will know how to look the other way like a good wife should. She will be beautifully behaved, herself, without requiring any kind of virtue from her husband. And that, my dear, might be just what the marquis would want in a wife. After a misspent youth, and some of the most dashing women in keeping in London, he could hardly be expected to change his habits overnight upon marriage. Unless, of course, he takes after his father or grandfather. But this cannot be thought likely."

To Lady Talboys' satisfaction, Juliana did not argue at this. It seemed, at last, that she was beginning to come to terms with the way the fashionable world went on. And quite time too, thought Lady Talboys. Although the girl was still insistent upon helping small boys or cats in the gutter, she had stopped some of her romantical notions. Lady Talboys was also pleased to note that Juliana was making progress in the social graces. Her dancing was now elegant and assured, and she had gone so far as to find pleasure in playing whist for pennies. Indeed, in one game with her grandmother she had won so heavily that Lady Talboys had run out of the copper coins. It was not that the old lady wanted to turn her protégée into a gambler, but some acquaintance with betting on games of chance was essential if the girl aimed to take her place in society.

Juliana had even acknowledged her pleasure to her grandmother explaining, "I am beginning to see why people become so partial to gaming. There is an excitement in the fall of a card, or the rolling of dice, which I now appreciate. Of course gaming in excess is a ruinous habit."

Well, thought Lady Talboys, that at least was a

more moderate view. One could hardly argue with the girl's conclusion in a year during which both Lady Alice Macready and Lord Wallis had committed suicide, after gambling themselves into bankruptcy. The other sign of Juliana's growing interest in the fashionable world was that she was beginning to enjoy the finery of her new clothes. Instead of sighing when it was time to shop for a new brocade, or stand while a new gown was fitted, the girl was beginning to take an interest. She had a tolerable eye for color and natural good taste. Even the redoubtable and always grudging Pinkerton admitted that much.

"She may not be a beauty of the conventional sort, my lady," confided the maid, "but Miss Quincey has a certain something about her looks which seems to me to be better. I enjoy turning her out to look her best."

Compliments from that source could come no greater.

But whatever the success of Juliana's looks—and several young gentlemen were showing themselves to be admirers—all was not yet well about her reputation. Lady Talboys continued to do all she could, but without complete success. At Lady Milgrave's assembly a few days later, the old lady could not help noticing that some of the matrons—including the hostess—were eyeing the girl askance. In an effort to make sure that Juliana was not left at a disadvantage, Lady Talboys went so far as to curb her love of cards, and so stay with the chaperons in the ballroom. She was determined to see that things went smoothly. She had told Juliana firmly beforehand not to do anything odd or eccentric which might draw attention.

"You must now guard all your behavior, child," she warned. "Be and look the innocent young lady, I beg of you. Control that hasty tongue of yours, and do nothing which could make people remark on you."

The evening, however, was not entirely unpromising. Despite the coldness of the atmosphere among the mothers of other debutantes, Juliana was looking her best. The child had quality and charm, thought Lady Talboys, looking fondly over her. She had left off the hair powder so that Juliana's natural chestnut locks curled deliciously round her cheeks, a cluster of curls falling behind upon her slender neck. Her skirt was made of silver floss, with twining roses, the petals all of foil. Above it a bodice laced with silver thread was of the same material. Heavy ruffles of Brussels lace fell from the sleeves, and more lace trimmed the bodice and the pink petticoat which was exposed by the silver skirt. Once again, Lady Talboys had made sure that the girl was dressed magnificently but very much *jeune fille*. A single rope of pearls round her neck was the only jewelry she wore, save for a pearl crescent in her locks.

Charlotte Milgrave, resplendent in green silk with emeralds and matching green French lace, might look more fashionable, thought Lady Talboys—but she could not match Juliana for freshness. Lizzie Reddington, in dark blue silk, was also looking vivacious and appealing. But to Lady Talboys's experienced eye both girls lacked something that her own protégée had in abundance—a certain charm. There was something unusual about Juliana. Lady Talboys considered that her air of naive innocence and unselfconscious enjoyment could not fail to please. It shone down even Charlotte Milgrave's faultless self-control.

She was not surprised therefore to see Sir William Goring Pelham approach. Sir William bowed to Lady Talboys, offered a few compliments, and asked Juliana to be his partner. It was a gesture that Lady Talboys hoped might go some way to offset his earlier unkind characterization of her as the Fair Fury. Perhaps Sir William was going to fall victim to her charm . . .

But Juliana, going through her part in the dance with greater confidence than the last occasion when she had partnered Sir William, was not so sanguine. She was conscious that her partner had done his best to blight her career at the outset by a cruel nickname. She longed to ask him why he had thought fit to ridicule her like that, and to ask him what she had done to gain his dislike. But she knew such frankness would be disastrous. The dance was, therefore, all the more an ordeal.

"Enjoyin' your season, Miss Quincey?" drawled Sir William. "Findin' us fashionable fellows a great bore, I suppose?"

A week ago Juliana would have answered without thinking twice, favoring him with her unvarnished views on the topic. But she was learning discretion. "Of course, I am enjoying myself, Sir William," she said quietly. "Why should I not be?"

"Seem to recollect you thought we might be better employed in good works," sneered the Golden Exquisite. "Philanthropy your special concern, you told me. Not much call for it though during the London season. Thought you might be bored, therefore? Eh, Miss Quincey?"

"I am not bored at all, Sir William. But I am sure that *you* would be if I told you my reasons for thinking that London needs more philanthropic persons. I am sure that such complicated subjects would not interest you in the slightest. Why don't we talk scandal and gossip instead? That, surely, is more your kind of thing, is it not?"

The Golden Exquisite looked uncomfortable. Juliana realized that he did not enjoy being given some of his own medicine. She had meant to be conciliating and to charm him, and here she was already disputing with him. Well, it was just too bad. Even for the love of Lady Talboys, she was not going to take Sir William's nasty remarks lying down. The damage to her reputation was done, anyway. She had acquired an enemy in this man. She did not know why, but she supposed that she must learn to live with it.

As these thoughts were passing through her mind, she was jerked back to the immediate present by Sir William's next needling remark. "I vow that the Marquis of Peterborough has graced us with his presence! I wonder when he and Miss Milgrave will make an announcement. Lud, what a fine couple they make."

"Their engagement will soon be announced, I imagine," said Juliana quickly, trying to make it clear that she had no expectation of anything different. "I am sure that they make an ideal couple. Do you not think so, Sir William? With so much beauty on her side, and so much —what shall I say?—breeding on his, I am sure it must make the ideal match." She fought to hide the bitterness in her voice. Sir William's remark had come as an unwelcome surprise.

The marquis was bound to be present. She must surely be prepared to be in the same room as the man. What more natural thing than that he should turn up at the Milgrave assembly and dance with his hostess's daughter? It was only to be expected. She must school herself to get used to the idea that the marriage would be on. She was thankful she had not blushed. Cautiously, she looked round. Yes, there was the marquis, dancing with Miss Milgrave.

Well, perhaps the gossips would turn their attention to his relationship with the beautiful Miss Milgrave, rather than herself. She told herself that she should be grateful if the marquis ignored her. She told herself that she should be happy that the odious marquis was going to settle down with Miss Milgrave. She told herself a hundred other suitable, useful, and soothing things—and still the sight of them together hurt. She was conscious that the marquis seemed to be looking intently into Miss Milgrave's eyes. She was conscious of his hand upon Miss Milgrave's, conscious of the way his body touched hers as they went through the motions of the dance.

She tried once more to put a good face upon it for the benefit of Sir William, whose malicious gaze was probing her face. She knew he would be delighted by any sign of unhappiness and jealousy on her part.

"I gather everybody is just waiting for the announcement," she said, and was glad that her voice had not quavered. "Miss Milgrave is a beautiful girl and I hope she will be very happy." Even as the words left her lips, Juliana knew that they were lies. She loathed Miss Milgrave, and never more than at this moment when she was dancing with the marquis.

"I believe you have some prior acquaintance with Peterborough. Did you not meet him on your journey down to London?" Sir William Goring Pelham was smiling a nasty little smile as he made this malicious remark.

She did not give him the satisfaction of showing any confusion.

"Yes, indeed," she managed to say casually. "I gather everybody knows about his shocking behavior then. As for myself I do not bear him malice. I was taught a valuable lesson—that country towns are not safe for ladies of quality, when there is a prizefight in the vicinity."

Make what you like of that, she thought to herself. She was put in mind of that old nursery fairy tale proverb —*Be bold, be bold, but not too bold*—and wondered whether such frankness had been wise. But what else could she have said?

Sir William did not seem enormously happy with her reply, but he managed to come back with another sneer. "A valuable lesson, indeed, Miss Quincey," he said.

It seemed an age before the dance was over, and Juliana could escape from her unpleasant partner to the relative security of Lady Talboys's side. She found solace there, indeed, for Robert Torrington was waiting to claim her hand in the next dance.

Lady Talboys did not look very pleased at this new partner, but she said nothing. As Robert Torrington led her out upon the floor, Juliana could not help noticing Lizzie who was also taking the floor with a young man. Her eyes could not help following the young man with Juliana, though she looked away as soon as she caught Juliana's eye.

"I believe we have a friend in common, Mr. Torrington," said Juliana, determined to raise the subject. She smiled at him warmly as she did so. "If there is anything I could do to help either you or my cousin, Lizzie, then I should be delighted to be of assistance."

"Thank you so much, Miss Quincey," he said, his face lighting up with unfeigned pleasure. "I had wanted to ask your assistance, but it is not the easiest thing in the world to ask one charming young lady if she will help forward a love affair with another. I was quite at a loss how to bring up the subject. Your offer has saved me the embarrassment of seeming churlish."

"Come, come, Mr. Torrington. I am not so vain that I need every man to be my suitor," said Juliana with slight impatience. "But I do have a plan, to which I hope you and my cousin will agree. I think that you and I should seem to flirt together. If it is thought that you admire me, and that I am not adverse to your admiration, then it will conceal the true aim of your affections. I have told Lizzie that I would be happy to be a go-between, but I have not yet suggested that I should seem to encourage *your* attention. But I think she will agree to the scheme, do you not agree?"

"I think so indeed. And it will be a pleasure to flirt with you, by Jove, Miss Quincey," said Robert Torrington. He followed his remark up with a languishing look, so exaggerated that it made Juliana want to laugh. Then he twinkled and added, "Should you not tell Lizzie about your plan before we set it in motion? I should hate to give her cause for even a moment's doubt of my love!"

Juliana had to admit that she found his handsome looks and his undoubted charm rather telling. She also liked his consideration for Lizzie. All in all, she thought that he was a very nice young man who would probably make a good husband. He seemed kind, as well as amusing. "You are right, of course," she agreed. "Besides, we had best start cautiously. My grandmother has already warned me that you are a younger son, and that I should aim higher."

"Oh dear, you cannot think how much I hate the sound of that phrase, 'younger son,' Miss Quincey," said her partner in mock dismay. "It seems to haunt me everywhere. I suppose I should own to you that I cannot offer Lizzie the kind of life I should like to. I am not a pauper, but I have nothing but my commission and a few hundred pounds to live on. I assure you that I know this looks bad, but I am not a fortune hunter. Nor would Lizzie's portion—were I one of that odious gentry—tempt me. We must content ourselves with living very modestly if ever we marry. I for one could be happy in a cottage with Lizzie. But I do not at the moment see any prospect of that happy conclusion. I fear that Lady Helen is not my friend."

"That's true, Mr. Torrington. Lady Helen has a great regard for money, and I fear that nothing but the immediate possession of a handsome fortune would make you acceptable to her. Have you no aunt, nor rich cousin, who can die conveniently and leave you an estate? That seems to be how the heroes of romances manage."

"I fear I have no expectations from any such source," said the young man mournfully. "The only way that I could become rich would be if—and God forbid it—my elder brother died. He and I are not bosom friends, but I should be most sorry to see ill befall Gerald. No, Miss Quincey, there will be no convenient legacy to soften Lady Helen's heart, I am afraid."

Juliana liked his frankness. His honesty about his prospects—and his refusal to make his condition seem a whit the better—pleased her. She felt that he was a man who was not afraid to face facts as they were. It was too bad that Lady Helen was so mercenary. "Do you think you could call on me tomorrow, Mr. Torrington?" she asked him diffidently. "I may have the chance of some confidential words with Lizzie this evening and then I can tell you if she agrees that I should become your go-between. I think it would be best if you did not dance with her this evening. Do not be anxious. I will tell her of the reason, and get her permission for your setting up as my admirer."

Young Mr. Torrington's face fell, when Juliana said she thought he should not dance with Lizzie. "That is too bad," he said ruefully. "However, I daresay you are right. Dear Miss Quincey, a thousand thanks. You have given me hope. I have been despairing of a way to further my love, but now you have come to make things easy. I shall rely on you utterly, and so, I know, will my darling Lizzie."

"I cannot promise miracles," Juliana warned. It seemed to her that young Mr. Torrington was placing inordinate faith in her. "But I shall do my best. There is nothing I would like more than to help dear Lizzie find true love and happiness."

As Robert Torrington took her back to Lady Talboys's care, Juliana reflected that her promises were easier to make than to keep. She realized that as a young lady who always needed a chaperon she had very little privacy. Though Lizzie was standing nearby she did not dare mention the subject of Robert Torrington to her. She was afraid that Lady Talboys might overhear. Indeed she was conscious that Lady Talboys had not ceased for a moment to keep an eagle's eye upon her during the whole of that last dance. She was already giving Juliana searching looks. She must have noticed that the two of them—Juliana and Robert Torrington—seemed to be getting on very well and drawn her own mistaken conclusions.

Suddenly Lady Talboys's expression changed. Juliana looked round to see what had caught her attention. She paled, and for a moment felt she might faint. Then a feeling of determination pulled her together. Toward them was strolling the Marquis of Peterborough with magnificent but careless grace. She had time to notice his clothes. He was in scarlet silk of an unusual plainness. Only a very slight embroidery on the waistcoat and round the button holes picked out its impeccable cut. But the lace at his neck, and at his wrists was priceless. Rubies sparkled on his fingers and at his throat, and he was carrying a silver-topped cane. This evening he did not wear a sword.

As always, he created a frisson of interest in all the ladies round about him, even among the matrons well into middle age. There could hardly be a female in the room, thought Juliana bitterly, who was not taking notice of what he was doing. No doubt they were all agog to see what would happen when he addressed her. She determined that she would not let her grandmother down this time. She *must* keep control of herself.

Even Lady Talboys looked somewhat alarmed, while Lizzie Reddington by her side looked curious, and James Reddington a little further away looked disgusted. Juliana hoped that her own pounding heart could not be heard by anybody but herself. The marquis came straight up to her, and said, with what looked suspiciously like a mocking glance, "May I have the pleasure of this dance, Miss Quincey?"

To give herself time, Juliana sank into a low curtsy, then she held out her hand to the marquis who kissed it without much enthusiasm. He bowed, too. Any onlooker would have thought it a scene of formal propriety. Juliana, however, was fully alive to the irony of it all.

He took her hand upon his arm, and led her out from her chaperon's side. It was rather like going out to meet the foe on a battlefield, thought Juliana. She knew that all eyes were upon her, and she felt that the marquis, too, must be well aware of this. Was he doing this to tease her? She wished she had the icy calmness of Miss Milgrave, whose color never seemed to come and go like her own. She could feel the hot blood running up to her cheeks, and the palms of her hands moisten with anxiety. She only hoped that the blush was not too fiery.

"Your natural feelings of embarrassment and anger do not show at all," said the ironic voice by her side. Like the Marchioness, the Marquis was something of a thought reader. "You look very well, Miss Quincey. Nobody

114

could tell that you were suffering from an insane wish to strangle me."

"You are insufferable, sir," said Juliana in a voice so low that nobody might hear. His words were teasing, and she felt in no mood to see anything funny about them. "Is this your idea of a joke? Have you asked me to dance so that you may insult me further at your leisure?"

"Cool your temper, Fair Fury," said the odious marquis. Although his tone was far from friendly, he wore a fixed smile on his face. He took his part in the dance with a kind of elaborate grace, so that the matrons round the side of the room could see only an apparently smiling good-humored figure. "You should be grateful to me, little termagant."

"Me! Grateful?" Juliana's voice nearly broke through her self-control. She managed to keep it down.

"Grateful! What else?" said the relentless voice of the man by her side. "Do not flare up so easily, Miss Quincey, else you will spoil all. The purpose of our dance together, you know, is not to cause another ill-bred scene to amuse the vulgar."

"I do not understand why we are dancing together at all," said Juliana roughly. "We are hardly friends. Indeed we obviously do not like each other. I find you quite detestable! And you, for some strange reason quite beyond my comprehension, seem only to wish to torment me!"

"The purpose of our dance," he explained patiently but with a note of exasperation in his voice, "is to restore your wounded reputation, Fair Fury. If it is seen that you and I can smile at each other, and generally conduct ourselves with self-control and self-discipline, then it is to be hoped that the scandal surrounding your burst of temper the other day will die down. You see, you should be grateful. I am not doing this to amuse myself, but in order to do *you* a favor."

"What exquisite thoughtfulness! What gallantry!"

mocked Juliana. "Has it not occurred to you, sir, that this would not be necessary, had you only refrained from insulting me at our first meeting?"

"How the devil was I to know that you were a lady of quality?" he retorted, still with the maddeningly fixed smile on his face. "You were dressed like a shopkeeper's minx. Besides, I don't consider that a kiss is an insult. Many females would have been only too pleased to be in your place, Fair Fury! I consider that I was excessively civil to you."

"Do you never consider anybody's feelings but your own?" protested Juliana. "Pray, think of my shame, my confusion!"

"I don't think of 'em. Why should I? Besides, it was not the action of a well-bred young lady to make a scene when I returned your glove. Fondness I did not expect; good manners, however, I did. You were singularly discourteous, yourself, Miss Quincey. No, do not frown at me! It will only set the gossip going again! Smile sweetly so that all the old tabbies think you and I are fast friends."

Juliana forced herself to smile. Through her teeth she muttered: "It is enough to make me feel sick. I detest you, you know!"

"That remark is not kind, Miss Quincey. I am, on the contrary, becoming quite fond of you. And when I think of the sweetness of our first encounter, I am minded to repeat the pleasure." His voice was as mocking as ever.

Juliana felt she was going mad with the effort of restraining her rage. She felt she could not bear this charade a moment longer, and tried to break away and run off the floor—only to find that her hand was held in a grasp of iron. She was forced to continue her part in the dance. It was like a nightmare.

"I would not run away like that, Miss Quincey," came the odious voice. "You will do yourself harm, and you will also disgrace Lady Talboys. She is an old lady who sets some store by appearances. *You* may be entirely impatient of courtesy and convention; but pray, think of your grandmother. Further scandal must distress her."

He was right, of course, Juliana had to admit to herself. But she would not give this teasing monster of a man the satisfaction of hearing her say so. She rallied her dignity and managed to say, "I am glad that you can, at least, consider the feelings of Lady Talboys, however careless you are of my own. I will endeavor to control my feelings of detestation for you. I see that, however natural they may be, they are neither profitable to me nor to my grandmother. When this charade is over, after all, we need see each other no further save at a distance. I shall no doubt find some congenial company of a more serious nature elsewhere, and you will no doubt soon be busy with the announcement of your impending marriage to the admirable Miss Milgrave."

"You are quite wrong, Miss Quincey," said the Marquis. "We will be seeing a great deal more of each other. I am beginning to get quite attached to your company. Your rudeness is refreshing, Fair Fury. It makes a difference from toadeating, at least. I am finding your hot temper quite stimulating. We are two of a kind, you know? Or perhaps you would prefer to pretend otherwise?"

Juliana did not quite know how to shrug off this gallantry which was so little to her taste. She decided she would fall back on politeness and insincerity. "Lud, sir," she said with a creditable imitation of a fashionable titter, "I do not know what you mean! You are too clever for me! Do you not find this assembly delightful? Is not this a charming evening?"

"You know very well that I find the assembly damnably boring, Fair Fury," said the marquis. "What is more I do not find fashionable small talk in the least amusing either, so spare me that at least. Besides, it is not your forte. You are not a simpering silly miss, Fair Fury, so do not pretend to be, when you are dancing with me."

Juliana smiled for the first time without any pretense. She could not help it. There was something very refreshing about his honesty, even if the man was a rake and a debaucher. "I am shocked at your opinions, Lord Peterborough," she said in the most simpering voice she could assume. "Fie, sir! And such language! 'Tis enough to make me cover my ears!"

"You're not shocked at all, Fair Fury," said the marquis with a grin. "You may think you are a virtuous little rustic, but I know better. You are no fonder of humbug than I am, Miss Quincey, though you've not yet discovered how much there is about. As I say, you may not like it, but we are two of a kind."

The music stopped. Juliana was glad. She felt that the conversation was getting on dangerous ground, and that her own defenses were slipping. Talking to the marquis was rather like treading on ice, she thought—you never knew whether it might not break under your feet, plunging you into his icy disapproval. She gave him one of her most graceful curtsies after he had led her back to her grandmother. "Thank you, my lord, for the dance," she said primly.

"Thank *you*, Miss Quincey," he said with irony. Then to Juliana's disappointment, he turned away, going back to a group of young men who were making a noisy game at one of the card tables. Although she disapproved of the sparring way he conversed, it had been stimulating, she thought.

The rest of the evening should have pleased her, since a number of young men danced with her. The faithful James Reddington was among these. Once again he entertained her by telling her of numerous interesting facts connected with assemblies both of today and of ancient times. His conversation was very educational, thought Juliana, but somehow it seemed rather boring. She found herself longing for a less conventional talk. The other young men were all polite, and she began to feel that she was quite a social success. But she found their conversation insipid. She thought it must be the frivolity of the fashionable world, perhaps.

She was glad, however, to see that Lady Talboys seemed pleased with her. "Kind of that rascal, young Peterborough," the old lady grunted in the coach back to Curzon Street. "I always said that he had a kind heart, for all his rakish ways. I would have thanked him, if I could. The marchioness must have put him up to it, should think. He's prodigiously fond of his mother. Wouldn't want to upset her. She's a good woman, Anne. You must remember to thank her, when you next see her, Juliana."

"Of course, grandmama," said Juliana obediently, suppressing a feeling of disappointment. "Do you think the Marquis only danced with me because his mother had asked him to?"

The old lady gave her a sharp look in the darkness of the coach. "Why not, child? Of course, there is another possibility. He may be seeking to attach you. He is devilishly charming, and it's well known that he has only to throw the handkerchief for any female to pick it up. He's quite unscrupulous with women, too. I don't say that's what he's doing, but as a conscientious chaperon I should remind you about that wager at White's. That set of young bloods may have put him up to it. There's nothing they'd like more than to see the Marquis laying siege to you, child. I can only warn you, Juliana, to make quite certain that you don't lose your heart to him."

"I wouldn't do anything so foolish," said Juliana fiercely. "I quite detest that odious Marquis of Peterborough."

Six

The next morning Juliana was able to forget the odious marquis. Lady Helen, with the delighted support of Lizzie, had arranged for her to join them in a charming expedition to St. Pancras Wells. It was fashionable to spend a morning in the rural surroundings of the town, either drinking milk fresh from the cows at Chalk Farm, or eating strawberries picked from the market gardens of Lambeth and Brompton.

St. Pancras Wells combined many delights. The waters, themselves, were advertised as "a powerful antidote against the rising of the vapors and a sovereign help to Nature," though even Lady Helen admitted that they were not very pleasant to taste. However there were other pleasures. For the gentlemen there were wines, a curious punch, and Dorchester and Ringwood beers. For ladies, set on a morning frolic, there was "new milk and cream and syllabubs in the greatest perfection" from the cows which were specially kept. Glasses of milk, frothing and still warm from the cow, were a specialty, as were cheesecakes. And the gardens were extensive with bowling alleys, fish ponds, and long straight walks amid avenues of trees. There was even, Lady Helen promised Juliana, a ladies' walk in which gentlemen were not permitted— "which is particularly convenient when one wishes to avoid the importunities of the rougher sort late at night."

Juliana, fresh from the real countryside, had found the idea rather amusing. She had consulted the expert Pinkerton on what she should wear, and had been told that this was just the occasion for her simpler dresses. "A milkmaid look is very in vogue," said Pinkerton seriously. "For that you should wear your *bergère* hat, the one without the silk trimming, and I suggest your pink and white striped lutestring with no hoop just panniers."

As always, Pinkerton had been absolutely right. As Juliana arrived she was greeted by the sight of fashionable London dressed in elaborately simple wear. Many of the ladies had taken the opportunity to don villager hats and generally appear in very fashionable undress. Aprons, often beautifully embroidered and trimmed with expensive lace, were much in evidence, as were lacy handkerchiefs at the bosom. Hoops had been discarded, and most of the ladies were dressed in nightgown frocks or *robes a l'anglaise*.

Fortunately for Juliana and Lizzie, Lady Helen soon met up with several matronly friends of hers, and settled down in the pump room to sip the waters, enjoy the syllabubs and talk of fortunes, settlements, family alliances, and dowries. "May Juliana and I take a stroll among the trees," begged Lizzie prettily. "There are some vastly pretty prospects which I am sure Juliana would find charming."

"Of course, my dear, but do not go too far, mind. At this time in the morning the rougher sort are not here, but I saw several cits in the gardens," warned Lady Helen.

"My dear Juliana, do not let my scatterbrained daughter take you too far. I rely on you to keep an eye on her."

"I will do my best. But I own I *should* very much like to purchase a drink of milk from the cows, Lady Helen." Juliana curtsied obediently. The two girls set off arm in arm, making a charming picture. As Lady Helen observed to her cronies, it was most convenient that not only should Miss Quincey have ten thousand a year, but she was just of the face and figure to set off Lizzie's black hair and tall figure to advantage. "I am sure that you must look far to find two such sweet girls," she cooed.

The sweet girls were having a conversation that would have shattered Lady Helen's complacency if she had heard it. "Dearest Juliana," sighed Lizzie, once they were safely out of earshot, "I am all eagerness to talk to you. I could not fail to see you dancing with Robert. Is he not charming? Do you not think he is handsome? And so noble in his thoughts and feelings. Did he confide in you? I fear that he may have felt our case is desperate, for he did not once ask me to dance."

"Why, I thought him a very handsome man, and what is more he is madly in love with you, Lizzie. 'Twas I advised him not to ask for your hand in the dance. For I have a plan. Indeed, I swear that he did not have a thought in his head, except for you, and he charged me with all kinds of sweet nothings to tell you. It was enough to make any right-minded young lady jealous. He avowed his love for you to me, and said he did not know how he could get your parents' consent."

Lizzie clasped her hands together in relief. "I am so relieved to hear it. I will own, dear cousin, that I had sensations of jealousy when I saw that he danced with you but never asked for my hand all evening. You can imagine my dismay! I knew, of course, that he was all goodness, all constancy, but I could not help the natural anxieties which arose in my mind!"

"Silly Lizzie," said Juliana affectionately. "I expect

you saw us flirting a little. Well, that is part of my plan. I have determined to set myself up as a go-between for you both, and Mr. Torrington agrees that it will look more natural if he is seen to turn his attentions toward me. Then your mama will be the more easily fooled."

"She has already been so, dear Juliana," confessed Lizzie. "Indeed the feelings of jealousy that I have mentioned were partly provoked by her. She told me that Robert was no doubt a fortune hunter, and that he had turned his attentions from me to you, because you have the greater fortune. Of course, I did not believe her! But I nevertheless felt qualms of uncertainty!"

"There was no need for it," reassured Juliana. "What both of you need, I think, is a plan of campaign. I have asked Mr. Torrington if there is likely to be any change in his circumstances, which might make him acceptable to your mama, Lizzie. He says there is none. He has no expectations. This you probably already have asked. Do you think, however, that you could persuade your father to give his consent to the marriage?"

"I do not believe I could persuade papa to go against mama's wishes. He always does what she says. If she would agree, then I am sure he would be delighted. I know that he thinks well of the Torrington family, and that he thinks Robert is a fine young man. Indeed, if I were safely married to him, I am sure that papa could help him rise to higher rank in the Army. Being so closely connected with the Admiralty, Papa has much influence in military circles."

"This is most promising," said Juliana with satisfaction. "The real obstacle to your marriage, then, is your mama and her determination that you should marry a rich man."

"She is a formidable obstacle," said Lizzie hopelessly. "I know that mama would *never* consent. If I so much as asked her, she would simply send me down to my odious old aunt in the country, and I should never be allowed to see Robert again."

"Well, if you do not feel you can even ask your parents, then what other course of action is left to you?" pondered Juliana, more to herself than to Lizzie.

"If only I could just run off and get married quietly to Robert. I should not want a rich wedding. The merest of ceremonies would be enough for me!"

A thought struck Juliana. "What about doing just that, Lizzie? Why not run off with Mr. Torrington and get married without your parents' consent?"

"Oh Juliana, do not tease me! Don't make me think of such tempting things! I am sure I could never manage it. Imagine trying to climb out of my bedchamber at night! Besides, my maid would wake for she sleeps next-door and is a remarkably light sleeper. Then the whole household would be woken and I would be undone! No, no! I simply could not face doing such a thing!"

"But, Lizzie, you exaggerate," said Juliana in exasperation. "There would be no need for you to escape from the house at midnight, I am sure. What is to stop you just getting married one morning in London? I have heard that such marriages are common in the Fleet prison. You simply pay the parson, and the marriage is done. I remember reading about it in a book about London. I never thought that it would be of the slightest use for me to know such things about the metropolis, but I was wrong."

"Do I dare?" asked Lizzie Reddington, nervously pressing her hands to her face. She glanced round almost automatically towards the pump room where Lady Helen and two or three other matrons were still talking. "What on earth would mama do to me, when she found out? We should have to tell her eventually."

"I don't see that there is much she *could* do," said Juliana stoutly. "I am sure she would be very angry, but, consider, Lizzie—will she not be anxious to avoid scandal? Will she not wish to hush up the whole affair? Once you have gone through a marriage ceremony, she will have little choice but to accept it. She will want to get through the whole thing with as little fuss as possible, I am convinced. Your mama is very keen on propriety."

"That's true, and so is James," Lizzie replied, thinking hard. "And my dearest Robert will surely be able to bring her round to the idea, once the die is cast. No parent could fail to be impressed with the nobility of his bearing and the real sensibility of his feelings! Besides, even if mama *is* unaffected, I know that papa will be on my side. He is all for the quiet life, and so he will wish things just to die down. Surely he will argue for me."

"I am sure he will," encouraged Juliana. Privately she considered that the virtues of Robert Torrington would have little effect on Lady Helen. But she also thought that the potential scandal would act powerfully for him, making it necessary for Lizzie's mother to come to terms with the clandestine marriage as soon as possible. After money, Lady Helen's next thought was propriety.

"But how can we do this?" Lizzie suddenly said. "As I have said, nothing will persuade me to elope at night. I am simply not fitted for midnight escapades."

This was what Juliana had been waiting for. She outlined her plan of campaign. It all hinged on the fact that any couple, who had the necessary guineas to bribe the parson, could get married in one of the many "wedding shops" near the Fleet prison by one of the several notorious clergymen who operated from there. No banns or licenses were required. Indeed the trade was so well established that marriage hawkers solicited in the street with the words, "Pray step in and be married" to any couple who passed. Such were the details Juliana had learned from *The Antiquities of London*. It made her want to giggle to think that the unsuspecting Miss Humphries, who had insisted upon reading the book to her, should thus help in a clandestine marriage. How shocked that worthy governess would be! At the thought, she laughed aloud.

"Pray, what amuses you?" asked Lizzie, rather puzzled and a little offended.

"Nothing save a private thought of my own, dear Lizzie," was the reply. Then struck by a qualm of uncertainty, Juliana added, "You do really want to marry him, don't you Lizzie? I mean, you would not regret his lack of wealth, would you? Or feel that you had been cheated out of a proper wedding ceremony?"

"Oh, I do not care a fig for ceremonies and suchlike," said Lizzie, her eyes shining. "It will be enough for me if I can join my life and my fate to my dearest one. I know that a clandestine marriage is a very shocking idea, and that I shall have a disagreeable time until mama forgives me, but it will be too late for her to bully me into changing my mind and that is all I care about. Love is what matters! What does Robert think of the idea?"

"I have not told him yet," confessed Juliana. "It seemed to me that I should first of all see what your feelings were, dear Lizzie. But I *have* asked him to pay a call at Curzon Street and so, if my plan meets with your approval, I can sound him out on the topic. What do you say?"

"I say that you are my benefactor, dearest Juliana," exclaimed Lizzie. "I think it is a marvelous scheme, and I am sure Robert will be as grateful as I am." And she fell to working out some of the details of the plan with Juliana.

Later that day, when Mr. Robert Torrington called at Curzon Street, he fulfilled Lizzie's expectations. Eager to follow Juliana's instructions he had already left his card, while she had been at St. Pancras Wells. With devoted determination, he had gone away and come back later.

Luckily for Juliana, Lady Talboys was out by the time he called the second time. Having spent a quiet morning in bed, while her granddaughter tasted the spa waters under the chaperonage of Lady Helen, the old lady decided it was time she paid a call on Mistress Medway, a retired children's nurse to the Talboys family, who now lived in a tiny cottage in the village of Kensington. Lady Talboys—as she herself had pointed out—was not charitably inclined, but she did her duty as she saw it. Without any great fervor, she made sure that family retainers like Mistress Medway were pensioned off with an adequate income, and about once a year she bestirred herself to visit them. If she often came to scold rather than to sympathize it was forgiven, since all the retainers agreed that Lady Talboys's sharp tongue and blunt manner concealed a warm heart. By now, she was as old as many of the retainers, but such was her energy and vigor that nobody thought it odd that she should be calling on them, least of all Lady Talboys herself.

It was as well that she *was* absent, since she would have disapproved of the way Mr. Torrington was received at Curzon Street. Hitchens the butler, who showed him into the morning room, very properly asked Juliana if he should call Miss Pinkerton to accompany her. It was a suggestion Juliana spurned, and it was therefore an uneasy Hitchens who showed her into the morning room where the young man was waiting. Juliana was gratified to see that Mr. Torrington was the very picture of the anxious lover, suitably pale of cheek and pacing up and down the room nervously. She immediately outlined her plan to him and waited for his response.

Like Lizzie, Robert Torrington was of a romantical turn, and so his enthusiasm showed itself in a flood of words. "What can I say to thank you, Miss Quincey? Can I, *should* I allow the dear girl to risk her happiness in this way? My dearest Elizabeth is so young and innocent! Am I not behaving like a scoundrel so to take advantage of that sweet innocence? Tell me that I am not behaving badly? Or is it my duty simply to go away and suffer in silence my broken heart, hoping against hope that she may one day turn her affections to a more worthy object?"

"You know your duty best, I suppose," said Juliana, rather affronted by these words, though sure in her own mind that they were only rhetorical musings. "But I think it would be the meanest thing in the world to give up Lizzie now. After all, you have won her affections. If she has no objections to a clandestine marriage, I cannot see why *you* should. I do not think it is taking advantage of her innocence. You did that when you made your love known to her. Now it is up to you to to put that love into being. I would have thought it was obvious."

"Ah, but she is so young, so pure, so good!" rhapsodized the lover in what Juliana privately thought was a rather tiresome fashion. She was glad that she was not beloved by Robert Torrington. She had no taste for such fantastic and belated scruples. The flood of his words continued, "But how shall we manage the deception, Miss Quincey? How can Lizzie slip away from her chaperons? She is always guarded by her dragon of a mother."

He looked expectantly at his mentor. Like Lizzie, he seemed unable to think up any schemes for himself, reflected Juliana. They were both rather happy-go-lucky romantics, and really suited each other down to the ground. Patiently she explained about the Fleet marriage to Robert.

Juliana and Lizzie had not yet run over *all* the details, but Juliana was confident that there would be some way in which the two girls could escape the vigilance of Lady Helen and Lady Talboys. No doubt some errand could be invented whereby the two girls could go out on their own, and then meet Robert Torrington at the Fleet prison. With a hackney carriage, there need be no tale-telling by servants. Mr. Torrington might leave all that to Juliana. Did he not agree that it was a plan which could not fail?

Robert Torrington was all enthusiasm, all compliance. After careful discussion, the day was fixed—in three days' time. The details of where to meet were agreed upon.

"And when the ceremony is over, Miss Quincey," said the young man, "we must leave two or three days while I post down to see my brother and engage his help. I dare not approach him before the event, lest a careless word from him should alert Lady Helen to our plans. After we are safely married, then I will find him and beg his aid. We will defer telling the admiral and Lady Helen until I have seen him—in case he can find it in his heart to aid me with a larger allowance. I do not expect it, but I think I should at the least ask him."

"That's a good idea," agreed Juliana. "In the meantime until we meet at the Fleet prison, I think you should not endeavor to communicate with Lizzie. I think in fact you should continue to flirt with me, Mr. Torrington. No doubt it will displease my grandmother, but it will hide your true affections. If Lady Helen can be persuaded that you have fallen in love with me, in the place of her daughter, she will think you sadly volatile, but she will not entertain suspicions of the true state of affairs."

"I am a lucky dog, Miss Quincey, being given *carte blanche* to flirt with you," said Robert Torrington gallantly, and suiting the action to the words, he lightly kissed Juliana on the cheek. It was a brotherly peck, and Juliana accepted it as such without embarrassment.

It was therefore more than a little unfortunate that at that precise moment in time, the door should open to admit a visitor into the room. Juliana could not suppress a slight gasp, followed by a blush of embarrassment, when she turned around and saw who it was. To her horror, she found herself looking straight into the eyes of the Marquis of Peterborough.

"I am interrupting a very touching little *tête à tête,* I see," he sneered unpleasantly. "I am *de trop,* I fear."

"Not at all, Lord Peterborough," said Juliana briskly in a rush of exasperation. How typically odious of the man to come in without being announced! "Mr. Torrington and I have concluded our business together and he was on the point of leaving me. I hope that we shall meet again soon, Mr. Torrington." So saying she gave Lizzie's young man her hand as an unmistakable gesture of parting.

He lingered for a moment. "I should not wish to make too precipitate an exit, Miss Quincey, if my staying here could be of any help to you," he offered, looking anxiously at the grim expression of the marquis.

"No, Mr. Torrington, there is no possible way in which your company could help me. I shall look forward to seeing you tomorrow." Juliana's tone was dismissive. Obeying her commands, Robert Torrington bowed and took his leave.

When he was no longer in the room, the marquis broke the silence. "Do you usually receive young men as visitors entirely without a chaperon, Miss Quincey?" he asked in a disapproving tone of voice. "I must tell you that you are running a risk with your reputation to behave in so unconventional a fashion. For a female who made such a fuss about kisses, I am amazed to discover your embracing that young sprig. *His* kisses, it seems, are acceptable to you. Am I to congratulate you on a betrothal? Or am I merely interrupting a fast and furious flirtation, Miss Quincey?"

"It is not what you think," said Juliana resentfully. She was mortified to be discovered in this way by the one man in all London, whom she disliked the most. She was also uneasily conscious—and it did not improve her temper—that she was in the wrong. Nothing could have been so ill-timed, she thought, as the marquis's interruption, and unfortunately there was nothing she could say to allay his suspicions. The plan to get Lizzie and Robert married depended upon her being willing to be thought Mr. Torrington's latest flirt.

"How do you know what I am thinking, Miss Quincey? Reluctant as I am to play propriety, for it is hardly my usual role, I must warn you that such freedoms are outside of enough. I cannot believe that Lady Talboys would permit you to encourage the pretensions of a younger son. And it is quite, quite wrong to allow gentlemen to kiss you, unless you intend to marry them. You will be put down as a flirt, Miss Quincey, and I need not tell you, I am sure, about the dangers of further scandal."

"It ill becomes you, sir, of all men, to lecture me!" exclaimed Juliana with a sense of outrage. "Who is the cause of the scandal attaching to me? *You!* Who should I blame but you, for the way I have been watched over, spied upon, and gossiped about since my arrival in London? *You!* For the sake of a wretched wager, you have destroyed my reputation! Anyway, I am not in love with Robert Torrington, nor do I intend to engage myself to him in marriage. Nor am I even flirting with him! But I tell you this—if I was to fall in love with him, I think it would not matter too much. He is ten times more agreeable and kind than yourself! He may be just a younger son, but he has feelings!"

There was a pause. Then the marquis said: "Have I your word on that, Miss Quincey? Do you promise me that there is nothing between you and Mr. Torrington, and that the embrace which I saw you accepting with so much compliance was nothing more than a *brotherly* one?"

"You have my word, sir." She was almost crying with vexation and shame. "I do not expect you to understand brotherly or sisterly affection. I daresay you think there only can be one kind of hateful love between a man and a woman. Your whole experience, your way of life, every action you have ever performed is clearly quite opposed to natural friendship between the sexes. For you every kiss is a seduction, and every kindness from a man to a woman part of an odious game of debauchery. But it is not so to everybody!"

"I accept your word, Miss Quincey. I am forced to do so," said the marquis savagely. By now his eyes were glittering and his mouth was twisted into a ruthless sneer. "Very well then, if you do not care for that sprig of a young man, if you have no feelings for the *brotherly* Mr. Torrington, prove it! *Marry me!* Prove it I say!"

Juliana looked up in astonishment from the handkerchief that she had been twisting nervously in her hands. It was the most unexpected thing she had ever heard. The tall man in front of her seemed to be towering in rage, and then she thought perhaps she understood. Suddenly she was icy cold. "Am I to take that choleric outburst as a proposal of marriage, sir? Or is this some new torment, some refinement of teasing, that you have invented for the purpose of plaguing me?"

"It is a proposal of marriage, Miss Quincey. I am not in the habit of joking upon such topics. Let me repeat it. Prove that you do not love Mr. Torrington. Marry me." There was an odd tone in his voice, and his eyes were very dangerous.

It flashed through Juliana's mind that he might be drunk, but she knew it could not be intoxication so early in the day. "Thank you, sir, but let me tell you that you are the last man in the world that I should marry. I detest you, sir, and even the temptations of your rank and wealth are not enough to outweigh that hatred." Ironically she curtsied, and as she rose back to her full height she felt frightened. For just a second she thought he was going to hit her.

But the marquis had himself under control. The mocking note had gone from his voice, which was now shaking with rage, but he was master of his anger. "May I have the pleasure of knowing what I have done to win such hatred? I have always heretofore considered that, if I made a proposal of marriage, the recipient would at least be courteous, even if she refused me. But since meeting you, I have discovered that you are a new kind of female—you cannot be relied upon to behave with either decorum or good manners."

Now Juliana herself was in a towering rage.

"Had you behaved more like a gentleman," she said, "and less like a rake on our first encounter, I might have done no more than dislike you, Lord Peterborough. But I take leave to tell you, sir, that I have now gained quite a settled hatred for you. Everything I learn about you—your gaming, your wenching, your opera dancers and other females that you are so notorious for keeping, makes me think that you are a thoroughgoing wastrel. Besides, there is another thing. Do not think I am ignorant of the disgraceful wager which you have caused to be entered in the betting book at White's. I am convinced that for a gamester like yourself, even marriage proposals are not sacred. I will not help you win your bet by being so obliging as to enter into a marriage proposal with you. This is one wager you will have to lose, my lord!"

The marquis stood very still, and Juliana felt a pang of dismay. His eyes were alight and glittering with anger. His long fingers were clenched against his riding crop so fiercely that the blood was driven from them. Those same white fingers twitched the crop restlessly against his polished boots, making a tapping noise.

"I thank you ma'am for your opinion of my character," he said sharply. "I shall not bother you by disputing it. Rather I will remove myself. But first let *me* do some plain speaking."

What this plain speaking was to consist of was never to be known. For at that exact moment Hitchens knocked at the door. "Miss Quincey," said the butler, and it was plain that his composure was severely strained. The morning's events, of which he already disapproved strongly, had now culminated in a new trial. "There is a female personage outside with an . . . an urchin in tow. She insists on seeing you personally. I have not promised her that you will see her, of course. I have placed her in the library. Would you like me to tell her to go away?"

"Why ever do that?" said Juliana. "Let her in now, if you please. The marquis is just taking his leave."

The butler looked at the marquis with a mute appeal. With maddening coolness the Marquis of Peterborough looked back at him, and a slight twitch of his

134

lips in what looked like the beginnings of a smile was the only sign he gave that he was responding to Hitchens' unspoken appeal. "I collect that the . . . er . . . personage is a lady, and that she has some kind of grievance. I will stay with Miss Quincey while she receives her to ensure that she is not troubled with impertinence."

"Thank you, my lord," said the butler gratefully. "I am sure you will be able to advise Miss Quincey on the best course of action to pursue with this tradeswoman."

The last remark was calculated to awake the sleeping demon in Juliana's breast, and her indignation must have shown on her face. Certainly the marquis correctly interpreted her emotions for he let out a smothered laugh, as the butler disappeared to bring in the mysterious visitors. "Come, Miss Quincey," said the Marquis of Peterborough, "It seems that your butler thinks you need my protection. The role appeals to me. Do not spoil it with one of your tantrums. I must own that I consider it a refreshingly odd sequel to your rejection of my suit."

To her own surprise Juliana found she could see the ridiculous side of it all, and so it was to find both occupants smiling that the butler returned, ushering in a stout middle-aged woman, who held by the arm a very ragged and dirty little boy. Juliana immediately recognized the urchin whom she had attempted to help a few days ago, after her drive in the park.

Before she could say anything to reassure the trembling waif, the middle-aged woman with him burst into a long and involved speech:

"I am sure I am not wishful to trouble you, miss, not being one to be always troublin' the gentry even when it *is* a matter of money owin', but I thought it no less than my duty to come 'ere and bring this 'ere rascal to you. The boy's a proper thief and no mistake and I ought to give 'im up to the beadles, but for what I'm a compassionate woman and I don't like to see children hungry. But I catches 'im pinchin' a loaf of bread as soon as my back was turned. With all the customers waitin' to be served, 'e thought I couldn't see 'im, but I does, and then when I was givin' 'im a right 'idin' with the back of my 'and, 'e pipes up with your name, miss, and says you told 'im 'e could call on you."

"He was speaking the truth," said Juliana quickly, just managing temporarily to halt the flow of words. "I gave him my name and address in case he got into further trouble. Can I repay you for the loaves he stole, mistress ... er ... ?"

"Mistress Bateman, miss. No I don't need the price of a loaf, miss, what with the business going well. Nor do I grudge the lad a bit of the broken bread or a bit of the stale, but it's thievin' I don't 'old with, and what I want to know is 'ow you're goin' to stop this 'ere lad doing it."

"Well, I am not perfectly sure, at the moment," said Juliana. "But I do know that the first thing to do is to find him something to eat, and then to get him some proper clothes. After that, I expect we must find him some kind of trade. Is there any kind of trade you would like to follow?" she said kindly to the small boy, whose mouth was open with amazement at the fine house and folk around him.

"I dunno, miss," he muttered.

"What's your name, child?" The marquis's tone was unexpectedly soft.

"Frank."

"Frank what? What is your second name, boy?"

"I dunno, sir. Don't rightly 'ave a second name wot I knows of," said the small boy.

Mrs. Bateman, the baker, intervened. "They 'aven't got names nor parents nor nothin' those street boys," she explained. "I don't know what you know about the way the other 'alf lives, miss, but these 'ere children 'aven't got nothin'. I'm sure I do my best, but that's not much, for I've got my own family and five of 'em all alive to think of. But it went to my 'eart to see the boy stealin', and I said to myself, I'll see if this 'ere fine lady wot 'e talks of can do anything to 'elp 'im. For else it'll 'ave to be the work'us for 'im and there 'e'll only learn some more to thieve."

"You did quite right, Mrs. Bateman. I thank you," said Juliana quietly. "I suppose you don't need a helper in your bakery? I'd be delighted to aid you—to pay for his apprenticeship, if you think you could find a livelihood for the boy."

"No, Miss, thanking you kindly, I'm sure, but I couldn't see my way to it. My older boy works with me, and there's 'is younger brother to see to, and Mr. Bateman wouldn't like it, wot with 'im wantin' to carry on the business in the family, so to speak. But something's got to be done about this 'ere Frank, 'cos 'e'll turn to thievin' if not. It's all the little beggar knows 'ow to do."

"Yes, indeed, Mrs. Bateman. I do understand. I shall take charge of Frank now, and you may go back to your family. It was kind of you to bring Frank over here, and I shall not be ungrateful. If you would like to leave your name and your direction with the butler then you may expect a visit from me in the future. In the meantime, perhaps, I can offer you this to cover the expenses of your time and money in bringing the child here."

She took a couple of guineas out of her reticule, and handed them to the woman, whose face had brightened at the mention of pecuniary gratitude. She bobbed a curtsy, setting free the arm of the boy for the first time; then turning to the child she said roughly but kindly, "Now, look 'ere, lad, you listen to what the lady says and do what she tells you. You 'eard 'er say it. You'll get summat to eat, and summat to wear." With that parting admonition, she took herself out of the room, to be shown to the door by a very disapproving Hitchens.

The small boy was now left alone with Juliana and the marquis. She felt rather at a loss. What on earth was she going to do with him? Slightly confused, she called for Hitchens, and asked him to take the child to the kitchen and get him something to eat. "Then return him here."

The butler bowed. "What shall I tell Lady Talboys

when she returns? I beg pardon for saying so, Miss Quincey, but her ladyship will not be best pleased. We had best give the child up to the beadle."

"Just get the child something to eat, Hitchens. I will explain to Lady Talboys," said Juliana firmly. The butler departed obediently. She was aware that he was correct. Lady Talboys would not be pleased to find the household staff augmented by the presence of a small, dirty, and—if truth be told—smelly urchin.

"You know you can't expect your grandmother to keep the child," said the Marquis of Peterborough in a casual tone. There was a twinkle in his eye which suggested he was finding considerable amusement in Juliana's dilemma.

"I know I can't," said Juliana impatiently. "I must think of something to do. If only papa was still alive, he would help me! He knew exactly what to do with small boys, and indeed the estate has a school on it which would be just the thing for Frank. Only what can I do? How can I contrive it? I cannot take him there myself. And I do not think that Lady Talboys would let me send one of the footmen with him. I suppose I *could* send him by stagecoach, but ten to one he would just run away or get into some kind of trouble. Small boys are extremely troublesome."

"So are older ones," murmured the marquis provocatively. "I think you are at a stand, Miss Quincey. You will not be able to keep young Frank here. Lady Talboys is a delightful and very unusual lady of the old school, but she does not believe in rescuing members of the lower orders of society. I know I have heard her say as much a hundred times to my own mother."

"It is very difficult. I suppose I shall just have to risk quarreling with her. I must do *something* for Frank. I cannot just let him go back to the gutter. Even if I do give him money, that is where he will end up. After all, you heard the woman say that thieving was all he knew. He is bound to return to his old ways, and then what will happen to him? I shall just have to *make* Lady Talboys understand. Or perhaps I should turn to James Reddington. He is a sober man, and would undoubtedly help me."

"James Reddington! That pompous bore concern himself with a child in the gutter?" The marquis laughed. "You will draw a blank there, Miss Quincey."

"Why do you say so? Just because you do not like Mr. Reddington! Let me tell you that he has often expressed himself very well on the subject of the poor in my hearing. He feels all he ought to."

"I don't doubt it, Miss Quincey. James Reddington is very good at expressing his views, but just see if he will actually *do* anything.

Juliana was about to quarrel further, but she saw it was of no use. "Who else could help me?" she demanded.

"I could," said the Marquis.

"You?"

He smiled rather grimly at her evident astonishment. "It must be difficult for you to imagine that I possess *any* of the virtues, but believe me, Miss Quincey, I have *some* vestiges of compassion. Let me do this one good act, if only to show you that I am capable of acting on the purest of motives."

"What will you do with him?" demanded Juliana suspiciously. "What do you know of poverty and small boys?"

"I shall give him to my mother," said the marquis calmly. "She knows all about such things. Has she not told you about the orphanage she runs? And her schools? I had thought she must have discussed such things. She has taken a liking to you, I know."

"We did not really have a chance of talking about them," said Juliana uncomfortably.

The marquis understood her meaning immediately. "Ah," he murmured, "you were both too busy deploring my evil ways, I collect. Well, let me tell you what my mother has failed to do. She runs one orphanage and three schools, and she will know exactly what to do with Frank. You may safely let me take him away, and I will promise to convey him without any delay to my mother. Does that set your heart at rest?"

"Yes, of course," said Juliana. She felt that perhaps she ought to apologize to the man in front of her. "I owe you some sort of apology, my lord. I am sure such benevolence must bore you to death, so it is extremely kind of you to exert yourself in this way. I am sure that Frank will join his thanks to mine, when he returns."

In this she was wrong. For, in a few moments, when the small boy was brought back into the room under the horrified eye of Hitchens, his mouth was full and he was beyond words.

The butler's air of agonized concern lightened when Juliana told him that the Marquis was going to take the child. It further lightened when the marquis discreetly put something in his hand and suggested that Lady Talboys need not be worried by anything more than a passing mention of the boy's presence. Juliana heard the chink of not one but at least several coins, and though she disapproved of bribery, she could not but be glad that the marquis had given a sweetener to Hitchens. She knew that she was in disgrace with the butler, who was bound to tell Lady Talboys of her behavior. Perhaps his tale would not be so bad.

"Come, Frank," she said to the small boy. "You are to go with this gentleman, the Marquis of Peterborough. You must be very good and obey him, and he is going to take you to his mother. She will find you somewhere to stay with regular meals and a proper bed to sleep. And you will learn a proper trade."

"Come, child," said the marquis firmly. "I want no trouble from you."

"Yessir," said the small urchin, recognizing the voice of authority. Though obviously confused by the program spelled out for him, he did not forget Juliana. Awkwardly he tugged at his forelock in her direction, and managed a

140

clumsy bow. Juliana's heart melted. " 'Fanks, mum," he muttered.

Juliana looked over the head of the boy at the tall man who had helped her out of this difficulty. For a moment she forgot his arrogance, and the proposal which had so annoyed her. She just saw him as a benefactor. "Thank you, my lord," she said with a smile.

"Miss Quincey, what a damnable thing it is," said the marquis, and the mocking tone was back in his voice. "When you smile, you make me want to kiss you again."

"Well, you can't," snapped Juliana. And it was in a turmoil of rage and confusion, she saw the strange couple —the fashionable buck and the ragged urchin—to the front door.

Seven

Lady Talboys was in a bad temper when she returned. Nanny Medway had been more than usually tedious, subjecting Lady Talboys to a rambling denunciation of the modern girl, the high price of flour, and the unhealthiness and extravagance of current fashions. With the tyranny of an old retainer, she had hardly allowed Lady Talboys time to get a word in edgewise. Worse still, Nanny Medway led a blameless life, confined to her bedchamber, knitting repulsive garments for the poor. Even Lady Talboys was at a loss to find anything she could scold her for.

And if the visit had not been tiresome enough, she had been greeted at the front door of Curzon Street by what she privately called Hitchens' "resignation face." Every so often when his propriety or his patience had been tried beyond endurance, the butler would offer to leave her service. It was an offer never accepted. Indeed Hitchens would have been both astonished and hurt if it had been, since he never really had any intentions of going. What his ritual resignation usually required, thought Lady Talboys with irritation, was either a rise in the already excessive wages he was paid, or at least an hour listening to his grievances. She was already tired, but she listened.

A tangled story of the willful misbehavior of Miss Quincey, the shocking appearance of a tradeswoman and a beggar boy, the interview with Mr. Torrington, and the kindness and nobility of the Marquis of Peterborough emerged. Lady Talboys, who gave only half an ear to the story, made a mental note that she must talk to Juliana. It sounded as if once again the girl had cast all thought of the conventions to the winds, and was behaving badly. Lady Talboys was particularly cross about Mr. Torrington.

Her irritation was further increased by her maid Pinkerton, who insisted on telling her how her services as chaperon, kindly volunteered by Hitchens, had been spurned by Miss Quincey. "I am sure that I don't mind, what with having an armful of sewing to do, not to mention putting mothballs in your traveling cloak, my lady, but what I say is that miss has just no idea how to go on in London. I would be the last person to accuse her of flirting with Mr. Torrington or the Marquis of Peterborough, but what I say is that to receive them without a chaperon goes beyond the line of what is prudent or pleasing, and such conduct will be misunderstood. Mark my words."

Lady Talboys was in complete agreement with her maid, but she did not say so, thinking it better that the household staff should believe that Juliana had her grandmother's support. But at the first opportunity, she summoned the child to her bedroom, and demanded in her blunt outspoken way, "What's this, miss? I hear that you have been seeing Mr. Torrington! And the Marquis of Peterborough! And with no chaperon! I know that you cannot have wished to have Pinkerton with you, child, for I will agree that she can be tedious in the extreme. But to receive gentlemen alone without any kind of female present is the outside of enough. It simply will not do, Juliana! You have behaved like a hoyden, and, what is more, a simple-minded hoyden."

Juliana hung her head. She was aware that her grandmother had right on her side, and that she was in disgrace. "I expect you had only a garbled version, grandmama," she ventured cautiously, wondering what exactly Hitchens and Pinkerton had said. "I always intended to tell you." She then launched into an account of the afternoon, suppressing the plan she had fixed up with Robert Torrington and making no mention of the odious marquis's proposal. Mention of either of these, she thought, would lead to trouble.

The version she gave to her grandmother was that Mr. Torrington had merely stopped by to pay a call, and so had the marquis. The tradeswoman and the small boy were more difficult to explain and Juliana felt she had to tell the truth. Lady Talboys had been giving Juliana suspicious looks all through the narration, particularly when it concerned Mr. Torrington. It was when she was telling her grandmother about the Marquis's offer to take Frank off her hands, that the old lady broke into speech. "Stuff and nonsense, girl! You can't expect me to believe that the Marquis of Peterborough went off with some grubby beggar from the gutter!"

"I will confess that it surprised me. But he did. He told me that his mother has schools for orphans and that he would give the child into her care. I would never have let him take the boy otherwise, only I am sure I can trust the marchioness to do all that is proper."

"Well, well," mused the old lady. Her face brightened. "Perhaps the marquis really has developed a *tendresse* for you, Juliana, and is doing this to fix his interest with you. That would account for it."

"I would not be flattered if that was so," said Juliana, thinking of the graceless proposal made by the marquis. "But I fear there is a more likely reason. Rather than having a *tendresse* for me, I think he is just trying to win the wager which has been made. He probably thought this was a way to persuade me to fall in love with him. He will not succeed, I need hardly tell you."

The old lady looked at her penetratingly. "Humph," she snorted, "I hope you can be sure of that. He's devilishly charming when he wants to be. You wouldn't be the first female to lose your heart against your better judgment."

"Believe me, grandmama, I am totally impervious to that famous charm of his. I find him thoroughly detestable."

"Well, I only hope that you ain't thinking of that other worthless young man, Torrington. It would never do, Juliana. As for the marquis, I dare say he is just amusing himself."

Later in the day, Juliana wondered whether Lady Talboys' words had been prophetic. It looked as though the marquis was already repenting of the moment's attention he had paid her. The Reddingtons had asked Juliana and her grandmother to make up a party to see the up and coming David Garrick in *Richard II*. All the polite world was there, since the young actor was already making a name for himself for his unusual style of acting. Unlike the other two principal actors, Quin and Macklin, Garrick was remarkable for his informality. Where they had gone in for weighty and ponderous delivery, Garrick seemed to live and breathe on the stage. Juliana had heard of him within a few days of arriving in London, and was yearning to see him.

The occasion was particularly favorable because, the actor, as well as performing in the Shakespearean play had, himself, written the farce which came after the main performance. It had to be admitted that Lady Talboys had shown little interest in listening to the tragedy, maintaining that Shakespeare was "sad stuff even though it is now coming back into vogue." But she said that she would look forward to *The Lying Valet,* the title of the farce, after the main play.

At the theater Juliana once again saw Charlotte Milgrave, cool as an iceberg, wearing pearls and a sacque dress in exceedingly fine white satin. She was seated in the box opposite the Reddingtons, and the two girls, Lizzie and Juliana, dutifully bowed and waved to her across the auditorium. The beautifully behaved Miss Milgrave inclined her head ever so slightly, and lifted one gloved and languid hand just enough to signify that she was returning their salute.

It was then that Juliana noticed in the shadows of her box, the familiar lounging figure of the marquis, accompanied by his friend, Mr. Ponsonby. The lovely Charlotte leaned back in her chair, making good use of her fan, and exchanged some kind of remark with him, in what was for her a very lively fashion. The marquis evidently responded, for he leaned forward and actually succeeded in provoking what was some kind of laugh or titter from her. Mr. Ponsonby was meanwhile entertaining Mrs. Milgrave, dutifully aiding his friend by keeping the matron amused, thought Juliana savagely.

Mr. Reddington had seen the wave exchanged between the girls, and tactlessly said to Juliana, "I am so glad that you have made the acquaintance of Miss Milgrave. I am sure that you must have found her as notable for her good sense as she is for her beauty."

"So everybody has told me," said Juliana tartly. She was getting prodigiously tired of hearing Miss Milgrave's virtues. Lady Talboys always seemed to be mentioning them, as did Lady Helen. Now James Reddington joined the chorus. Perhaps Lizzie had been right, and he had paid court to the beauty.

"I hope I do not detect a note of envy in your voice, Miss Quincey," said the serious James Reddington by her side. "I must tell you that I do not consider you deficient in good sense, and it is clear to me that you have had a superior upbringing to Miss Milgrave in one respect at least—that of seriously devoting thought to some of the important aspects of the times we live in."

"Your paean of praises is almost too much for me," said Juliana crossly. Goodness gracious, she thought, I am beginning to talk like he does. She regretted having been surprised into incivility toward him, and wondered if he would notice the blighting irony of her remark. But Mr. Reddington merely looked slightly puzzled. To take his mind off it she said, "Has my grandmama told you about the extraordinary kindness of the Marquis of Peterborough? The Marquis has actually been so obliging as to help me with one of my charitable projects."

James Reddington did not smile, though Juliana had expected he might. She had after all related it as a joke.

"Your grandmama did tell me and, I feel it my duty to warn you, Miss Quincey, against allowing your sentiments to override your prudence," he said heavily. "I am quite at one with you in deploring the condition of the poor in London. But I do not think it is a suitable occupation for a young lady of your age to throw convention to the wind and involve yourself in rescuing a child from the gutter. You cannot be sure you were acting in his best interests, Miss Quincey. Sometimes the suffering of the poor is the inevitable result of a dissipated and feckless way of life—and produces a lesson for those that see it. If you intervene in the irresistible workings of natural law by injudicious charity, you may be acting against divine providence."

"What on earth can you mean?" asked Juliana in dismay. She was genuinely confused by his attitude. She had thought that James Reddington would have been supporting her in her attempts to rescue little Frank. "I thought you would have approved of me. Why, I well remember when I had first met you, that you praised my father's work as a great philanthropist. I had thought you must favor what helps rescue the poor from degradation and starvation."

"That is true. I had been made aware of your father's excellent work," Mr. Reddington replied with

148

complacence. "I believe that even my greatest enemies would allow that I have taken an interest in the charitable and philanthropic works that are now on foot. But that is very different from the *individual* and imprudent exercise of charity, Miss Quincey. I do not mean that I am against the giving of alms, within reason, to worthy people who live a godly and sober life—but I do not think that we should extend this indulgence to those who live in idleness and sin. To aid a boy who makes his living thieving in the street is to encourage dishonesty."

Juliana was silent, digesting his words. It seemed that she had misjudged Mr. Reddington. True, he was of a serious, even a pompous, nature. True, he disapproved of gaming and fashionable excesses. He knew a little about charity, too, but this did not seem to be something he practiced as an individual. No doubt he was one of the worthy subscribers to various schemes set up to help the poor.

Sir Basil had often taken a dim view of such schemes, saying that they were frequently ill-advised associations of fashionable people who wanted to make a display of their noble feelings rather than to do practical good. His view was that every single individual who was comfortably circumstanced should practice individual acts of charity. "Only in that way, will the shocking conditions of the poor be truly alleviated," he maintained.

She wanted to question James Reddington further. Perhaps she was being unfair.

"Does that mean, Mr. Reddington," she asked, "that you think I should not concern myself with such actions? How could you approve of papa? He actually ran the almshouses on the estate. He did not get somebody else to do so."

"My dear Miss Quincey, your papa is notable in certain circles for setting out a system of almshouses, which I believe to be most effective. However, I have never ventured before to criticize him, since I was not acquainted with him, but I believe that his own involvement in such projects *was* misguided. 'Twould have been more proper for him to hire some worthy man to administer such schemes for him."

"What about the Marchioness of Peterborough?" parried Juliana with growing indignation. "I gather she runs various schools and patronizes an orphanage."

"I would not like to criticize any lady of fashion who is unfortunate enough to marry into the St. John Family," said Mr. Reddington stiffly. "Nor can we judge your conduct by hers, Miss Quincey. You are a lady only just out in society; she is a married woman of an age which must be expected to be secure from the backbiting of the scandalous or the wonder of the ignorant. It is entirely different in your case."

It was perhaps fortunate that the curtain rose just as Mr. Reddington finished. Juliana felt so out of sympathy with him, that she could have slapped his face. Such tedium, such intolerable prosing on, made her want to scream with frustration. She had entirely misunderstood him, she realized. What she had taken for the strong principles of charity and warm feelings of philanthropy, were nothing but the arid and boring views of a man who had a better opinion of *himself* than of the rest of mankind. She had agreed with him when he had condemned gaming as extravagant and time-wasting. She had not realized that it was more in his nature to condemn others, than to do anything himself. The Marquis of Peterborough had warned her that Mr. Reddington was all words and no actions. It seemed that he was right.

The performance was everything Juliana had hoped it might be. It was a new departure for the London stage to present the plays of Shakespeare more or less as the Elizabethan playwright had written them. For the fashion had been to rewrite the plays, till they were barely recognizable. Macklin, one of Garrick's rivals, had started the new trend by reviving *The Merchant of Venice*. Garrick continued the trend, adding to it his new acting style of foregoing formal stage declamation in favor of entering into the characterization. Juliana was enraptured by his performance as the unhappy King Richard II. She had never before seen a stage performance, though she and Sir Basil had often amused themselves by reading the works of Shakespeare to each other in the library of her old home. She gave herself up to the tragedy, ignoring the restless fidgeting of both Lady Helen and Lady Talboys, and the whispered comments of Mr. Reddington who took it upon himself to make sure that the ladies thoroughly followed the plot by adding little explanations to almost every scene.

In the interval before the start of the farce, James Reddington favored the company with his views on the performance of Garrick, the propriety of performing Shakespeare's plays, and the character of the tragic King Richard II. These views passed imperceptibly into his now familiar criticisms of the gambling set. Juliana could not help but see that he was repeating himself, and was gloriously unaware of how much he was boring the womenfolk.

"Take the Marquis of Peterborough," he said gravely, and Juliana, who had rather allowed her attention to drift off, came quickly back to full alert. "He is universally acknowledged to be of good family, well-liked by his contemporaries, admired by his intimates. Altogether he cuts a fine figure in the fashionable world. Yet it is well known that he is a reckless gamester and that he has the reputation of having had numerous opera dancers and actresses in keeping. I will not sully the ears of Elizabeth or Miss Quincey by saying more. Suffice it to say, that he is a man better known for his vices than his virtues."

"That's true," said Lady Helen, giving the conversation a twist in the direction of her own preoccupation. "'Tis said that he squandered two thousand pounds a year on that actress he had in keeping last year. As for his losses at play, they are not to be thought of! 'Tis a wonder that the estate can bear it, though 'tis well known that the St. Johns are shockingly rich."

"I heard that the marquis had been a good friend to Ponsonby," said Lizzie quietly. She had been silent for most of the evening, her natural high spirits smothered by the nearness of her mother. From the way she had cast several anxious glances, Juliana realized that she was worrying about Robert Torrington and the planned elopement. With the close proximity of her family, there was at present no way that Juliana could reassure her.

"Yes, Ponsonby was bankrupt—nothing but ruin or the Fleet prison left," said Lady Talboys. There was a note of malice in her voice which Juliana thought was aimed at James Reddington. "It's well known that the marquis bailed him out, and a pretty penny it must have cost!"

"As much as five thousand pounds 'tis said," Lady Helen interjected with unfeigned awe.

"Such generosity was no doubt inspired by the fear that he had been responsible for encouraging Ponsonby into extravagant habits in the first place," James Reddington stated grimly. "Ponsonby follows the marquis's lead. The least that Peterborough could do would be to rescue him from the consequences of his own bad influence."

"It sounds like a kind action," said Juliana heartily. Her remark fell on hostile ground. Lady Helen looked frankly incredulous, Lady Talboys bored, and Lizzie anxious. A change of subject seemed desirable, not least because Mr. Reddington looked ready to go into a prolonged sulk. "What do you think of the play, Lady Helen?" she ventured to ask that formidable matron.

"Garrick is an actor who must always please," said her ladyship without very much enthusiasm. " 'Tis said that he is so well liked that Fleetwood, the manager, has to pay him double what he pays Peg Woffington. Of course, this new fashion for Shakespeare is prodigiously profitable. It saves the cost of a new play."

The conversation then became general and less charged with emotion. Juliana could not help noticing that the Marquis of Peterborough was still in the box with the Milgraves. He had seen the play from there, and seemed to be planning to see the farce as well. Perhaps it was as it should be, she told herself. *She* could not find pleasure in his company, but she supposed that the calm and less emotional Miss Milgrave might enjoy what she, herself, detested. There was, after all, no accounting for tastes.

In the cheaper stalls below, she caught sight of Robert Torrington gazing up toward their box. Lizzie, from the look of the blush on her face, had seen him too. He made an unmistakable wave in their direction, to which Lizzie, heedless of discretion, responded. Hurriedly Juliana diverted attention by waving too. Her gesture caught the eye both of Lady Helen and Lady Talboys. Lady Helen merely looked down her nose with disapproval, but Lady Talboys, less tactfully, gave a snort of disapproval. Juliana guessed that if James Reddington had not been present, her grandmother would have fabored her with a piece of her mind.

It was becoming vital that she should somehow get five minutes private conversation with Lizzie. Fortunately, Lady Helen, showing signs of incipient boredom, asked her son to accompany her to the Milgrave box. "I must have a word with that sweet girl," she said. Something in her voice made Juliana think that this was an indirect snub to her. "Shall you come too, Elizabeth?" asked Lady Helen. "James, I know, will accompany me."

"No, mama," said Lizzie quickly. "I wish to consult dear Juliana about the ribbons on my tabby silk frock. Do you think, dear cousin, that they should be changed for a crimson? I have a mind to brighten up the garment, and I thought new ribbon might do the trick. Molly my maid says that crimson would look too bright, but I think it might suit extremely well."

Juliana was well aware that this was just a conversational gambit. She responded with unusual earnestness. "Crimson ribbons! Never! My dear Lizzie don't be so provoking! I am sure that they would make you look fast, if I have the right frock in my mind. Besides, 'tis silver which is all the rage. Bring your chair a little closer to mine, and I will show you what I mean. Do you see that lady down there? The one with the powdered hair, and the prodigiously fashionable silk?"

With all the ingenuity at their command, the two girls talked silks and ribbons, brocades, calicoes, velvets, muslins, and trimmings until Lady Helen had left, taking with her at the last moment Lady Talboys. The old lady had heaved herself to her feet and said rather rudely, "If the two girls are going to talk fashion, I'll come with you, Helen. I never could abide mercers' talk and I'd better be bored by Charlotte and Amelia Milgrave than by an endless discussion of ribbons."

"There is nothing that grandmama finds more tedious than talk of shopping and fashions," said Juliana with satisfaction. "It is odd in a way, because she says that clothes are of first importance. But when it comes to buying them, then she usually sends me out with Pinkerton, her dresser. Still, I did not mean to bore you with these details. Now at last we are alone and I can tell you all! No, Lizzie, do not look at Mr. Torrington like that! I am sure the expression in your eyes will give you away. Remember your mama can see us from the Milgraves' box. Fix your eyes elsewhere."

"Very well, Juliana," breathed Lizzie, "but quickly tell me what plan has my dear Robert thought up? Is it to be a clandestine marriage?"

With real nobility, Juliana refrained from reminding Lizzie that the marriage was her plan, and that all dear Robert had done was to agree with her ideas. Instead, she outlined the marriage scheme, this time in greater detail.

"Mr. Torrington," she said, "thinks that it will be best if you do not tell your family for the first two or three days after the marriage. He wishes to inform his elder brother, who I believe is in the country on his estate, and beg his help in supporting a wife. He is not sanguine about his elder brother's generosity, but he believes it is worth an attempt, at least.

"Meanwhile, Lizzie, you will need the help of somebody in your household. I have considered and come to the conclusion that your mama and my grandmama will insist upon some kind of chaperon. Even if we say we are going to choose ribbons, they will want to send somebody with us. Unless you can bring one of your household, Miss Pinkerton will be foisted upon us and that would never do. She is firmly attached to my grandmother and could neither be cajoled nor bribed into helping us. Indeed I think she would disapprove most strongly, for she is very fierce about conventions."

"Oh that is all right, Juliana. I shall bring my maid, Molly. She used to be my nursemaid when I was still in the schoolroom, but when I came out, mama said I needed a lady's maid and that Molly should become it. She is completely dedicated to my interests. When we were young she would never tell tales of either James or me to mama. Besides she is a great reader of romances, and is fond of all kinds of tales about lovers. I think, if I tell her about my love for Robert, she will be captivated by the idea of helping a clandestine marriage."

"You are quite sure that she is trustworthy?"

"Quite certain. Besides, whom else can I trust? Certainly I cannot rely on James, you know. He would immediately inform my mother, if he knew what we planned, and he would tell me he was doing so for my own good. Though he may be my brother, and though you may like him, Juliana, I consider him very stuffy indeed. He has no idea of what it feels like to be in love, and I truly believe that he has very little sensibility, himself, and so cannot recognize it in others."

"He is a good man in some ways," said Juliana thoughtfully, "but I will own to you Lizzie, that I cannot escape a certain tedium in his conversation. He is always so improving! He reminds me a little of that odious Miss

Humphries, the governess who accompanied me to London."

"You know, Juliana," said Lizzie, speaking rather awkwardly, as though waiting for Juliana's disagreement, "I think that Miss Humphries was a prodigious liar. She blamed you for encouraging the marquis's advances, and she has spread the story round the whole of London, thanks to Mrs. Milgrave's efforts to secure the marquis for her own daughter. Yet there was no truth in it, was there? He may have kissed you, but you did not encourage him. I can tell that you would not do such a thing, even if you had a feeling toward him!

"But, I was going to say that there is one good thing about it. I do not believe that the Marquis cares a rap for Charlotte Milgrave, and this story may disgust him with her. I know that he flirts with her, as much as a man may flirt at all with such a lump of ice. But there is no emotion in his eyes. Have you ever noticed how cold they are when he looks at her?"

"I am not in the habit of keeping a careful watch on the Marquis of Peterborough," said Juliana stiffly. "I do not give a damn whether he cares for Miss Milgrave. I detest him utterly."

"Oh," said Lizzie Reddington. For a moment it looked as if she would continue the subject but she thought better of it. She changed the conversation back to her own affairs. What dress should she wear? Did Juliana think she ought to carry a mask so that the clergyman should not recognize her? Would a cloak help her to avoid being looked at by passersby?

Juliana had quite some difficulty in persuading her cousin that a mask would attract just that curiosity she wished to avoid. Nor would it be a good idea to wear any one of her particularly fine dresses. True, she would be wearing a dress for her wedding day, but it was vital that it should not arouse suspicion at home. If Lizzie left on a shopping expedition wearing her finest gown, it would look more than a little odd. In this case, fashion must give way to discretion. "After all, Lizzie," said Juliana, "you said you did not mind missing the finery of a proper wedding."

Lizzie then devoted herself to explaining to Juliana how she would give up anything for the right to wed her dear Robert. Their discussions might have continued for several more minutes, but for the return of Lady Talboys and the rising of the curtain. Lady Helen and James Reddington came back into the box a little later disrupting the moment on stage when Kitty warns her mistress Melissa not to marry Mr. Gayless, who is head over heels in debt.

As the farce proceeded Juliana found herself even more out of charity with James Reddington, as he continued his habit of explaining the plot and making critical comments throughout the play. She found this extremely distracting and more than a little irritating. She was grateful eventually to her grandmother, who in withering tones told Mr. Reddington to be silent as she did not need his help to follow the plot of as silly a farce as ever she had seen.

Indeed the old lady continued to grumble about James Reddington all the way home after the farce had ended, and the farewells had been made. Having arrived at Curzon Street, she told Juliana firmly, "I only hope that you don't decide to marry him. He is the greatest bore in all nature, forever prosing on about every subject under the sun. I am convinced that any woman who married him would be quite mad with it all within the week."

"But I thought you approved of the Reddingtons," said Juliana with some amazement as she watched her grandmother having her hair combed out by Pinkerton in the privacy of her bedroom. These late night chats that the two of them sometimes had were the times when Lady Talboys was at her most outspoken. "You have encouraged me to be seen in their company often enough," Juliana added.

"There's nothing wrong with the Reddingtons. Your mother and the admiral were first cousins, you know. The admiral's father was my poor brother, Frederick. I could never approve of the way he allowed his only son to ally himself with the daughter of a tradesman. Well it was a foolish thing. I told him he was dishonoring the family, even if she did have a good dowry."

"Grandmama!" cried Juliana with amazement. "What is all this? Why even I know that Lady Helen is a lady in her own right. She is the daughter of an earl."

Lady Talboys was obviously in a supremely grumpy mood. "She may be the daughter of an earl, child, but even your father had better blood in his veins. There are titles which cover a multitude of sins! Lady Helen's grandfather was not better than a tradesman. Made his money in the time of Charles II probably in a dashed smoky way. 'Twould be more genteel if the title had come by way of one of Charles's mistresses. Less vulgar by half."

Once again, Juliana was thrown into confusion by the odd way Lady Talboys and the fashionable world thought. Here was another example! It was more genteel, apparently, to have acquired a title in the family by an illegitimate love affair, than to have acquired it by honest trade. "You rather surprise me," said Juliana slowly. "I thought you were in favor of my being friendly with the Reddingtons. I have become bosom friends with Lizzie, I declare. She and I plan to go shopping together on Friday. I wish to show her some ribbons for her new sacque."

"I'm not saying that the Reddington children won't do. They go everywhere and for that matter so does Lady Helen. Don't get me wrong, Juliana. I like the woman and I'm grateful for her kindness to you. For all that the tone of her mind is mercenary. She not only thinks of pounds, shillings, and pence, she talks about 'em! It's the whiff of trade in the blood. The girl's different. She has quality. As for the son, he's a dead bore. Not that he wouldn't make a better husband than that other young fribble you have dangling after you. What's his name?"

"You mean Mr. Torrington?"

"That's it! Nothing wrong with the Torrington blood. It's an old family, as old as ours. But he's as poor as a church mouse. If you're imagining love in a cottage or some such shocking romantic nonsense, I can only tell you that there's nothing enjoyable about living in penury. It may be all right for the stage but it won't do in real life."

"Why do you say that Mr. Torrington is dangling after me?" asked Juliana guardedly. She was anxious to know how far her deception had succeeded.

"It's as plain as the nose on your face. Don't be sillier than you need," said her grandmother robustly. "Don't think I didn't notice him making sheep's eyes at you in the theater box, because I did! Besides he was here that afternoon and you refused to have Pinkerton with you. If that isn't encouraging a young man, well then you tell me what it is. I wasn't born yesterday, you know. He's a handsome sprig, I grant you, and looks well in his uniform, but looks ain't everything! He's got an eye to your fortune, I'll wager. Why, he was casting his eyes at Lizzie Reddington before you arrived in London. I can only suppose he switched his attentions when he heard that you were worth a great deal more than her."

"How horrid you make it sound. Why can't you allow for the idea that people fall in love?" asked Juliana impatiently.

"I do allow for that fact, child, and it accounts for some very odd younger sons and daughters. But I have always maintained that a woman should be virtuous, or at least should not have a connection until she's given her husband an heir, or better still two. Then she may please herself, as long as she is discreet. But you must not be thinking that love has anything to do with marriage! After all, for us poor females marriage is a way of life. If we do not marry where money is, then we can expect very little

159

from life. Marriage is our only venture in life and if we get shipwrecked by it, then we are ruined indeed."

"I think that's hateful," said Juliana mutinously.

"I'm sure that you do, child. But for all that I'll lay odds that you have some sense somewhere. If your papa taught you how to run almshouses, he must have taught you the value of money. Where do you think you get all those pretty dresses that have been bought for you? And how do you think I have a carriage and a coachman and a pleasant house? Marriage brought me all these things. If I had married a mere younger son, I'd be living on the fringes of fashion in Chelsea or Kensington, I dare say, and going to shabby genteel assemblies given by cits. Or I'd be cooped up in some muddy manor in the Thames valley, with only the parson's wife for company, and a visit to London once every five years when there's been a good harvest."

Though Juliana was shocked at the thought of taking lovers after marriage, she had to admit that there was *some* sense in what her grandmother had to say about marrying for money. There was no denying that marriage was more important for a woman than a man. So much more depended upon it. She decided, however, that she had better try to continue the deception over Robert Torrington. She must leave her grandmother with the impression that it was she, not Lizzie, who was interested in that young man.

"Well, I think love is more important than riches when it comes to marriage," she murmured. It was true in that she did believe it. Despite all that her grandmother said, she had no intention of marrying where she could not love!

"Oh what silly sentiments, girl. You put me out of all patience! Come now, give me a kiss and be off to bed. I'll wager you wouldn't think so much of that milk-and-water Torrington boy, if you'd ever known what it was like to love a real man. He's handsome, but just a bread-and-butter youngster. Give me something stronger any day, though I probably shock you by saying so," said the old lady. With this dark and ambiguous remark, Lady Talboys clutched her wrap around her, and placing a very becoming nightcap frothing with lace on her head, she tottered to her bed, aided by the faithful Pinkerton. Juliana kissed her dutifully, as she settled onto the pillows, and went off to her own bedchamber.

There in the darkness and the silence of the night, after a maid had helped her off with her gown and into her nightclothes, she pondered. Was she doing the right thing for Lizzie Reddington? Perhaps marriage *was* rather an adventure. Could Lady Talboys be right, when she said that it ought to be an alliance of money rather than love? Was she—*Juliana*— helping Lizzie ruin her life?

Eight

The Fleet prison, with its three melancholy gates, was a gloomy place. It was London's principal prison for men and women who could no longer compound with their creditors. They were thrown into the Fleet, and had no chance of seeing the outside world again, unless through fortune or friends they could strike a bargain with the creditors or pay their debts. Whole families— men, their wives, and their children—lived there, and in many ways it was a little world in itself. There was a chapel, a coffee room, a tap room, billiard tables, and other amusements inside its walls. Debtors who were still able to beg or borrow money would patronize these establishments, and could also secure favorable apartments on the upper floors. As for the miserable debtors who had no cash, their main reliance was the so-called begging grate, where they clustered against the bars begging alms from the passersby.

It was a street near the prison, Fleet Lane, that was so famous for its marriages. Juliana had instructed Robert Torrington to meet her and Lizzie by the Hand and

Pen, nextdoor to the china shop just before Fleet Bridge. It was an establishment run by one of the Fleet parsons, a Reverend J. Lilly whose handbills, which he distributed as advertisements for his services, described him as being "bred at one of our Universities and lawfully ordained according to the institutions of the Church of England."

The two girls had found very little difficulty in slipping away from their respective homes. Lady Talboys had accepted Juliana's story without question, and had not pressed the attendance of Pinkerton, once she heard that Juliana and Lizzie would be accompanied by the latter's maid. Lady Helen—still apparently anxious to see the Quincey fortune in her family—was still expressing her delight at the two girls' friendship. When it was explained that Molly would accompany them on their shopping expedition, she had raised no objection beyond warning Lizzie not to outrun her allowance. The Reddington carriage had then picked up Juliana from Curzon Street, and the three of them had alighted in Bond Street, at the mercer's shop of Mr. Talbot, giving the coachman instructions to pick them up from there two hours later.

The next step in the deception had been to find a hackney cab which would take them to Fleet Lane. Molly, the maid, secured one quickly and Juliana was thankful for her competence. It surprised her when she discovered that Molly was middle-aged. Somehow she had expected a younger, flightier maid, rather than such a matron. But she was soon to discover that Molly was young at heart—indeed as foolishly romantic as any young girl. With much clucking she fussed over Lizzie, making sure her curls were in order, and she showed an alarming tendency to burst into sentimental tears at the least opportunity. Juliana could only be grateful that her own maid was not so emotional, and—for the first time— she began to see advantages she had not before perceived in the dour Miss Pinkerton.

Lizzie sat pale with trepidation in the hackney carriage, and when the little party alighted at the Hand and

Pen she looked as though she might faint. Molly was still clucking, and even Juliana felt rather nervous as they made their way up the drab stairs of the public house to the upper room where marriages were solemnized. She was thankful to see that Robert Torrington had got there earlier and was awaiting them. Looking pale and tense, he too was obviously suffering from nervous anxieties, but his color returned as soon as he set eyes upon Lizzie. The two lovers ran to each other and clung in an embrace for a second or two under the benevolent eye of the Reverend Lilly. Juliana could not help noticing that the clergyman, for all his University connections, looked sadly shabby and, she suspected, a little the worse for wear for drink.

"My dearest one," Robert asked urgently as he relaxed his embrace, "are you sure that you want to make this sacrifice for me?"

Privately Juliana hoped that they would not be too long in discussion, for time was running out if they were to complete the ceremony and make their way back to Bond Street, without keeping the Reddington carriage waiting too long. So she was considerably relieved when Lizzie, making no objections to such a romantically phrased question, merely replied, "Dearest Robert! I trust you utterly!"

Fortunately for that trust, Robert Torrington had not been idle. One of the public house tapmen had been roped in as a witness. The promise of a guinea had made his eyes brighten with anticipation, and he played his part with attention if not with elegance.

The Reverend Lilly, too, had been paid, thought Juliana, realizing that fees were the attraction which brought clergymen to perform these irregular but legal marriages. She did not much take to his looks which were of a greasy nature, nor to his red complexion. She was glad, too, that neither of the lovers seemed to notice the distinct smell of brandy on his breath. They had eyes only for each other and any imperfections in either the marriage ceremony or the parson were not noticed.

The actual wedding ceremony was a makeshift affair. Juliana recognized the familiar words from the English prayer book with difficulty, for the Reverend Lilly rushed through them at a great pace, as if he hoped to be able to finish the business and be back to the bottle. She, herself, could not be a witness for fear that her age might affect the legality of the marriage. But the young couple gave their responses firmly and with such obvious devotion that she could not prevent two stray tears stealing out of her eyes. Molly, one of the witnesses by her side, was a positive watering pot of liquid sentiment, so much so that Juliana feared she might go into a fit. Even the tapman, Juliana could not help noticing, seemed to find Robert and Lizzie affecting for he blew his nose very loudly at the end of the ceremony as if the sight had affected even his deadened sensibility.

To Juliana, who was used only to the weddings of village folk in the parish church, this marriage seemed a shocking affair. There were no weeping relatives, no neighbors bent on jokes and jollifications, and no well-wishers to crowd round after the pair had signed the register—a large book which the Reverend Lilly produced from his robes. True, Robert kissed Lizzie with as much feeling and fervor as any bridegroom, and Lizzie—blushing and a little nervous—looked as beautiful as any bride Juliana had seen. But the officiating clergyman hurried and bustled them, no doubt so that he could clear the room for another profit-making marriage. In the marriage shops of Fleet Lane there was little time for the niceties of social behavior, and once a marriage had been paid for and delivered, the cleric had no time to waste for the young couple he had so carelessly launched into the seas of matrimony.

At the bottom of the public house stairs, Robert Torrington took both ladies by the arm. "My dearest Lizzie," he said, his voice taut with emotion, "I must leave you now and we must pretend for a time that this has never happened, while I see if I cannot persuade my

166

brother to give us his support. Juliana, I will be relying on you to keep my darling safe and well."

The three of them stepped outside, with Molly following a few steps behind. "I shall pay you an afternoon call in two or three days time, Lizzie, and then I will talk to your mother and your father. I hope to come before them with my brother's promise of an extra allowance. When they know that we have taken this irrevocable step, then I am sure that they will come to terms. But I do not wish them to know, until I am there to defend and protect you, Lizzie. I will not have you bullied and made miserable even by your own mama and papa."

"Dearest Robert," was all that Lizzie could manage to say. Her voice was suffused with tears, and she was struggling to control them. She turned her face from him, as though she could scarcely bear to look at him. Then slipping her arm out of his, she fell back a pace or two to borrow a handkerchief from Molly.

It was left for Juliana, still on Robert Torrington's arm, to nod wisely, to promise her aid, and to reassure the anxious young husband, as they walked back up Fleet Lane to where the hackney cab had been instructed to wait.

Just at this moment, an uproar started from the direction of the Strand. The noise of shouting and revels was heard, and down the hill of Fleet Street swept a coach with a party of drunken young bloods on its roof. Juliana looked up, and to her horror encountered a quick glance from the driver, who had obviously wrenched the reins away from the coachman. It was the Marquis of Peterborough, who had shouldered the man aside, and was holding the reins, urging the horses into a reckless pace while beside him sat the terrified servant. In the same horrified glance, Juliana recognized the ever-present Ponsonby among the passengers on the roof, and the familiar sneering face of the Golden Exquisite. Sir William Goring Pelham had his quizzing glass at the ready, and Juliana thought she saw him give her a little ironic bow, as the coach rattled past them at a reckless pace toward St. Paul's Cathedral.

Her heart sank. This was a disaster! What on earth was going to happen now? The marriage would be all over the town within minutes! "Did you see?" she asked the others. "I could swear that we were recognized by at least two of those men. Worst of all, it couldn't be more horrifying! It was that frightful Sir William and the marquis! I fear that all is discovered and that Lizzie and you are totally undone."

Both Robert and Lizzie sprang together in an instinctive reaction. They both looked very alarmed. Neither had really looked carefully at the coach, both being preoccupied with their own thoughts. "Well, they cannot know what we have just done, even if they did recognize us," said Robert Torrington slowly. "After all they could simply think that we have made up an expedition to see the debtors. Many people do visit prisons, you know, for pleasure, and the sights of Bridewell, the asylum for the mad, are recognized as one of the attractions of the Metropolis. Why should we not simply have done the same in the Fleet prison? After all, Molly has been with us to chaperon you two girls. There need be no impropriety for all that the marquis knows."

"But surely they will think it odd of us? How can people do such a thing as go to gloat at the unfortunate? I fear that the Marquis of Peterborough will not put such an innocent explanation on our presence," said Juliana. "He delights in thinking the worst of me, and has already taxed me with a fondness for you, Mr. Torrington."

"Well, perhaps that is just as well!" Lizzie remarked. "After all, Juliana, you won't mind if people think you are flirting with Robert. It was your own scheme, remember? It is an excellent ruse to distract attention from *us!* Besides, I'm sure I can't think why it should be thought so shocking that both you and I should visit a prison with him. The main thing to remember is that the men in that coach will not immediately perceive that Robert and I have been married. How could they?"

"I suppose not," said Juliana reluctantly. Of course, she didn't mind if the fashionable world thought she had a fondness for Robert Torrington. It was not entirely pleasant to be scolded by Lady Talboys for her folly in encouraging a mere younger son, but that did not really matter. Lizzie's happiness must be put first. But somehow the idea that the Marquis of Peterborough should think that she was a flirt, that she made assignations with Robert Torrington, was something far more grave. She remembered that horrid scene in Curzon Street, when the marquis had warned her in a horridly interfering way about the dangers of arousing further scandal. He had asked her to give him her word that there was nothing between her and Mr. Torrington. She had given him what he asked. But now he would wonder. He might think that she had broken her word, that he had been made a game of.

She felt she could not bear *that*. She hated the marquis, but she did not want him to think she was the sort of female who did not keep her word. She also had a shrewd idea that the Marquis of Peterborough was not the kind of man who would believe a tale that she and Mr. Torrington were merely visiting prisons for amusement. He surely would make the connection between Fleet Lane and secret marriages. He would have his suspicions, and then he would have good reason to suppose that she had allied herself to Robert Torrington. What then? Would he tell Lady Talboys? Or would he simply turn from her in disgust, keeping silent but blaming her in his heart? She found herself losing the thread of her thoughts in a tangle of fears and anxieties. And always and ever surfaced the question: *what will he think of me now?*

"Cheer up, Juliana," said Lizzie seeing her friend's worried looks. "After all there are not many days to be gone through, and then we can be open and tell the world what has happened. Then there need be no more confusion. It is only for a little while that you may be misjudged."

"Of course, Lizzie. Don't fear! I shall not desert either of you now. As you say, it is only for a few days that there may be a little disagreeableness." Juliana felt ashamed of herself. It was not much to bear. All she had to do was to be willing—if it became necessary, and it might never be—to take any blame that might come from this escapade.

She would manage to tell some kind of story, she reflected. Perhaps a tale about her interest in prison conditions, and her determination to see for herself? Yes, that sounded far more plausible than a mere jaunt to gape at the unfortunate inmates. After Frank, and the stray cat, her grandmother might well believe it. She would tell anybody who asked, or anybody who might have seen them, that she had had a desire to inquire into the misery of prison inmates, and that Mr. Torrington had volunteered to accompany her there.

She was grateful nonetheless when they safely reached the hackney cab, and could be out of sight again, away from the prying eyes of casual passersby. The couple made their fond farewells, and Molly sniffed for the final time, before the three females all climbed into it and were shortly on their way back to Bond Street. Luckily they got there before the Reddington carriage turned up, so that they were able to go inside and purchase some ribbons hurriedly to give color to their story of a shopping expedition.

Juliana had been the more confident than Lizzie at the beginning of the day; now she was beginning to feel increasingly nervous. Just the opposite had happened to Lizzie. Before the marriage, she had been nervous and worried. Now she was confident, and glowing with happiness. Juliana saw her shining eyes and flushed cheeks with envy. Lizzie seemed to have decided that the world was well lost for love. She was feeling no regrets about a step which could land her in trouble with her parents, and perhaps in trouble with society. She looked up to Juliana and smiled, as if reading her mind.

"I am so happy," she admitted, "because I don't really mind what happens now! I have married my dearest Robert, and I know that eventually we will both be very happy. Perhaps mama will rage at me, and perhaps papa will reproach me. But I shan't care. All that I care about is my future with Robert."

They climbed into the Reddington carriage without apparently arousing any suspicions in the Reddington coachman. When the vehicle stopped at Curzon Street to set down Juliana, she asked her cousin if she would like to come in for some refreshment. Lizzie felt she would do best to go straight home. "The sooner I face mama the better," she whispered as she embraced Juliana farewell. "It seems terrible to deceive her, but Robert says I must do so. I just hope my happiness doesn't show too much in my face."

It was just as well that Lizzie had not alighted, thought Juliana, for when she was let into the Curzon Street house, she found a visitor there awaiting her. This time she was expected to see him without a chaperon apparently. Lady Talboys, though undoubtedly in, was nowhere to be found, and there was no offer of Pinkerton's services. Hitchens the butler seemed to be in the plot, too, for he was full of good humor, delicately conveying his approval of the visitor.

It was Mr. Reddington, said the butler. He had had a word with Lady Talboys and was now anxious to have a few moments with Miss Quincey. Lady Talboys had instructed him that the young lady might see Mr. Reddington alone.

Perversely Juliana found that she did not wish to be alone with Mr. Reddington. "Do you not think I should have Miss Pinkerton?" she said to Hitchens, lingering in the hall before going into the morning room.

"No, miss," said the butler. "Mr. Reddington has, I understand, requested the pleasure of your company alone."

Mr. Reddington reinforced this explanation. With an arch smile he came forward to kiss her hand, saying, "You will no doubt be wondering, Miss Quincey, at my temerity. I have of course got Lady Talboys's permission to see you thus, without any chaperon. I should like to hope that perhaps you can guess what it is that I am going to ask you."

Juliana's mind was a blank. She could think of absolutely nothing secret or private that she had to discuss with James Reddington. Then a horrid suspicion came over her. Had James Reddington discovered the secret marriage? Was this going to be an interrogation about Lizzie and Mr. Torrington? A second look at his beaming face made her think again. He did not look either angry, or even worried. It *could not* be about Lizzie's love affair. Juliana felt a wave of relief. She said gaily: "I cannot for the world think why you should wish to see me alone, cousin. But I am happy to bid you good day, and to talk to you at any time."

James Reddington looked even more arch. "Miss Quincey," he said with a touch of pomposity, and cleared his throat. Then he continued, "Miss Quincey, it will no doubt not have escaped your notice that I have found no little pleasure in your company. You have entered into my sentiments about society in such a way as to make me confident that your principles are fixed, and that your character is one of which I cannot disapprove. There is a tendency to levity, perhaps, and a lack of discretion, but these are the faults which are natural to one as young as you are."

"Thank you, Mr. Reddington," said Juliana, trying to remain serious.

"My mother, of course, has given me her blessing in this action," went on Mr. Reddington. "I thought it proper to consult her, and she was of the opinion that your

172

faults are those of inexperience. Time and the guidance of one older and wiser than yourself will put them right, she is convinced. I know that you will be relieved to know that she considers you are most prettily behaved. Those unfortunate lapses from proper conduct which may have arisen she opines are due to your upbringing. I believe that once you have overcome a tendency to hotheaded and impulsive action, you will be a pattern for your sex. Union with somebody who is preeminent for stability of mind and worth of character will, I venture to suggest, cure any unsteadiness of disposition. Do you now perhaps have some idea of what I am leading up to?"

"Are you being so obliging as to offer for me, Mr. Reddington? Juliana asked bluntly. She found herself irritated with this solemnity, and the way he seemed to be uttering carefully rehearsed sentences. She would prefer to get the whole thing over as quickly as possible.

James Reddington wagged a playful finger at her. "Now Miss Quincey that impetuous manner again! But perhaps it may be excused when such a matter, so vital to your future happiness, is at stake. Yes, my dear Miss Quincey, I am asking for your hand in holy matrimony."

"I am very indebted to you for your good opinion and to your mother, Lady Helen, for hers," said Juliana slowly, "but I am afraid that I must refuse your obliging offer."

"I had anticipated that you would feel the need to answer my request in the negative, Miss Quincey," said Mr. Reddington, not a whit put out. "I know that it is the custom among you young ladies, to feel a natural reluctance to give up your maiden state. A certain disinclination, an affected indifference, a natural feeling of delicacy —these are to be expected from your sex, and I honor you, Miss Quincey, for them. Your hesitation becomes you. Scruples and qualms about the thought of matrimony are the privilege, indeed the glory, of a young lady. I am content to wait for you to put these natural feelings aside, confident that your good sense and your amiable disposition will exert their influence in my favor."

"No, Mr. Reddington, you misunderstand me," said Juliana firmly. "I do not feel any scruples or qualms. I must refuse your offer once and for all. I find that my heart is not yours, Mr. Reddington."

Mr. Reddington's face acquired a look of solemnity mingled with a certain distaste. "Am I to understand by this extraordinary statement that you have entered into an engagement with some other suitor? Or do you feel you have formed an attachment, Miss Quincey? Your grandmother was confident that you were free to entertain my proposal, otherwise I should not for a moment have dreamed of making it."

"No, no, Mr. Reddington!" exclaimed Juliana impatiently. "There is no question of a prior engagement or a prior attachment. It is just that, although I am sure that I have the highest regard for you, I cannot love you."

Mr. Reddington permitted himself a discreet laugh. "You set my mind at rest, Miss Quincey. I had for the moment feared some imprudence, some infatuation . . . I shall say no more. You need feel no embarrassment in admitting that you do not—as you choose to say—love me. I would never be so indelicate to require that kind of love for a betrothal such as ours. Such an improper emotion can have no place in the life of a well brought-up young lady, no place at all in the heart of a woman of quality. That you should feel respect and a proper regard for me is all I ask."

"Do you mean that you do not believe that an affianced couple should love each other?" asked Juliana in amazement. "Do *you* love me, Mr. Reddington?"

He looked acutely embarrassed and cleared his throat for the second time. "I feel a very tender regard for you, Miss Quincey," he replied, "and I have, as I have surely made clear to you, the highest opinion of your worth. Otherwise I should not have wished to join your fate with mine in marriage. I am not aware that a man could feel anything better than this. As I say, I have no time for the vulgar emotions which I believe the lower classes call love."

"What an extraordinary thing! Well, I cannot marry you, Mr. Reddington and that is all I have to say!" said Juliana. She smothered a desire to argue further with him. There was such a gulf between them that an argument would not be helpful. Besides, she wished to draw the interview to an end. She rose from the chair on which she had sat.

Mr. Reddington rose, too, and looked round for his cane. "I shall of course renew this offer, and shall hope that when you have duly considered it, after taking the advice of your grandmother, you will see that it is to your advantage to accept it, Miss Quincey," he said stiffly and not altogether good-humoredly. "I am persuaded that further reflection will banish both your maidenly fears and your misplaced ideas about love. I am convinced that you may expect considerable happiness from marrying me."

Juliana thought that further reflection was unlikely to do anything of the kind. It was only likely, she decided, to show her that Mr. Reddington was a pompous ass! She found herself wondering how on earth she could ever have thought she liked the man. He had never once said how happy he would be in marrying her, only how happy she would be. It was as if he saw the advantages of the match mainly on her side. All in all, it was with great relief, she heard the front door close on him.

Lady Talboys must have been listening for the door, too, for no sooner was the visitor shut out than she bustled into the morning room, all agog to hear Juliana's news. "Well, girl, am I to wish you happy? Will you have him?"

Juliana was offended by her plain speaking. "Not at all, grandmama," she snapped crossly. "You have no need to wish me happy. I have refused Mr. Reddington's offer, but I cannot get him to understand it! He thinks it is all maidenly reserve and that I shall change my mind, if only he persists."

Lady Talboys gave a cackle of laughter. "How very like him! I dare say he simply cannot believe that you should not jump at his offer. Well ... there's no saying but what his offer might not come in useful later, Juliana. A suitor who keeps on persisting does one's reputation nothing but good. It can only add to your credit. But what made you turn him down? I had thought that your approval of his moral attitudes was secure. I thought you liked the man and that it was only dreadful old ladies like myself who thought him a bore."

"I think you are a lovely old lady, grandmama, and that you were right all along. He *is* a bore!" said Juliana penitently. "Somehow—I don't know why—I seem to have lost my taste for his kind of conversation. Mr. Reddington may be of a serious turn of mind, but he does not seem to *enjoy* life at all. I think I would be bored to death within a month of marriage. I don't know really what's happened to me, grandmama, but I seem to have changed since I came to London."

"The truth of the matter is, child, that you're more of my granddaughter than you know! I can see that you've got a taste for the frivolous and frolics of fashion —as well as having a warm heart and a charitable disposition. It is just as well too, that you *have* changed. For this afternoon I am taking you to a card party at Lady Sefton's and there's no dancing—only gaming. No gentlemen, either, so we ladies may play as high as we please without fear of incurring their censure."

It was the first time that Juliana had been to one of the private card parties, which were increasingly being held by London hostesses. While assemblies were, of course, still essential for the business of proper entertaining, with routs, ridottos, and masquerades being fashionable, card parties were growing in popularity among the wealthy set. Lady Sefton's party was very select for, as Lady Talboys pointed out, it would never do to take a girl in her first season to anything but the most carefully chosen parties. It was known that some ladies of quality, the younger married set in the main, played very high, and some had even considered the idea of opening their houses as gambling dens. Still, it was generally agreed that that sort of behavior was fast, and could only gain the disapproval of society. Even the most dashing matrons, however high the stakes at their card games and however deep the play, were careful about whom they invited.

For a girl just out, like Juliana, not yet permitted the freedom given to married ladies, card parties were only permissible if they were of the most sober kind. "I might go anywhere and play, even at Lady Archer's," said Lady Talboys, "but such jaunts would not do for you, Juliana. There will be no gentlemen this afternoon and nothing served stronger than tea or chocolate. Even so you will be the only young person present and I am relying upon your good behavior. I have asked dear Lady Sefton if I might bring you along and she has said very kindly that you may make up a fourth at her table. Under her aegis, there can be no objection to your taking part, I think."

So for the first time in her life, Juliana found herself playing a serious card game for real money. She had for a second or two wondered if she ought to refuse the outing, mindful of what her dear papa might have said. But she thought better of it, realizing that Lady Talboys would not have suggested anything outrageous. Better to learn how card games were played and how money was staked under the protection of her grandmama and Lady Sefton, then to find out later in life when perhaps there might be no older women to tell her how to go on.

She was naturally nervous as she sat down by the side of Lady Sefton for her first game of whist played in company. By now, from playing for counters with her grandmother, she had a grasp of the essentials of the game. But she nevertheless felt some qualms when Lady Sefton said casually, "Five guineas a game? Are you in agreement ladies?" The other two ladies at the table, Juliana was relieved to find, were both amiable. One was the Marchioness of Peterborough on her left who had smiled warmly when greeting the girl; the other was Mrs. Molton, a friendly widow in her fifties.

Lady Talboys was not in attendance. She had deserted her granddaughter for the pleasure of playing basset at another table. It was a much deeper game, as she promptly admitted: "I cannot ask you to join me, child. The stakes are too high, and you do not properly understand the game. Do you mind? You have company enough at this table. Lady Sefton will help you if you have any difficulties." At this Lady Sefton, the amiable hostess nodded. She was a fat good-natured woman whose chief passion was cards—though she had an indifference either to winning or losing. Lady Sefton was one of London's most popular hostesses, being kindly disposed to everyone as long as she was not expected to put herself out.

After a half hour or so, during which Juliana had excitedly won a considerable sum from the kitty, Lady Sefton turned to her saying, "You do not seem to need my assistance, Miss Quincey. Let me say that you play your cards creditably. Why, I vow I have not seen such a performance for ages! I only wish that the luck would turn in my direction for a little time, and I might be dealt a reasonably good hand."

The marchioness was also encouraging. "I am glad to see you winning, Miss Quincey," she said agreeably. "Indeed, it is as well perhaps since I see your grandmother may be drawing the bustle at that other table. Basset is all very well, but I should not like to play it for such high stakes. Let us hope she is not fleeced!"

"How is the Peterborough luck holding for you?" asked Lady Sefton of the marchioness as the cards were dealt out again. "My son tells me that he was cleaned out by the marquis t'other night at White's. He vows that Auberon has the devil's luck and plans his revenge some day at the tables."

The gossip became general, while the game waxed serious. Juliana noticed with dismay that her pile of guineas, which had seemed so large, was beginning to dwindle. The cards simply would not fall right. Lady Sefton was fortune's favorite, and was soon playing from behind a heap of gold on her right. As Juliana pushed forward her last five guineas, she wondered whether she should ask to leave the game. It went through her mind, as Lady Sefton on her right opted to go solo, that she could perhaps consult her neighbor—but then a feeling of embarrassment stopped her. She did not wish to look foolish in front of the marquis's mother. Besides, she should not withdraw *now* just because she was losing. Perhaps I will win this hand, she thought.

As Lady Sefton won trick after trick, she knew that she was going to lose again. Soon her neighbor was pulling in the heap of guineas from the table and it was her turn to deal the cards, while Juliana's turn to call. It was the moment when she would have to think quickly what to do. Opposite her at the table Mrs. Molton was happily scrawling IOUs, which were now making an increasing flutter of paper over the table. The marchioness still had several rouleaux of guineas in front of her.

Only Juliana had nothing, and had not yet resorted to the paper. She looked at Lady Sefton with a look of dismayed inquiry, and Lady Seflton gestured towards a notebook which for the first time Juliana noticed had been placed beside her. This was for her IOUs. A nervous qualm hit her. Her papa had always said that half the evils of gambling were to be attributed to this practice, which encouraged gamesters to bet well beyond the guineas in their pocket. Juliana dithered, as Lady Sefton dealt the cards. Should she write a piece of paper? All the ladies seemed to expect it. Somehow she felt she could not. Yet she could not back out of the game now. What should she do?

A sudden inspiration hit her, and without stopping to think, she stripped off a sapphire bracelet from her arm and threw it onto the table. "I will use this as my stake, ladies," she said with an attempt at gaiety.

"It is rather an extravagant gesture, is it not?" Lady Sefton's smile was a little forced, but she completed dealing out the cards. "May I remind you, ladies, that hearts are trumps for this game."

It was Juliana's turn to call. She looked at her hand. It was a good hand, almost a spectacular one. She had two aces, diamonds and clubs; three kings, diamonds, clubs, and spades; and no less than three queens of the same suits. It was a hand, she thought, with which she ought to be able to win. "I will go solo," she said cautiously. Surely the luck would be in her favor now?

But it was not to be. Mrs. Molton had been happily chuckling opposite her. Now she triumphantly threw her hand on the table for all to see, declaring, "I vow, ladies, there is no point playing this game further. I hold a hand to beat you all." Her scattered cards revealed that she had the five highest hearts. "I can trump you off the table, my dear," she laughed, exulting.

Juliana did her best to keep her face impassive. She was about to push forward her bracelet into the heap on the table, when from her left, the marchioness put out a restraining hand. "My dear," she said quietly, "you cannot stake that bracelet else you will have us all in confusion. I will frank you for this afternoon, and you may settle up with me tomorrow. See, I have plenty of guineas to lend. I expect it will be easier for you to remember play, than if you start writing IOUs."

Juliana mumbled her thanks. She felt terrible. A rich

blush had spread over her cheeks, and she looked down at her cards barely daring to raise her eyes. Her confusion was further increased by Lady Sefton's saying, in a kind voice but a touch critically, "That is much better! 'Tis thoughtful of you, Anne. I should have done as much. My dear, it will never do to get into the habit of throwing your jewelry about the card table. If the gentlemen were here, they would make a game of it, and it would scarcely redound to your credit! Such impulsiveness has a very off appearance. Of course, amongst us females it is of no consequence, and we all perfectly understand that you are new to the ways of the card table, child. You may forget it, and play on."

After such a rebuke, however kindly intentioned and gently delivered, Juliana could take no further part in the conversation. She continued to play, borrowing guineas from the marchioness. Fortunately the cards seemed kinder, and she won a hand or two so that by the time the game finished, she found she owed the Marchioness only ten guineas.

Juliana was grateful for the marchioness's kindness. For when the game came to an end, she patted the girl's hand and said in an amused tone of voice: "My dear child, do not concern yourself with what you owe me. I shall be visiting your grandmama tomorrow and will collect it then. Depend upon it, we all three of us at this table were amused by your trying to stake your bracelet, but we shall not mention it to anybody outside, shall we, Lady Sefton? Or you Mrs. Molton?" The two ladies nodded their agreement. " 'Twould have been a great deal better to have written an IOU without further ado, than to throw your jewelry upon the table. I vow you are more of a gamester than you know, child."

To Juliana's relief, that was the end of it. She saw her grandmother coming over from the table where she had been playing basset. "We must make our *au revoirs*, Juliana," said the old lady in a grump tone of voice.

" 'Twas a most agreeable party, Lady Sefton, even though I vow I've had a run of bad luck enough to try a saint. 'Twas kind of you to look after the child, and I am sure that Juliana is very grateful. It is not often that she will have the chance to play in such good company."

Nine

It was not just her losses at hazard which had put the old lady in a bad temper, Juliana learned quickly. During the journey back to Curzon Street, Lady Talboys was in an irritable mood, saying practically nothing, abruptly rude in her commands to the coachman, and sparing Juliana barely a smile.

When they had first seated themselves on the leather cushions of the coach, Juliana had permitted herself a sympathetic question about the sum involved. Lady Talboys had snapped her head off with: "Five hundred guineas, Miss, and I want none of your moralizing about the evils of gaming."

Juliana was not in the mood to moralize about such a subject any more. For she realized that her own conduct, in staking her bracelet, was well beyond the line of what was pleasing. As the old lady did not seem disposed to conversation in the coach she kept silent, ruminating on what had happened. How could she have been so bound up with the card game, that she would forget herself in that way? The Marchioness had been right. It would have been better simply to write an IOU. But perhaps it had been her duty to have risen from the table and ceased from play? And yet that would have ruined the other three ladies' enjoyment.

It did not seem a simple question of right and wrong. Juliana could not help remembering how easy it had all seemed when she had first arrived in London. She had felt then, that gambling for money was all wrong. Now she was not so sure. Perhaps it was all a question of how much money was involved? One thing was certain—she had learned that gaming *was* enjoyable. When she had first arrived in town, she had just thought that gambling must be the result of an evil character. Now she knew that gaming held quite a lure for many people, *including herself*. She could condemn others no more. Now, she could begin to understand why they got involved in such deep play, and with understanding must go forgiveness.

Originally, the plan for the evening was for her and her grandmother to pause at Curzon Street, and then make their way to the Ranelagh pleasure gardens for a supper of the thinly sliced ham which was the specialty there. Juliana had been looking forward to the evening, knowing that the Ranelagh pleasure gardens were one of the most fashionable, and amusing places to spend an evening. Now she was not so sure. With Lady Talboys in an ever blacker mood, it did not look as if there would be much enjoyment in it.

As she followed her grandmother into the drawing room of the Curzon Street house, she said rather tentatively, "Grandmama, do we *have* to go to Ranelagh? I have the headache, and would prefer to go to bed early tonight."

The old lady looked at her suspiciously. "It's not like you, child, to have the megrims. What is this new trick? I have been hearing things about you, miss, which

184

make me wonder whether you are the bread-and-milk girl you seem to be. Yes, you may well color up! If they are only partly true, then you deserve to blush!"

"What have you been hearing?" was all Juliana dared ask. She was uncertain what it would be. Would her grandmother simply rebuke her for trying to stake her jewelry in an unladylike fashion? Or was it something worse? To judge from the old lady's countenance—all frowns and thunder—it was something worse.

"Lady Betty Coke tells me, when I was at basset, that you are like to disgrace me, Juliana. I hardly knew what to do, or where to look, and all that I could say to her was that I was sure that you were doing something quite innocent. But I want the truth. Are you married, child?"

Juliana paused. Obviously her grandmother had been told about her visit to Fleet Lane. Now the fat was in the fire! She had not before considered that this might happen! All her fears had centered round Lizzie's reputation, rather than her own. "How did you know?" she asked cautiously, evading the direct question.

Her evasion infuriated Lady Talboys, who banged the floor with her cane. "Come, miss, I will have the truth! It *will* out! I *must* know! Are you married to that puppy?"

Juliana's mind went blank. She wanted very much—oh, how much!—to tell her grandmother the truth. But there was Lizzie to think of. She must, above all, give Lizzie and Robert time to sort out their lives before the storm broke. She compromised, stating, "I cannot answer that question, grandma. All I can do is to assure you that I have done nothing wrong."

The old lady seemed almost dumbfounded by this lack of a direct answer. She snorted, and then—in a kindlier tone of voice—said, "Come, Juliana. Don't be sillier than I think you, girl! If you are married, then it must come out some day, and 'tis better you tell me now so that I can do my best for you."

"Grandmama, I cannot discuss it with you," said Juliana desperately.

Lady Talboys continued to urge her, in carefully measured tones which suggested that she wanted to control her irritation. "Lady Betty Coke told me, while we were playing cards, that you had been seen in the company of Robert Torrington in Fleet Lane, and that the general gossip was that you had engaged yourself to him in a clandestine marriage ceremony. Apparently you had brought Lizzie Reddington along to lend you countenance. Now Juliana, be reasonable! It is not enough simply to tell me that you have done nothing wrong.

"Of course, I told Lady Betty that it was all a hum and that I knew about the expedition. I said that you had had an interest in the condition of debtors, and that you had asked your cousin and Mr. Torrington to accompany you to see the wretched inmates of Fleet prison. Well, a sillier tale there could not be! But I was at a loss to know what to say. I do not think she believed me, but she smiled and said very handsomely that *she* would not spread the story further. But I know the worth of that promise! Lady Betty is a very charming woman, but she is the most indiscreet creature. Try as she may to button her lip, all London will know in two or three days' time. Lud, girl you have gone too far this time. I am not a mealymouthed person, as you know, but this bids to be the greatest scandal of the season. I must know the truth of it!"

Juliana longed to deny all this, but she could not. If she explained the true state of affairs, she would only get Lizzie Reddington into trouble. And that would be against her promise to help them. She hung her head and looked distressed. She felt extraordinarily guilty about deceiving her grandmother, and her guilt made her flush. She realized she must look far from innocent.

"Well, miss?" demanded Lady Talboys getting crosser by the minute, "are you married, or ain't you? If 'tis done, I had best know so that I can try to lessen th damage. If not, then we must scotch this rumor. Come, pray tell me. I want a truthful answer, miss, and no more beating about the bush!"

Juliana remained mute. She did not know what else to do. It made her grandmother even crosser. Lady Talboys began to look red in the face, and she gave the sofa a blow with her cane which suggested she would have very much liked to have hit Juliana instead of the inanimate object.

"Pray speak out, girl," said her grandmother. "Else it will be bread and water and no more gallivanting about for you, miss! I will not have you stay in my house unless I know the truth! Pray speak out and shame the devil, miss!"

Juliana was still silent. She did not dare even to look at Lady Talboys, and she was full of sorrow for what she knew was shockingly bad behavior. She knew very well that she owed Lady Talboys an explanation. It could not have been pleasant for the old lady to hear vicious gossip about her granddaughter over the gaming table.

Eventually, Juliana managed to find something to say. "Grandmama, it is not what you think!" she said with an imploring tone. "I cannot say more now, though you will think it very odd of me. I know it is rude of me, and that it is a bad return for all the kindness you have shown me. I hope to tell you the true story in about two days' time. But all that I can tell you now is that it is not what you think."

"Hoity-toity, miss! How do you know what I think? I think you are a fool, child, but there are others who will think that you are something worse than a fool. Lady Betty said that you were seen by the Golden Exquisite *and* by the Marquis of Peterborough, and that Sir William is going round saying that the Fair Fury has thrown herself away on a worthless younger son. He has very little love for you, Juliana, and his odious tongue is one that is widely listened to. I tell you that you are in deep water and apt to sink unless you confide in me.

"I will engage to do my best for you, child, even if it does mean letting you throw yourself away on a younger son. I am not a monster, child. But I must have the truth before I can deal with this tangle. It is a damned imbroglio, and I find myself wishing that you had accepted that bore, James Reddington. He may be as prosy as a windbag, but at least none of this could have happened! Now you are in worse case, I fear."

Juliana almost wanted to cry, save that the situation was too grave. Lady Talboys was being so kind. She was really trying to help. Only Juliana could not cooperate—yet. She frowned, as she thought of the odious Sir William Goring Pelham. And no doubt the Marquis of Peterborough would contribute his share of gossip against her. And Mr. Ponsonby, too.

Also she could imagine that Mrs. Milgrave would enjoy the rumors. The whole subject of her bad and wild behavior would be discussed between her and her daughter—and probably their governess, the odious Miss Humphries! She felt the whole world was against her.

"Well, miss, you give me no alternative. Were you younger I should whip you for this! As it is, you may go to your bed. We will not go to Ranelagh, for I will not take about such a willful girl. I am excessively displeased with you. I hope you will reconsider your conduct, and will see that you are failing in your duty. Perhaps an evening on your own will bring you round to a proper way of conduct.

"No, no, do not kiss me good night," she added, as Juliana approached to do so. "I am not in the mood for your kisses, only for your obedience. Off you go."

There was nothing for it, but for Juliana to retreat to her bedroom. There she found the maid waiting to help her dress for Ranelagh, and had to tell her that she was not going. She knew that the news would spread rapidly to the rest of the household, who would immediately know about the row. Servants always did. She was only grateful that Pinkerton was not waiting on her. She did not think she could have borne that worthy woman's disapproval, which most certainly would be freely expressed.

She knew that she had been unfair, disobedient, and undutiful toward Lady Talboys. The old lady had been absolutely justified when she said that it was Juliana's duty to tell her the truth. Did Lady Talboys really think it was a secret marriage? Juliana had a great respect for the old lady's wisdom. Surely, she would realize that it was no such thing. But obviously her grandmother had been dismayed by the magnitude of the scandal that threatened her grandchild. Yet again, it seemed that the world of fashion was somehow against Juliana. Forgetting that she had been carried away herself by the delight of card playing, Juliana condemned society for the unfeeling pursuit of pleasure. When men and women of quality were not losing huge sums at the tables, it seemed that they had nothing better to do than to gossip among themselves.

It was that horrid set of young bloods who were the worst, Juliana told herself. The Marquis of Peterborough was an odious rake, and the Golden Exquisite was a creepy little rumormonger. Juliana thought she would have liked to run through Sir William with a sword. If only she were a man and might fight a duel and so silence his horrid tongue!

As she lay in her bed, it came into her mind that perhaps the rumors were not just the creation of Sir William. Perhaps the marquis had had a hand in them. Piqued by her refusal of his offer, and suspicious of Robert Torrington (whom, after all, he had actually found *kissing* her), he might have jumped immediately to the conclusion that she had married him. Juliana remembered how she had given the marquis her word that there was nothing between her and Robert Torrington, but— ten to one—that would mean nothing to him. He would probably think she was just another deceitful female. Yes, that was probably it. No doubt the marquis had told his cronies that he had found Miss Quincey and Mr. Torrington in a *tête à tête*—and then the hateful Sir William had taken up the tale and was even now spreading it around the ballrooms and the gaming clubs that made up high society. It was in this mood of despair and resentment that she had drifted off to sleep.

Sir William Goring Pelham *was* spreading the tale. Such a juicy piece of gossip was calculated to afford him considerable pleasure. He had told Lady Betty Coke, whom he had met in Bond Street, only an hour after the incident had occurred. He had passed the story on to several of his cronies that afternoon, dropped dark and interesting hints about it to several matrons during the evening's entertainment at Ranelagh, and now he was discussing it over cards with friends in the ground floor of a small gaming den a few streets off Piccadilly.

It was a snug but obscure little establishment where vast sums passed over the felt-covered card tables nearly every night. Some gamesters maintained that the cards were fuzzed and the dice loaded, but the den was enjoying a brief spell of popularity for all that. The gaming set, led by Charles James Fox and George Selwyn, had favored it with their presence, and the Marquis of Peterborough had publicly said that he found it an amusing establishment. With that kind of endorsement, the den had rocketed into fashion and Sir William was one of those who could be counted on slavish adherence to fashion. He liked to be seen in the right places.

The Golden Exquisite had gathered round him several of the younger spirits and was telling them his latest piece of scandal. "Imagine her discomfiture! I vow that the Fair Fury turned quite pale with fear when she saw me, and saw that *I* had rumbled her scheme," drawled the dandy, as he dealt out the cards. " 'Tis a runaway match to be sure, as I was tellin' Lady Betty Coke. Lud, the girl has outraged every canon of society within a sennight or so of arriving in London. *My* sympathies lie with poor Lady Talboys. The girl's nothing but a rude and rustic country miss."

Sir William's back was to the door, and so he could not see the latest arrival at the den—the Marquis of Peterborough, accompanied by the faithful Ponsonby.

Unaware of their presence he continued in high pitched voice which carried throughout the room, since the rest of the company had fallen silent. "Why, 'tis the most shockin' scandal since Lady Coke was held up by the highwayman."

"Pray enlighten me, Sir William. What is this shocking scandal which you are so evidently enjoying?" said a voice behind him. The Marquis was speaking very gently, very calmly.

Sir William swiveled round in his chair, and with something of a shock, noticed who had arrived. His voice trailed off into silence and he gave a nervous titter. The faces of his cronies round the table were avid with curiosity. They sensed something dangerous in that gentle voice.

By the side of the marquis, Ponsonby was similarly alert. He had shared several bottles with his friend and was in prime order—but not so drunk that he could not detect the anger bottled up in the marquis. Ponsonby had been friends with him for years. He had never before heard him sound so . . . so in earnest. What the devil was this all about? he wondered.

"Come, Sir William. Let me share your latest piece of enjoyable gossip," persisted the marquis. His voice was still deceptively reasonable, but beneath the tones of sweet reason lurked the indefinable air of a threat.

"I am sure I do not have to tell *you*," twittered the Golden Exquisite, now looking thoroughly alarmed. "I was merely remarkin' upon the singular sight of Miss Quincey and Mr. Torrington this morning. In Fleet Lane, no less! We know what that means."

"And what does it mean? I must be growing very dense with age, but I do not seem to be able to draw the quick conclusions at which you are so apt, Sir William," said the marquis with elaborate politeness. Nearly all the men in the room had ceased to pay attention to their cards and were watching the scene which unfolded before them.

Sir William seemed to gather up his courage. In defensive tones, he declared, "It can only mean that the Fair Fury has decided to give her hand and fortune to young Torrington, and they have made a match of it. No doubt about it. Plain as the nose on my face. You surely must have realized that, Auberon."

"I do not recollect giving you the right to call me by my Christian name," said the marquis in sudden blighting tones. Sir William flushed. The marquis, however, paused for a moment's silence and carelessly took snuff. Then turning to Ponsonby he said in light, almost carefree tones, "It is remarkable, Ponsonby, how vulgar this place has become. 'Twas a mistake, I think, to bring it into fashion. I fear I shall have to cease honoring this place with my presence. It has grown too full of jack-a-dandies for me."

Ponsonby grinned. The wine was beginning to make him feel reckless. The devil had got into Auberon and no mistake. It looked as if there must be trouble. He helped fan the flames. "You are right, as ever, my dear Auberon," he said, placing just the faintest emphasis on the Christian name, " 'Tis vulgar, monstrous vulgar!"

Sir William paled at the undoubted insult. He looked round the room, as if for some kind of escape but on all sides he met the pitiless eyes of the onlookers, most of whom were enjoying the row. "Fie upon both of you," he tittered, trying for a light tone which would dampen the tension. "You must be disguised. Too many bottles, I daresay. A trfle too much wine, eh, Ponsonby?" He did not try to address the marquis directly after the cruel snub about the name, but his voice quavered slightly as he tried to shrug off the whole affair.

"Yes," said the marquis in musing tones as if there

had been no interruption, "devilish vulgar, Ponsonby! I am surprised I did not notice it before. Speaking for myself, Ponsonby, I cannot bear the tedium much longer. Odd, isn't it? I never thought to hear ill-bred remarks about the amount of wine I might choose to drink. Foolish of me, I suppose. Drunk, did you say, Sir William? I am not so drunk that I cannot recognize a malicious little punk when I see one."

There was an audible indrawn hiss of breath from one of the onlookers. Sir William paled even further. This was an insult he could not, dare not, swallow, if he were to save his face. Ponsonby looked at the Golden Exquisite's white fury, and wondered where it would all end. It was clear that the marquis desired to force a quarrel on the man! That was not like Auberon. True, he had fought his man in a duel twice before now, but Ponsonby had never known him to start a quarrel so deliberately. This time was different. It was as if . . . as if the mere mention of Miss Quincey had set Auberon off. Lies the wind in *that* quarter?, wondered Ponsonby.

Sir William was now fairly bubbling with rage. "I will not hold with such insults. Outrageous to insult a gentleman . . . choose your seconds, Sir, or else I must ask you to withdraw your remarks."

"I do not think I shall withdraw my insults, Sir William," said the marquis with maddening calm. "You forget that I warned you about spreading tales that concern me. Miss Quincey concerns me. I do not choose to have you mention her name, Sir William. Do I make myself clear?"

Frightened though he was, the Golden Exquisite could not resist his habitual sneer. "Oh. So the Fair Fury has conquered *your* heart, has she? Well, I wish you well. Perhaps you will be able to curb her desire to outrage society. Or perhaps not. I fear you may be disappointed. The lady seems to prefer Mr. Torrington. I shall win my wager yet."

His words struck home. Ponsonby noticed that the marquis went white. Otherwise he seemed still in control. With deliberation he picked up a glass of wine that was standing nearby and threw it full into Sir William's face.

With the red liquid still dripping from his face, Sir William drew out his sword. Anger had made him momentarily forget his fear. "I will avenge *that,*" he declared dramatically.

"Avenge it, *if* you can. We will settle it here and now," snapped back the marquis with what seemed to Ponsonby to be indecent promptitude. "I can count on you, Ponsonby, not to let anybody in."

Ponsonby nodded. He looked round the small gaming room. " 'Tis damned irregular, Auberon. There's precious little room. We must pull back the tables. And we need more light. More candles! Bring more candles!" he ordered a frightened-looking servant. The duel was against every rule of honor! Auberon must be mad! He only hoped that he would not kill Sir William, but looking at his friend's intent face, as the two opponents carefully tied back the ruffles at their wrists, he could not be sure. Auberon looked in a killing mood. But a death in such shocking circumstances! It might be too much of a scandal even for the Marquis of Peterborough's reputation.

With a hiss of steel the two blades were out and glittering in the candlelight. The card tables had been dragged back against the wall, and the cardplayers had left their games and were standing round the outside of the room, eager onlookers to this addition to the evening's entertainment. A couple of white-faced footmen had brought up two extra candelabra which were placed on the tables. There was just enough light for the two swordsmen to see, though the flickering wax candles cast strange twisting shadows on the walls and ceiling of the stuffy room.

They fought silently, with only the occasional grunt of effort, or gasp of exertion to be heard over the clash and slither of the blades. Sir William, like most of his contemporaries, was no mean swordsman. He thrust and parried with a certain neat competence which showed that he had been creditably taught—and all the time the buckles on his shoes, the jewel at his throat, and the spangles on his waistcoat flashed and sparkled in the candlelight.

But he was no match for the marquis. His build was more slender, his skill was less absolute, and he fought with competence rather than with fire. The marquis, on the other hand, was fighting with a savagery that surprised the onlookers. Though his whole body was under masterly control, as his blade flashed hither and thither seeking out Sir William's weakest point, his grimly set mouth and glittering eyes told their own story. It was nothing less than a massacre, thought Ponsonby. He noted that Sir William's breathing was becoming heavier, and his defense was more and more strained. Whatever was his opponent about? This was no way to kill a man, thought Ponsonby, looking round at the crowded gaming room by the light of the hurriedly fetched candles.

If Auberon had wanted to kill the man, he should have done it properly with a formal duel at dawn, with seconds, in one of the many open fields round the town. Such an affair was recognized as part of the way fashionable society behaved. It was good *ton*. This was not. Society would not forgive even the fifth Marquis of Peterborough if he killed his man in nothing less than a gaming den brawl. Ponsonby found himself getting worried.

The marquis was feinting with his sword to draw Sir William on. It looked as if he would not be satisfied with just a flesh wound. He had passed up at least once a chance for that. No, he was fighting as if he meant to go for the heart itself.

The marquis's blade flashed forward suddenly, halted for a second while Sir William's sword tried and failed to strike the blow away, then thrust forward again.

Sir William gasped, wavered, staggered on his feet with a look of surprise. He threw down his sword and clutched both hands to his chest where the marquis's sword had thrust. A thin trickle of dark blood oozed through his fingers. With a noise like a sigh, Sir William fell to the ground unconscious.

His opponent stood looking at the body for a moment. Then the marquis pulled a napkin from one of the tables. For a moment Ponsonby thought he was going to bandage the wounded man, but it was no such thing. Coolly, he wiped the blood off his own sword before sheathing it. "Shall we go, Ponsonby?" he said casually.

"The devil you'll go," shouted one of the cardplayers, crouched by the fallen man, endeavoring to stanch the flow of blood from the wound. "You've killed him, by Gad."

"By Gad, so I meant to," said the Marquis unemotionally. He turned to go.

"I can still feel his pulse. Fetch a doctor," shouted another bystander in the group round the body.

The marquis turned to one of the footmen. "It seems I have been a trifle premature in my claims. Do you hear that, man. Fetch a doctor and be quick about it."

"Auberon, you can't just leave," protested Ponsonby urgently. "The man may still die. That thrust was devilish deep, unless I'm mistaken."

"Not deep enough, it seems," said the marquis. "I have nothing further to do here, Ponsonby. What use would I be to a wounded man, assuming I wished to be? Come, I am leaving this very unamusing establishment."

With a helpless shrug of his shoulders, Ponsonby followed the marquis through the small hall and out down the steps into the cool streets of Mayfair. Once they were safely out of hearing, he nerved himself to say, "Auberon, you'd best make speed to leave the country. I wouldn't lay odds on Sir William lasting the night, and there'll be the devil to pay if he dies. It was damned irregular, you know. You could find yourself standing trial for murder."

"I think not," said the marquis. "I meant to kill him, but it seems I missed just a fraction. The light was poor. Besides, I have no intention of leaving London yet. I have unfinished business with Miss Quincey."

"Auberon, don't be foolish. It's a terrible risk. Do not tell me you want to risk standing trial in a court of law."

"No, no, friend. I am not that mad. I will get me to France just as soon as I have had words with Miss Quincey. There is plenty of time, I assure you. But since you are so worried for my safety, I will warn my household that my departure tomorrow could be somewhat . . . er . . . precipitate."

Ponsonby sighed. He knew that he could do no more. He only hoped that the marquis was right, and that Sir William would not die. If he should not survive, it looked grim for Auberon. Such a hasty ill-planned fight would not look good.

"Stop worrying, Ponsonby," said the marquis with a grin, reading his unspoken thoughts. "I shall brush through this all right. Never fear. Oh, and you may wish me happy."

"I did not know that . . . that Miss Quincey was accepting your attentions," said the bewildered Ponsonby. "Sir William gave the impression that her affections were already engaged. You made her a proposal of marriage, I take it?"

"I did, and the girl refused me," said the marquis calmly. "But she gave me her word her affections were not engaged. I have a shrewd idea of what Miss Quincey was doing in Fleet Lane, and I fear she is about to plunge herself deep into scandal again."

"The duel tonight will not help her reputation," said Ponsonby cautiously. "It is bound to be all over London by tomorrow evening."

"This evening, you mean. It is well into the early hours," said the marquis. "I'll lay odds that the news will be all over London by breakfast time." He looked so grim as he said this, that Ponsonby fell silent. The two friends then walked companionably home together, as the first streaks of dawn began to lighten the London sky.

By the time the sun was high enough to light the whole city, Juliana was awake. She had still not shaken off the depression and resentment of the night before, and she got out of bed in a listless mood. She was not looking forward to the day ahead. Lady Talboys would reassume her interrogation. She was bound to be very cross and her anger would be justified.

Lady Talboys *was* cross, but Juliana did not have to face her immediately. The old lady, as at other times of crisis, had taken to her bed for the morning, leaving a message that on no account was she to be disturbed by her granddaughter before noon. Pinkerton had relayed the message with one of her most devastating sniffs of disapproval. Juliana could see that the maid knew all about the disagreement and was naturally taking Lady Talboys's part.

Further trails awaited her downstairs. Visitors had arrived to see Miss Quincey, reported Hitchens the butler, adding that he felt it his duty to have a few words with her before she saw them. The request was so unusual that Juliana thought it must be disapproval of the visitors. She asked who they were.

"It is Lady Helen and Mr. Reddington," said the butler, adding awkwardly: "And I very much fear, miss, that they may be wishful of seeing you because of a tragical occurrence last night."

His words pulled Juliana up short. "Come into the library and tell me what you mean," she said urgently to the butler. "Lady Helen and Mr. Reddington can wait a few minutes."

In the library, the butler cleared his throat with embarrassment. "I hope you will forgive the liberty, Miss Quincey," he said with an unwonted lack of confidence. "I am very well aware that it is not my place to convey gossip about unfortunate mishaps to you, but I believe it is no less than my duty on this occasion. You see, miss, I cannot help but know that Mr. Reddington has been particular in his attentions to you."

"I do not welcome those attentions," said Juliana quickly, anxious to set the butler right. "My affections are engaged in a quite different quarter," she added, unable to stop a blush. Even as she said the words, she wondered at them. They were true. With a shock, she realized that she had fallen in love—with the Marquis of Peterborough.

So amazed was she at this sudden revelation of her own heart, that she barely heard the butler's next words. "Well, miss, it's the housemaid's sister who is employed in the Peterborough household, and she took it upon herself to bring us the news. It seems that her master has fought a duel, and it's said it's along of a wager about yourself, miss. That's the Marquis of Peterborough," he added, anxious to make things clear.

Juliana came back to earth with a bump. The shock of hearing that name made her heart bang uncertainly. "What was this?" she said anxiously. "A duel? Over me? Pray with whom?"

"With Sir William Goring Pelham, miss. 'Twas last night in a low gaming den, and both of the gentlemen drunk, they say. He was wounded right in the heart, and fell down dead among the cards."

"The marquis dead?" Juliana staggered. She only stopped herself from falling by catching at one of the leather armchairs. While the room swirled round her, she steadied herself against the chair.

From far away she heard the butler's story continue: "No, miss, not the marquis. He had not a scratch. 'Tis Sir William who is dead. Not but what the marquis will have to fly the country or stand trial for murder, which I do not think he will do. He has told his household he will go abroad to the Continent."

Juliana found that she had to concentrate very hard

to take in what the butler said. Her nerves were shattered by the succession of shocks—first the news, as she thought, that he was dead, now the news, less horrifying but still horrible to her, that he was a fugitive from justice. "Oh Hitchens," she murmured. "I do not feel I could face visitors at a time like this."

"I'm sure, Miss Quincey, that I wish I could spare you the ordeal of seeing them. But I cannot. Lady Helen has insisted she speak with you, and when I told her that you had barely left your chamber she said she would wait until you were down. She says she will not leave without seeing you."

"I suppose I shall have to see them," sighed Juliana. She was beginning to be mistress of herself again. She told herself that it was all over now . . . she would never see the Marquis again. He would be leaving for the Continent even now, and she, left back in London, would have to ride out the scandal.

She tried to push the dull ache of pain into the back of her mind. Nothing mattered now. The marquis was the only man she loved, the only man she *could* love. She realized, belatedly, that she had fallen passionately in love from the moment he had first kissed her so disgracefully in the stableyard.

Suddenly Juliana understood what had been happening. From the moment of that kiss she had been fighting her own heart. She had tried to persuade herself that she hated him. But the hate she had felt had been the other side of love. Now that it was too late, now that the marquis would be on his way to the Continent, she realized . . . she had loved him all along.

"I must see Lady Helen," she murmured, as Hitchens opened the door of the library for her to leave. The butler looked anxiously at her. Miss Quincey looked pale, he thought. News of the duel had hit her hard. Was it simply the fear of the scandal?, he wondered. Or had she fallen for the Marquis? Hitchens had a soft spot for the Marquis of Peterborough who had tipped him so generously and who was a real gentleman of the proper sort. He might be wild, well everyone knew he was, thought the butler, but what he needed was a wife to settle down with. Would this shocking duel put a stop to all that? Miss Quincey could hardly get betrothed to a fugitive from the law. And what part would be played by that young Mr. Torrington? There were rumors about him and Miss Quincey. Hitchens sighed as he opened the door for Juliana into the morning room, then turned back to the servants' hall.

"Miss Quincey, we have come about this!" exclaimed Lady Helen as soon as Juliana entered the room. She stepped forward and thrust a piece of paper into the girl's hand. Her voice was icy with disapproval and she made no move toward the usual courtesies of greeting.

Juliana bobbed a hasty curtsy, and opened the paper. She recognized Lizzie's writing at once. The fat is truly in the fire, now, she thought, as she turned her attention to the words.

"Dear Papa and Mama," read the letter. *"When you see this, I shall be far away with my Husband, Robert Torrington. We were secretly married, as I proposed to tell you in a day or two. But circumstances have decided us to fly to Robert's brother in the country, whom we hope will take us in. Please tell my dearest Juliana that we are doing this so that she will not be plagued by false rumors about her and Robert. Please forgive us, Mama. I know Robert is poor, but with Papa's help he will rise in his profession. Trusting that you will not cease loving me, Your most affectionate daughter, Lizzie.*

Before she could properly assimilate what the letter had said, James Reddington addressed her in formal tones. "I am amazed, shocked, and deeply wounded by your perfidy, Miss Quincey. Oh, do not deny it! We know all! The wretched maid, Molly, has told us how you encouraged my sister to run off with this worthless young man. I leave you to imagine the full horror of *my* feelings, Miss Quincey. I count myself blessed that you did not accept my proposal of marriage, and I have come this morning to tell you that I wish, formally, to withdraw that offer."

"Well, Mr. Reddington, thank you for making things clear," said Juliana briskly. In her horror at the news of the Marquis's duel she had almost forgotten about Lizzie and Robert. Thank goodness if they had decided to run off together sooner than planned. It simplified matters. "I am very glad that Lizzie has found happiness," said Juliana defiantly. "Mr. Torrington is a worthy young man, Lady Helen, and I know—for Lizzie has told me—that the admiral considers his character above reproach."

"My father is too softhearted," said James Reddington in a disapproving voice. "I am shocked to discover that he will countenance the match. I have advised him that it is tantamount to sanctioning his daughter's disobedience and encouraging other young females to elope. Lizzie must pay the penalty, in my view. She should be cast off from the family without a penny. No good can be served by further intercourse between her and the parents she has disobeyed."

"James, you have told us your views a hundred times this morning," said his mother tartly. "I have heard enough of them. Like you, I am distressed by the marriage and by Miss Quincey's outrageously ungrateful attitude. But I cannot and will not cast off my only daughter. Not only would it be repugnant to my motherly feelings, but it will cast us all into worse scandal. We must hush up the marriage as best we may. You, Miss Quincey, can best help us and Elizabeth by keeping a still tongue in your head."

"Of course, I will, Lady Helen," said Juliana eagerly. "I am so glad that you are going to accept the marriage. I knew you would. I told Lizzie that you must come round."

"That is quite enough, Miss Quincey," said Lady

Helen, bitterly. "It is only because I wished to engage your silence that I have visited you this morning. You must be aware that I am most severely displeased with you and that in future our relations cannot be cordial. In short, I am here to tell you that Lady Talboys must look for another chaperon for you. I do not choose to be responsible for a girl who has brought scandal, not only upon herself, but upon our family too. No," she added, holding up her hand, "do not seek to exculpate yourself, Miss Quincey. You have promised your silence. That is all I came to seek. Come, James, we will leave immediately."

With those parting words, she swept out of the door.

Ten

"Lud, Miss, you are enough to try the patience of a saint, instead of an old sinner like myself," exclaimed Lady Talboys, entering the morning room only a few moments after the visitors had left. "What new disaster has occurred? I have just passed Lady Helen and her ass of a son in the hall, both of 'em with faces like thunder, all but cutting me dead in my own house. And Hitchens tells me some idiotic story about a duel and your fair name, as if he'd been reading romances instead of drinking port late at night."

"Oh, dearest grandmama. Now I can tell you," said Juliana with relief. " 'Twas not I who married Mr. Torington, but Lizzie Reddington! That is why Lady Helen and Mr. Reddington looked so angry. Lizzie has run off early this morning with her new husband. They have been in love with each other for months and it seemed the only way to make sure they weren't separated."

Lady Talboys was taken aback. The news caught her entirely by surprise. She gaped at her granddaughter. She had been standing near the elegant Adam fireplace of the morning room, and she placed her hand upon it for support. Looking round as if for succor, she spied out the Sheraton settee and with the help of her cane hobbled over and sank down upon it. Juliana was alarmed. The old lady looked very pale. She hurried over to her. "Can I get you some smelling salts?" she asked.

"Smelling salts be damned," said the old lady rudely, panting a little. "I'd sooner have need of a medicament against disobedient children. Lizzie Reddington! Why that little miss . . . butter wouldn't melt in her mouth. Unless . . ." she looked fiercely at her granddaughter. Then she continued slowly, "Yes, that would be it. 'Twas not little Lizzie's scheme. Don't tell me that girl's got enough brains! As for that handsome hulk of a Torrington boy, he would never have the nerve. I'll wager my diamonds to a bone button that 'twas you, Juliana. Aye, and so that was why you would not tell me about it last night. You gave me a terrible fright. I could not sleep a wink for thinking you had married that man. You sly little puss! And all the time 'twas Lizzie Reddington you were protecting."

Juliana looked at her grandmother with caution. The old lady sounded half admiring, but it might be the calm before the storm. She ventured to add, "It is not such a bad match, grandmama. The admiral will be able to use his influence in Mr. Torrington's favor at the War Office. Lizzie says that he has considerable military connections and approves of Mr. Torrington's character."

"What care I what sort of match it is?" said her grandmother impatiently. "Don't waste your reassurances on me, Juliana. I'll bet you ten to one that Lady Helen doesn't think it a good match. She had her eye on bigger game for the girl. I'll wager she has taken the news hard, and that you are not her favorite at the moment."

"That's true," admitted Juliana. "She was very cross indeed. She is having to accept the marriage, because she does not wish to cause further scandal in the family. It is just as I thought. She cares about propriety. She came to demand *my* silence in the affair. I think the Reddingtons will dream up some tale to account for the marriage's haste."

"Well I'd give a monkey to have seen their faces when they first found out," cackled Lady Talboys, maliciously taking pleasure in her relatives' downfall. Like many old ladies, the misfortunes of others gave her a certain warm feeling. "Mind you, if I were her, I'd be wishful to do you a bad turn, child, for having helped." She sniffed, and thought for a second or two. The smile on her face was replaced by rather a grim look. She pursed her lips, as if considering things.

"Lady Helen's anger is not going to do *you* very much good, child," she said warningly. "Why it seems to me that you have antagonized the whole fashionable world in the space of two or three weeks. You have caused a scene for the old tabbies to gossip over. You have had your name linked with that of the Marquis of Peterborough which cannot but harm *any* female. And now you are involved in encouraging a clandestine match. True, you are not the bride, but it might almost have been no worse if you had been. Ten to one Lady Helen will lay the blame on you rather than on her own daughter. Well I am sure that I would do so, if 'twere me. She will have no cause to love you, Juliana, and I'll go bail she'll not hesitate to blacken your name whenever she gets the chance. For one thing, it will make her own daughter's conduct the easier to excuse."

"Well, it doesn't really matter, grandmama," said Juliana tiredly. "I don't seem to be able to do anything right. At least I have helped Lizzie. Friendship *is* more important than fashionable success."

"High-flown sentiments, indeed!" mocked her grandmother. "But they won't help you find partners next time we go to a ball, nor will they stop the gentlemen trying to flirt with you."

Juliana shivered with apprehension. It sounded a horrible fate. She had a glimpse of what it would mean— a crowded ballroom, in which she and her grandmother would have nobody to talk to. Gentlemen might solicit her hand for a dance, but then they would be odiously free in their attentions. She would find a twitter of gossip following her every move. Disapproving eyes would always be on her. No doubt some of the matrons, like Mrs. Milgrave and perhaps even Lady Helen, would cut her completely. Perhaps even her grandmother might find social ostracism at the card table. And all this because she had tried to help Lizzie and Robert! No doubt *they* would stay friends, but they would probably be too bound up in their own happiness to have much time for her. James Reddington would certainly make it his business to ignore her as publicly as possible.

Sir William Goring Pelham would have horrid things to say . . . no, at least she would be spared that! Sir William was dead, or dying.

Her thoughts inevitably turned to the tall dark figure of the marquis. She loved him. But there was more pain than joy in that love, and it was mixed with fierce anger. *He* was to blame for her troubles. She thought again of how her whole London season had started off badly. It had been *his* fault. *He* had forced his odious hateful kisses on her, and had started off the whole scandal with that horrid governess's tittle-tattle. Then *he* had provoked her to anger publicly by returning that glove, and had followed up that by insulting her with an off-hand proposal of marriage which no woman of sensibility could ever have accepted.

And to crown it all, it had been the marquis who had been drunkenly driving a coach past the Fleet prison on that ill-fated morning when she and Robert Torrington and Lizzie had been standing in Fleet Lane. That had started this latest scandal which boded to overwhelm her entirely. Everywhere she looked, it seemed that one person, and one person only had been responsible for her ruin—the Marquis of Peterborough. She choked back a sob, and said, "Will it be very bad for you, grandmama? Should I not go back to the country perhaps? 'Tis not fair that *you* should suffer for *my* mistakes. Besides, I have nothing to live for in London. It does not suit me. I would do better to go back to obscurity. I was happy then."

"There's no question of your going back home, child," said her grandmother rather grimly. "Oh I know I threatened you with it, when I was angry. But you cannot go now. The Talboys family never turns tail. We face the enemy and fight—or die in the attempt! No, we must *force* the polite world to accept you. I have some credit, which I do not believe is entirely extinguished. There are some I can count on—Lady Sefton for one, Lady Betty Coke perhaps, Mrs. Molton for certain. Lady Helen will be furious with us, of course, but I do not think she will cut me for she is proud of the connection and would not like it if *I* were to cut her. The admiral will put in a good word for you, pet. He has a soft heart. Yes, and if I can think of a way of putting it to her . . . if I can persuade Lady Helen that it is not in her best interests to cut *you* . . . We will brush through somehow. It will not be easy and it will not be amusing, but it won't be the first time I have taken on the world and won."

"You know, grandmama," said Juliana tentatively, "I don't know whether it will be worth the effort."

"Nonsense, girl! You can't run away now! You must fight and help *me* fight. *You* may not care but I am damned if *I'll* see my granddaughter cold-shouldered by the *ton,* without at least struggling to set it right. What is more, child, I doubt if you'd be so happy in the country now. You are not the simple country girl you were. You have got a taste for the gaieties of town. Is it not so?"

Juliana was about to deny this, until second thoughts made her pause. There was something in what her grandmother was saying. The old lady had put a finger on the truth. She, Juliana, was taking an interest in fashionable clothes, for instance. She had just been beginning to enjoy the round of gaieties—the balls, the threaters, the card parties. And that was another thing. She remembered the fierce pleasure she had discovered in whist, and the way she had wanted to gamble her jewels.

She was not the girl she had been when she had arrived in London. She was corrupted, she thought miserably. "But I still care about poverty and misery and distress," she said out loud. "And I have discovered that people like James Reddington, though they keep *talking* about virtue and so forth, seem entirely unfeeling. You know, grandmama, I am grateful he has withdrawn his offer. It made me feel really sick the way he suggested poor Lizzie should be entirely outcast from her family."

"Humph, I have been trying to tell you, girl, that James Reddington is a frightful prosy windbag, but at first you wouldn't believe me. You just set him down as a good man because he doesn't touch the dice. Gambling isn't the sign of somebody being all bad, you know. What about me?"

"I'm truly sorry, grandmama," said Juliana penitently. "I see that I was completely wrong from the start. I thought that gaming was such a sin, that only truly bad people would do it. But now I know that some qualities are more important. You have a kind heart, grandmama, and that is much more important than simply not playing cards."

Lady Talboys looked embarrassed at the compliment. She was about to make some cynical remark to brush it off, when the ubiquitous Hitchens knocked at the door to tell the ladies that the Marchioness of Peterborough was calling on them.

"The marchioness?" exclaimed Lady Talboys with surprise. "Whatever can Anne want? I beg of you, Juliana, get upstairs quickly and change your dress. That cotton one will never do. Put on your blue silk with the hoop, child and wear the white embroidered petticoat with it. You must look neat and pretty. You look a perfect romp at the moment. And now's the time to make sure you make a good impression. Hurry, girl!"

"I beg Miss Quincey not to hurry away," said the marchioness, who had picked up the last few words of the conversation as she entered the room. She was simply dressed herself, in an informal striped lutestring with no hoop. Her hair was unpowdered and she wore a simple straw hat. Not for the first time, Juliana marveled at the way that the marquis, who was top of the trees for fashion, seemed to have rather an unfashionable mother.

"It is Miss Quincey that I particularly want to see, Lady Talboys. Please forgive the intrusion. I will explain all later. But at this moment I am in search of five minutes alone with Miss Quincey, if she will be so good as to spare me the time."

Juliana dropped a curtsy, blushing nervously. She could not think what the marchioness should want in seeing her, unless it was to rebuke her about her faults in the card game. But the marchioness did not look cross. Indeed she was smiling kindly. "Do you wish to come up to my room?" Juliana said doubtfully, casting an anxious look at Lady Talboys for her permission.

"No, child, stay where you both are," said Lady Talboys briskly. " 'Tis I shall leave you. You are kind to bother with the girl, Anne. Now, Juliana, mind your tongue and try for a little conduct. I do not know what this is about, but you are very honored by the marchioness's visit and I am sure that it is more than you deserve."

"Lady Talboys can be formidable at times," said the marchioness in sympathetic tones, once the old lady had left the room. "I remember that she used to scold me when I was a girl at my come-out. It was a sign that she liked me. She has a very kind heart, but rather a rough tongue."

"I know that," said Juliana. Then daringly she added: "Have *you* come to scold me for trying to wager my jewelry yesterday? I am truly sorry. I fear that I seem to have very little conduct and *that* action was the outside of enough. I know I go beyond the line of what is pleasing, though I try not to. I promise that I shall not do *that* again. Oh, and here is the ten guineas I owed you. I should not like you to think that I had not paid promptly. I would not wish to play and not pay."

"Why, child, thank you. I am not come to scold you. I found it vastly amusing to see you so carried away with the game, though it was good that no gentlemen were present. 'Tis refreshing to see wholehearted and innocent enjoyment. No, child, it is nothing to do with that. I have come to beg a favor of you."

"Beg a favor of *me?* I think you must jest," said Juliana with astonishment. "Why you know that you have only to ask. You have been so kind to me, I am delighted to serve you in any way I can, though I cannot think how."

"When you hear what favor it is, you may not be so ready to offer your services, Miss Quincey," said the marchioness. She paused. It seemed that she was having difficulty in finding the words for what she wanted to say.

"Please call me Juliana," said the girl quickly. "It sounds so formal to call me Miss Quincey, and I should very much like it if you would call me by my Christian name."

The Marchioness smiled gratefully. "Well, that is kind of you, Juliana. In a way, it links with what I wanted to say to you. You see, I should like the right not just to call you by your first name, but to think of you in a closer relation—as a kind of daughter."

"You mean . . . that . . . you would like me to marry . . . No, you can't mean what I am thinking," murmured Juliana in perplexity.

"I should like you as my daughter-in-law," said the marchioness quietly. "I should like you to marry my son. You see, Auberon has told me that he proposed marriage to you but that you refused him."

"Yes, but did he tell you *how* he proposed? Do you also know that he has insulted me in every possible way? Do you know that he made me the subject of a vulgar bet at his club? It is true that he asked me to marry him, but in such a fashion I cannot think that he was serious. I do not like to say this to his mother, but I concluded from the tone of his proposal that he was speaking in jest, or that he had some idea of winning his wager. He is the kind of man who might think it vastly amusing to try and win my affections without seriously meaning to return his own."

Juliana was panting by the time she got to the end of her speech. All her indignation, all her anger, and all her misery which she had pent up in her breast seemed to break forth.

"I know that he has not always been fair to you, Juliana. I know that he insulted you in the stableyard of some inn, but that was before he knew you . . ."

"Well, do you also know that he has not once spoken of love to me?" Juliana interrupted. "His proposal was the most graceless insulting thing imaginable! Why, believe me, only a girl at her last prayers would have— *could* have—accepted it! Besides, he is promised to Miss Milgrave, as all the world knows, and I am sure that they will suit admirably." Two tears strayed down her cheeks and with an abrupt little sniff she wiped them away with the back of her hand.

"My dear, I think you do not understand my son . . ." the marchioness said.

"I understand him only too well! I understand that he is a libertine! I understand that he is a gamester! And

213

I understand that he does not seem to have a heart for any female!"

"My dear, listen to me for a moment. Just for a moment, let me speak," said the marchioness quietly. Juliana gave another sniff, and fumbled for her handkerchief. The slow tears *would* keep coming. She stayed silent while the marchioness continued: "You owe me your attention, child. My son may have offended you, but what have I done that you will not listen to me?" The marchioness's voice was still kind and soft.

Juliana found the handkerchief, and with relief began mopping up her tears. She was angry at herself for displaying her emotions but she managed not to interrupt again. She supposed she would have to hear the marchioness out, though nothing could make her change her mind about the odious marquis.

"My dear, you are right that my son is a libertine and a gamester. That is what most people think of him, and indeed up to a few days ago I would have reluctantly agreed with them. I will not hide from you that his career as a rake has saddened me, and made me anxious for him. But I also know that it does not *have* to continue like this. Auberon was the most loving, charming son you could wish to have and he has continued to be loving to *me*. If now he is wild, well, it was not always so. Nor do I believe he will continue to be wild in the future.

"It will make you sneer perhaps, but I must tell you that he has some very romantic ideas about women, and that he has told me more times than I can remember how he longs to be able to fall in love. Up till now, he has not loved any woman. He told me two months ago that he had concluded he would always be a stranger to the tender passions. He had decided that it was time for him to settle down, and despairing of falling in love he was considering marrying Miss Milgrave in a marriage of convenience. I do not like the girl, myself. She has no sensibility and no feelings. But I will allow that she might make a very proper bride—for a man who wants beauty, fortune, but no heart. As I say, my son had concluded that, since he could not love, he must settle for a marriage without love."

"What has this to do with me? He did not mention that he loved me!" said Juliana bitterly.

"My dear, he *does*. He may not have said so to your face, but he has told me that he has fallen head over heels in love with you. He was in despair that you had refused his offer. He knew that he had not said the pretty things he should have. Did it not strike you as odd, Juliana, that a man who has so much experience in flirtation, should so make a mess of his proposal? It was because his feelings outweighed his judgment."

"But why did he not *say* that he loved me? And what about the wager? I do not see how I *dare* believe you," said Juliana. Her heart was a tangle of conflicting emotions—anger, impatience, a desperate longing, and a wild, but halting, joy.

"I am coming to the wager. I do not know who told you about it, Juliana, but you seemed to have misunderstood. My son did not make the wager. It was between Lord Mountford and Sir William Goring Pelham. I believe that Sir William made the bet to anger my son. I assure you, Auberon could not have it expunged from the book, without risking plunging you in further scandal. He had seen that his interest in you was already providing food for the gossips. Had he intervened in the bet, it would have been all over town within the evening. Besides, there is something else you should know."

"What is that?" Reluctance and eagerness warred in Juliana's breast.

"The duel he fought with Sir William was for *your* sake. My son has put it about that he was drunk, so as to avoid bringing your name into it. But the truth of the affair was that Sir William was spreading an evil story about you and some clandestine marriage. My son thought to silence him. It was not wise. I do not, myself, approve of duels. I do not condone his hot temper. But, however mad his folly, 'twas for your sake, Juliana."

"But why are you telling me this now?" asked Juliana. "It is surely too late. Your son has fled the country, I have been told. What is all this to me now?"

"He has not yet gone, my dear. I could not persuade him—though it is dangerously late. While Sir William lives—and for the time being he does—my son may linger. 'Tis mad folly, I do not deny, but he has an overwhelming desire to see you before he goes."

"Why have you told me all this? Why not let him speak for himself?" asked Juliana in some confusion. She did not want to surrender yet.

"Because I have made him wait outside, my dear. I was determined that you should know, lest you refuse to let him tell you. Was that so foolish of me? It seems to me that you are struggling against him, and that you have not allowed yourself to do him justice. I assure you that he is desperate for your love. May I fetch him to you?"

"I do not know what to do ... Lady Talboys ... a chaperon," Juliana murmured in a state of unholy confusion. The marchioness noted the rich blush in her cheeks and smiled. Without a further word, she left the room.

It seemed like an age that Juliana stood there, her cheeks red with confusion, her breast heaving, and her heart beating ... beating. There was such an emotional turmoil in her, that she did not know ... could not think how to react. Did she love him? Yes, but ... she hated him, too. He was altogether too much for her. It would be madness to take the risk of marrying him, madness to try to reform a rake and a gamester as hardened as himself!

Could she rely on his mother's word? After all he was a gamester who had killed, or almost killed, his man in a duel, and must flee the country. Prudence suggested she should forget him. Wisdom counseled her to refuse all thoughts of marrying him. Good sense suggested it would be a disaster to link her fate with one whose conduct showed plainly that he was a rake. And yet prudence, wisdom, and good sense could go by the board.

She tried to fight that small voice inside her which was whispering for her to marry him. She knew it was madness and folly, yet the voice kept on whispering how much she loved him, how in his arms she would be in heaven, how he would reform once he had her love. She struggled, and yet she could not overcome it. All her father's training suggested it would be a mistake. Or did it? Had not papa himself said that love was important? Had he not said that she should not give her hand without giving also her heart?

In the middle of this inner debate, she sensed that the door had opened, and that *he* was in the room. She looked up fleetingly but a kind of shyness broke into the glance, and she could not bear to rest her eyes on his. With three quick steps he was across the room and somehow—she never did know how—she was in his arms, and he was kissing her. His lips were powerful, urgent, and could not be denied.

Juliana started to struggle. Then again she felt that strange surge within her. Her body, her flesh was responding to his touch, against the counsel of her mind. She was powerless to resist the feeling inside her. It was as though her inmost being was calling out for him. His strong arms were round her, and her body was melting into his. Somewhere near her heart that same small voice was singing . . . singing, until a surge of flaming emotion turned into a roaring fire which drowned everything but him.

The marquis lifted his lips from hers and, holding her fiercely—she was no longer struggling, though—he looked down on her. His dark eyes, that glittered so wildly, seemed to look her over ironically, mockingly—and yet tenderly. Juliana found her own eyes meeting his, drowning in his, with an intensity that almost frightened her.

"Will you marry me, little prude?" he said, laughing

217

a little. His voice was as arrogant as ever. "I find you shockingly responsive in your kisses, you know. Yes, even in the stableyard I could taste the fire under that ice, Fair Fury."

"Don't call me that," exclaimed Juliana. She was still trying to hold back against complete surrender. "That horrid nickname reminds me of that hateful Sir William. I wish *I* could have fought a duel with him. I should have loved to run the Golden Exquisite through like you did!"

"He will not bother you again, my dear," said the marquis in a bored tone of voice. "Whether he lives or dies, I do not care. He may live, if he wishes. So long as he keeps his tongue still about my wife, I have no reason to trouble him further."

"Oh!" Juliana could not help the exclamation. As always, he was so arrogant! He was assuming her consent! "You have not yet asked me to be your wife," she pointed out crossly. "For all you know, I may yet refuse you!"

"What a troublesome wench you are," said the marquis still mocking her. "First you outrage society, then you take up gaming at Lady Sefton's—yes, I know all about it, child! You *have* given the matrons something to talk about. Next you cause me to fight a duel. And now you have kissed me like the veriest trollop, and you say you will not marry me. Let me tell you, my dear, you *will* marry me, even if I have to abduct you to the altar. I am perfectly capable of it, you know."

He looked down at her with an odd expression of mingled tenderness and grimness. Juliana could feel her heart pounding. She loved him and she feared him—or was it her own heart she feared? "And you, sir," she said in mocking tone trying to match his own, "what about you? Have you not been the *cause* of all my misfortunes?"

"Am I not trying to right the wrongs I have done you?" he replied. "I am being virtuous now. You do not have a monopoly of good conduct. After all, I am offering you the protection of my name."

A horrid thought entered her mind. Was this his

motive? Had his mother prevailed upon him to make the offer? "You have no need to marry me, I am sure," she said stiffly. "If that is your motive, then I cannot accept you. I do not need the protection of your name, and I would not have it merely to save my reputation. You had better by far marry Charlotte Milgrave, who I am sure will make you a far better behaved wife than I should."

The marquis threw back his head and laughed. He was still holding her, though he now had clasped her by the shoulders so that she was at arms' length from him. "Spitfire," he teased. "Do I detect a note of jealousy? Is this the Fair Fury feeling angry because I have paid attention to Miss Milgrave? You are quite right of course. She *would* make me a much better behaved wife than you will. I expect I shall be forever pulling you out of scrapes, rescuing odd ragged children, and paying your gaming debts. Charlotte would never make such a bustle."

"Well then, you had better marry her," said Juliana sulkily.

"There is only one problem," said the marquis pulling her close, so close that she could feel the buttons on his waistcoat pressing against her bodice. She could smell the faint perfume of his body. "Why do you think I want to marry a girl whose pranks will cause me so much trouble?" said the voice above her head.

She fixed her eyes upon one of the mother-of-pearl waistcoat buttons. She noted that the satin of the waistcoat was embroidered with flowers, and that a red rose was growing out of a yellow honeysuckle near the button. It must have been an expensive waistcoat, she thought idly. A little higher, her eyes could see the lace of his cravat, and the glimmer of the diamond pin which he always wore in the middle of its frothing folds.

"Why do you think I want to marry you?" said his voice.

"To make up for what you did to me," said Juliana in a small voice. "I suppose you want to right the wrongs you did and save my reputation."

"Folly! You foolish little prude! Silly child! Do you think that rakes like me marry women they have wronged? Why, I'd have had to marry a whole bevy of opera dancers were that the case! I *am* a libertine you know. Or rather I have been."

"I know that," said Juliana, still in a small voice.

"Well, then," he said, "get this clear in your mind— I do not give a damn about your reputation, or giving you the protection of my name. That sort of nonsense has never weighed with me. But since a certain troublesome minx erupted into my life, causing so much trouble for both herself and for me, I have had no thoughts of other women. I find I have no more time for the well-behaved Miss Milgrave, nor any time for opera dancers and the like. I do not, and never did, *love* them, you see. Those females will no longer be in my life. I shall no longer have time for them, for I shall be busy looking after you, my dear."

He bent down, and with his fingers forced up her chin so that she had to look him in the eyes directly. "Do you understand me, Juliana? I love you. I am mad for you, and I *will* have you."

With a little cry, Juliana flung herself against him, burying her face in his waistcoat. Her heart had given a great leap of joy, and she could not keep back the hot tears. She had at last surrendered to love.

At this inauspicious juncture, the door opened. In came Lady Talboys and the marchioness, both wreathed in smiles as they saw the couple in each other's arms. Juliana tried to pull away from the marquis. Reluctantly he let her go. She tried to regain her composure with her fan. The man she loved, however, seemed impervious to embarrassment. Carelessly he adjusted the ruffles at his cuffs. "You must wish me happy, mama," he said casually.

"My dearest Auberon, I am so glad! We *also* have good news," said the marchioness in a rush. "Your valet arrived not a moment ago while you were with Juliana and I did not like to interrupt you so he gave me the message. Sir William Goring Pelham will live!"

"What is that to me?" said the marquis, brushing a piece of fluff off his immaculate coat. "He has my permission to live, I suppose. I do not care one way or another."

"My dear Auberon, it means you need not fly the country," said his mama, disappointed at the cool way her son had received the good news. "It would never have done had he died. You would have had to stay abroad perhaps for a twelvemonth. I thought you would be glad to hear of his recovery. He will be laid up for several weeks, but the doctors agree that his life is no longer in danger."

"I am indifferent," said the marquis. "Indeed I had a mind to marry this wench of mine out of hand and take her to Paris with me. Should you have liked that, child? I wager you'd have cast all the French beauties into the shade." Smiling he held out his hands to her.

Juliana longed to run to him, but shyness held her back. "Paris ..." she said wonderingly. "I had not thought of that. I should love to go there." Then looking at her grandmother, she saw the old lady was looking rather disapproving. "I think I had better be wed from home, sir," she said thoughtfully. "After all, it would make a change for both of us to do the correct thing this time. I think perhaps I have outraged society enough for a time."

"If I thought you meant that poppycock, I'd withdraw my offer," said the marquis promptly. "And don't call me Sir like that. My name's Auberon."

"Yes, Auberon," said Juliana meekly.

"You must be married with all pomp and ceremony," said Lady Talboys decisively. "No, don't either of you argue. I'm an old lady, child, and you're my only granddaughter and I will have my way. And as for you, sir, you can for once listen to your elders and betters. I can bully as well as you can and don't you forget it. I say that Juliana shall be wed properly, and that is the way she will."

"I know when I'm beaten!" said the marquis with mock dismay. "I can see I shall have to go through a lot of tomfoolery with a good grace."

"Come child, and kiss me. Now you are my daughter, indeed," said the marchioness to Juliana, who promptly did as she asked. "I am so glad that you and Auberon have made a match of it. I vow I saw from the first that a living piece of marble like Charlotte Milgrave would never capture his heart. But I feared he might marry her, having given up hope of finding a real woman he could love."

Juliana hugged the Marchioness. "I am delighted with my mama-in-law," she said, "but I cannot help pitying poor Charlotte. I own I can't like her, but will she not be heartbroken? After all, Auberon, she has lost *you*."

"She never for one moment *had* me," he said rudely. "Besides she never cared a jot for me, only for my title and fortune. I daresay that la belle Charlotte will console herself rapidly enough."

"What do you mean?" asked Juliana.

"My guess is that Charlotte will console herself with that windbag, James Reddington. Who else?" said the Marquis. "I have eyes in my head, even if you haven't. What could be more natural than that the two of them should console each other? Besides, they will suit so well."

"You're right," said Juliana thoughtfully. "They're made for each other. And that will be nice for Miss Humphries, the Milgraves' governess. When the younger girls are grown up, she'll be able to help educate Charlotte's family. But tell me, Auberon, why have you not asked me about Robert Torrington?"

"Why should I? You gave me your word, do you not remember? That was enough for me. When I saw you and Robert Torrington and Lizzie Reddington in Fleet Lane, I put two and two together. I knew that you and *he* could not be in love; so I have assumed that he has wedded

222

Miss Reddington. Am I not right? Of course that poisonous worm, Sir Williams, was putting it about that yours was the clandestine match. That is why I had to stop him."

"You trusted me all along?" Juliana was deeply moved.

"Come here, Juliana, and stop doubting me," commanded the marquis.

Juliana stayed where she was. "Will you always order me about like this? I do not think you are going to make a very good husband," she said teasingly.

"In that you are correct, Fair Fury. I shall make a devil of a husband," admitted the Marquis. "Come here."

"I do not think it is proper that you should bully me," complained Juliana with spirit. She had forgotten the existence of the marchioness and Lady Talboys who were both smiling at this byplay from the lovers. "There is one more thing I must ask you. What have you done with the little boy, Frank?"

"He is with my other orphans," put in the marchioness. "He is quite well, and settling down nicely. I must tell you, Juliana, that I am looking forward to your help with the orphanage."

Lady Talboys intervened brusquely: "This is no time to be worrying about boys from the gutter, Anne. You and I must get our heads together and see what we can do to prevent the scandal which will otherwise attach to this wedding. Pray join me in the library where we can have a comfortable chat without interruptions from my romp of a granddaughter."

"Or my rake of a son!" laughed the marchioness, as she left the room.

"Now, girl, you have no excuse. Come over here," ordered the marquis.

"If I do that you will only kiss me," said Juliana, moving toward him.

"Exactly," said the Marquis, suiting the action to the word.

ABOUT THE AUTHOR
Caroline Courtney

Caroline Courtney was born in India, the youngest daughter of a British Army Colonel stationed there in the troubled years after the First World War. Her first husband, a Royal Air Force pilot, was tragically killed in the closing stages of the Second World War. She later remarried and now lives with her second husband, a retired barrister, in a beautiful 17th century house in Cornwall. They have three children, two sons and a daughter, all of whom are now married, and four grandchildren.

On the rare occasions that Caroline Courtney takes time off from her writing, she enjoys gardening and listening to music, particularly opera. She is also an avid reader of romantic poetry and has an ever-growing collection of poems she has composed herself.

Caroline Courtney is destined to be one of this country's leading romantic novelists. She has written an enormous number of novels over the years—purely for pleasure—and has never before been interested in seeing them reach publication. However, at her family's insistence she has now relented, and Warner Books is proud to be issuing a selection in this uniform edition.